FIND
MY
DAUGHTER

BOOKS BY JENNIFER CHASE

DETECTIVE KATIE SCOTT SERIES

Little Girls Sleeping

Her Last Whisper

Flowers on Her Grave

Last Girls Alive

The Fragile Ones

Pretty Broken Dolls

Silent Little Angels

Three Small Bones

The Rose Girls

Her Dying Kiss

The First Girl

Count Their Graves

EMILY STONE SERIES

Compulsion

Dead Game

Dark Mind

Dead Burn

Dark Pursuit

Dead Cold

JENNIFER CHASE

FIND MY DAUGHTER

bookouture

Published by Bookouture in 2025

An imprint of Storyfire Ltd.
Carmelite House
50 Victoria Embankment
London EC4Y 0DZ

www.bookouture.com

The authorised representative in the EEA is Hachette Ireland
8 Castlecourt Centre
Dublin 15 D15 XTP3
Ireland
(email: info@hbgi.ie)

ISBN: 978-1-83525-634-3
eBook ISBN: 978-1-83525-633-6

For all Search and Rescue Teams

PROLOGUE

Darkness shrouded the old cellar, causing a continuous chill to trickle down her spine. The dirt floor felt cold against her bare feet and her hands were dry as she rubbed them together. She could smell the musty remnants of what had been stored there in the past and the earthiness of being underground. The four walls seemed to be old stone or brick and they crumbled beneath her fingernails as she tried to claw her way out—but to no avail. Her exhaustion ultimately took over and she sat still, alone with her overwhelming fears. She had been left isolated and abandoned—in the pitch-black.

She hadn't heard the man in hours, or maybe it was days—she wasn't sure. In her bones, she knew this time he wasn't coming back. The plastic-bottled water and peanut butter sandwiches were almost gone; her mouth was constantly dry. Her memory seemed to play tricks on her. How long had it been since she'd gone to the casting call for young aspiring models? She hadn't told anyone where she was going, not her mom or even her best friend. She'd wanted to wait until she got the job to tell them the great news. It had been exciting; she dreamed of being a model and actress.

Her hands touched the dress she had been given to model—a yellow silk sheath wrap that made her feel beautiful, grown-up, as if she was finally someone who mattered.

She didn't know how many times she had crawled up the wooden stairs to the small opening into the cellar, checking to see if he had left it open. But it was always the same—bolted shut. She had memorized each stair, which ones were sturdy, which were creaky and unstable. There were nine steps in total.

As hard as she tried, she couldn't remember how she got there or what the house looked like. Even if she had a cell phone, she wouldn't have been able to describe where she was—or even what town she was in. She felt a million miles away from home.

But she wasn't giving up. Though weakened from lack of proper food, she dropped to her knees once again and crawled slowly toward the stairs. Her knees were bruised and scraped from the dozens of times she had attempted to escape—hoping that each time would be successful and she would be free.

As she paused at the first stair, feeling the familiar outlines in the darkness, she used her hands to steady her ascent; each time a stair ahead. Her knee pressed against the first stair, then the second, and the third. The creaks and groans were a disturbing symphony that reminded her of her situation: she was a prisoner in an empty basement and no one was coming back for her.

She stopped halfway to the top; her breathing quickening; feeling lightheaded. Her stomach grumbled. Her hope dwindled. Each time she'd gathered the strength to go up the stairs, it had turned out to be disheartening. She was never going to be free again. How stupid and selfish she had been, thinking she would become a model. She wondered if any of the other girls ended up like this. Or was she the only one whose fate was sealed?

Looking up toward the opening, she thought she heard footsteps. Yes, she had heard something. They were faint, but steady. He was coming. She froze. Her knees and hands were almost numb—her fingers hurt. Should she go back down or keep going?

What did she have to lose?

The footsteps were getting closer. They sounded like a pair of work boots hitting old hardwood floors. There was a strange echo to the movement, which was now above her. She could hear the creaks of the uneven planks; a mismatched harmony.

The distinct jingle of keys, then the rattle of a heavy lock.

She was going to stand her ground and push past the man to make her escape. It was all she had.

She could barely breathe.

The heavy creak of hinges.

Her body numb. She tried to stand up, ready to fight.

The doorway opened a crack at first, then wider, and finally pushed all the way open.

The blinding light overpowered her. Trying to escape it, she fell backward, flailing her arms in an attempt to catch her balance. She couldn't focus on anything. She felt every step hit her back and ribs as she tumbled down to the dirt basement. Her head struck the floor. She lost her breath and closed her eyes.

ONE

The large conference hall had standing room only. The California Law Enforcement Conference (CLEC) in Sacramento was at full capacity, with guest speakers from all areas of the law enforcement community along with information booths, recruitment, and representatives from various police departments. The overcast, showery day didn't dampen the annual event.

Detective Katie Scott from the Pine Valley Sheriff's Department was finishing up her talk on the importance of criminal profiling and how effective it was for her cold-case unit. Dressed in a navy pantsuit and a white blouse, Katie crossed the stage while giving the audience her bullet-point summary, photographs on the large screen behind her.

"Criminal profiling isn't about guesswork, wasting detectives' time on theories. It's about identifying the perpetrator by building a solid, evidence-based background for them, which is created from crime scene behavioral evidence, victimology, forensics, and the autopsy report. This is what's going to assist detectives to move forward in specific directions. It will also help with time management, which is especially useful with staffing stretched thin these days. Profiling can help the investigator keep on the right path and move ahead accordingly."

Several photos scrolled across the screen behind Katie as she concluded her presentation. She glanced at the clock on the wall.

"Are there any questions?" she said, gazing out at the attentive audience.

Several people raised their hands.

"Yes," she said, indicating a man in the second row.

"I'm Sergeant Kevin Randall, LAPD. Based on your hundred-percent solve rate for cold cases, what do you believe is the most important component to a successful investigation along with profiling?"

"Sergeant, it's multifaceted, and I can only speak from my own experience. I believe it requires exceptional teamwork, not only from me and my partner, but with forensics as well. And then it depends on the evidence available. If there's not much evidence, that's when it's crucial to put together a profile, or at least a basic threshold assessment as the blueprint for the case."

Katie glanced toward the back of the room where a tall man stood—her partner, Detective Sean McGaven. He smiled broadly as he watched the presentation.

"Thank you," said the LAPD sergeant.

Katie saw a woman enter, impeccably dressed in a tan suit. She had dark shoulder-length hair and carried herself with purpose. Something about the woman gave Katie pause. She was definitely agitated; her body rigid and her hands fisted. She was angry.

Another audience member stood up and said, "Detective Carey Dayton, SPD. Detective, what if there's very little or no evidence at the crime scene? For example, if the body was washed clean and there's no other evidence."

Katie loved this question. So many people didn't see the obvious clue. "If there isn't any of the usual evidence, as you stated, then that's actually a *big* piece of evidence." She walked across the stage and brought up a photo on the big screen of a minimal crime scene. "A crime scene lacking in physical evidence is a *key* piece of evidence and says quite a bit about the perpetrator. It says that this particular crime was planned, organized, and the killer thought of everything. Well, almost everything. You see, most crime scenes are generally sloppy, but this type of perp shows skills and that can tell you a lot. But, in my experience, no criminal is perfect and mistakes will be made. What mistakes are made will help you profile the killer."

Katie answered a few more questions before the talk ended.

. The audience filed out, with the exception of a few law enforcement personnel who shook Katie's hand and expressed that the seminar was helpful.

McGaven made his way to Katie, joined by a dark-haired man with intense eyes, forensic supervisor John Blackburn.

"Hey, partner," said McGaven. "I think you missed your calling as a teacher."

"I don't know about that."

"Great stuff," said John.

"Thanks. Hey, I don't know what your schedules are, but I'm starving. Lunch?" she said.

"Yeah, sounds great," said McGaven.

"I'll take a raincheck," said John. "I'm heading to one of the forensics seminars about cutting-edge procedures."

"Okay, see you later," she said, and he headed out.

The woman who Katie had seen enter the room at the end of her talk passed John. He too seemed to notice that the woman appeared agitated and angry. He waited at the door, watching.

"Excuse me, Detective Scott?" the unknown woman called.

"Yes?"

The woman walked up uncomfortably close to Katie. "You should be working on cases and not giving these feel-good seminars to law enforcement who don't have anything better to do than to attend this conference. People need your help…"

"Ma'am, please take a step back," said McGaven as he moved closer.

Katie wasn't sure whether the woman's behavior was going escalate, but she watched her wringing her hands and couldn't help but notice a deep sadness in her eyes. It appeared she had been crying as her face was slightly puffy and her eyes red.

Katie put her hand on McGaven's shoulder. "It's okay, Gav." Turning to the woman, she gently said, "What are you referring to, ma'am?"

"What am I referring to? I want justice. I want you to do your jobs."

"Please sit down. Tell us your name and what you're referring to," said Katie.

"You're a detective with Pine Valley Sheriff's Department, right?"

"Yes."

"Then why can't you tell me why you haven't found Anna Braxton? My daughter! Why?!" The woman lunged and then retreated. "I don't know why I'm wasting my time!" Her frustration exploded as she paced—every muscle in her body tense.

"Please…" Katie tried to calm the woman, but it was clear her emotions were boiling over and her anxiety was pushing her to retreat.

Two security guards entered the conference room accompanied by John.

"Ma'am, we're going to have to ask you to leave," said one of the guards.

"It's okay," said Katie holding up her hand. She truly wanted to help the woman. "Mrs. Braxton?"

"No, it's not okay!" the woman said as she began pacing.

The security guards took that as their cue and approached the woman again. Katie and McGaven watched them escort the woman out.

"Wow," said McGaven.

"We need to check on that case," Katie said. She walked up to the podium and grabbed several files and her laptop.

"I'll see what I can find out," said McGaven.

"Okay, I'll meet you at the restaurant. I have to put this stuff away and I have some outlines in my car."

"See you in a bit," said McGaven as he left the conference room.

As Katie hurried toward the parking garage, she couldn't help but think about Mrs. Braxton's appearance. The look in the woman's eyes was so powerful and it was obvious she was at breaking point. How could she blame her if her daughter was missing?

Katie stepped into the elevator. As she pushed the parking lot button, she kept hearing the woman repeat in her head, *Then why can't you tell me why you haven't found Anna Braxton? My daughter! Why?!*

The elevator doors opened. Katie stepped out and headed into the covered garage. It was full of cars but unusually quiet. The only sound was Katie's heels echoing as she walked quickly to her car. The name *Anna Braxton* resonated in her head as she tried to remember if she had heard it before.

Katie suddenly heard muffled voices, a scuffle, and what sounded like anguished pleas for help.

"Hello?" she called. Her voice resounded eerily around the garage, bouncing off the cement walls. She quickly looked in every direction to make sure that she wasn't walking into an ambush.

More voices. One female voice kept saying: *"Help... please help..."*

Katie dropped her files and laptop near a black SUV and

ran toward the voice. She hated not having her weapon but rushed toward the disturbance anyway. As she ran around a tight turn, she saw a woman lying on the ground in a vacant parking spot. She was still, her hands outstretched. Even from a distance, Katie could see spatters of blood along the ground and around the body. The woman was wearing a tan suit.

Katie took a quick survey of the area and didn't see anyone and she didn't want to leave the victim. Within seconds, she was at the woman's side, having recognized her immediately.

"Mrs. Braxton? Stay still," she said as she retrieved her cell phone and dialed 911, reporting the incident and stating that she was a police officer.

Katie noticed the blood patterns across the woman's abdomen. It appeared there were several knife wounds. The front of Mrs. Braxton's blouse was soaked in blood and her breathing was rattled and short. "No, *please... please* find her. Find my daughter."

"Don't try to speak. Try to relax and breathe." Katie shed her suit jacket and used it as a makeshift bandage, pressing it firmly against the woman's abdomen to try to slow the bleeding. "Help is coming." She kept a watchful eye for anyone who might be loitering or coming back to the scene. She felt vulnerable; the attacker could be hiding. She kept vigilant even while her heart was breaking.

"Please..." The woman grabbed Katie's arm. "*Please...*" Her grip was strong, her eyes expressing her desperation. "You have to find her..."

"Did you see who did this to you?"

She shook her head. "No... never saw... him before..." Her voice was weakening. "He's still out there."

"Is there anything you can remember?"

"No, but Anna... she's all I have..." Her breathing became unstable as her strength wavered.

"Hang on. Help will be here," Katie said. She could hear sirens in the distance.

The woman slowly pulled Katie closer. Katie realized she wanted to tell her something, so she leaned in close.

"Find the million-dollar man... you'll find my Anna..."

At first Katie didn't think she'd heard the woman correctly. But when she looked at her the woman's stare was powerful as she slightly nodded, as if to confirm what she had said. Katie decided then she would find her daughter, no matter what.

"Who is the million-dollar man?" Katie asked.

"He's who's behind this... there will be more... please find Anna before it's too late..." She could barely speak as her breathing became shallow.

Katie kept the pressure on the wounds until the ambulance and fire truck arrived and took over, stabilizing the woman before putting her into the ambulance. She felt helpless with the fact there was nothing more she could do and no leads on who had attacked Mrs. Braxton, as she stood in the parking garage covered in the woman's blood, watching the ambulance speed away.

TWO

Katie had finished her statement with one of the patrol officers at the scene. She watched as two other officers were securing the area, rolling out yellow tape to keep people away, and marking the location where the victim had been found. It seemed strange to be watching a crime scene unfold and not be part of working it.

"Hey," said McGaven as he approached. She had called her partner to let him know what had happened. "You okay? Where's your jacket?" He looked at his partner's bloody white blouse.

Katie nodded. "I'm fine. I think they thought it was Mrs. Braxton's and took it with them."

"It was the same woman who had asked you to find her daughter?"

"Yes."

McGaven didn't immediately respond. He seemed troubled as he stared at the area where Mrs. Braxton had lain on the cold cement. There were bright blood pools left behind.

"I don't know what else we can do right at the moment without looking into the missing person's report," she said.

"When's your next lecture?"

"Four," she said. "But I'm thinking I should cancel it so we can get back to Pine Valley and dig into the case."

"The case is in Sacramento's jurisdiction," said McGaven.

"But the missing person's report for her daughter and residence is in Pine Valley."

A white SUV slowly pulled in and parked nearby. There were no identifying numbers or a name of a police department, but Katie knew it was most likely a detective from Sacramento PD. She turned her attention to the garage, looking for video cameras and areas for the attacker to have escaped. She paused and moved toward the exit.

The detective got out of the SUV. He was handsome, medium height, muscular build, and dark crew cut with slight facial stubble. He moved with the ease of an athlete.

"Katie," said McGaven.

Katie heard an awkward pitch in her partner's voice. She turned to face him and saw the man walking toward them from the white SUV. It was Detective Evan Daniels. He had been Katie's K9 training officer when she was in the Army. They had worked a previous dual jurisdiction case in Pine Valley when Chad, Katie's ex-fiancé, had been missing, and had been thrown into some very precarious and dangerous situations together over the years.

Evan smiled at her as he approached. Katie wasn't exactly sure how she felt but realized they would most likely be working together again. She would have to stay focused. Mrs. Braxton was adamant her daughter Anna could still be alive.

Evan stopped in front of McGaven and they shook hands. "Nice to see you, McGaven."

"Same," McGaven said and nodded.

Turning to Katie, Evan said, "When I heard there was an

officer first on the scene, I couldn't believe it was the amazing Detective Katie Scott."

"Evan, nice to see you," was the only thing Katie could say. It was no secret they were attracted to one another, but seeing him at the crime scene stirred up all kinds of emotions and put her slightly off balance.

"Can you wait a moment?" said Evan.

"Of course," she said.

Evan talked with patrol officers to obtain more information for his investigation. Soon the CSI van arrived with two forensic technicians.

"So is this going to be a problem?" said McGaven quietly to his partner. He raised an eyebrow out of curiosity.

"No," she said flatly. Although, she wasn't so sure. Her life had been turned upside down recently and she was only just beginning to reroute her emotions, trying to be at peace again. Seeing Evan again made her feel uncertain and she hated that feeling. "I'll do whatever necessary to find Anna Braxton."

McGaven studied his partner closely. "I put a call into Detective Alvarez so he can forward us the reports and give any updates or leads on the girl's case."

Katie nodded. She could see in her peripheral vision that Evan was finished with the patrol officer and was approaching. He answered his cell and, by his grim expression, she knew it could only be bad news. He walked to the detectives.

"Mrs. Braxton?" she said.

"She didn't make it. Her wounds were too extensive. It was miraculous she was still alive when you found her."

Katie's mind replayed everything the woman had said to her. Even if they found Anna alive, her mom was gone. It was such a tragic situation.

"Any word on other family?" she asked.

"We're checking on that."

Katie looked away from the crime scene. She forcefully pushed off the emotions that were trying to overcome her.

"Gav has a call into the missing person's detective and requested the report. Right now it seems we're in the dark," she said.

Evan's cell phone rang again.

"Detective Daniels," he answered, and moved away from the detectives.

"You know, Katie, it wouldn't be impossible if we wanted to stay out of this case and go back to the cold cases we already have," said McGaven.

Katie looked at her partner with determination.

"I guess that's a no?" he said.

"Gav, Mrs. Braxton came to me specifically. I don't know why, but she tracked me down. This was a mother desperate to find her child. I can't turn away from this case."

McGaven nodded. "Then I'm with you a hundred and ten percent."

"I'm glad to hear you say that," said Evan. "I just got off the phone with Sheriff Scott."

Katie was surprised. How did her uncle, the sheriff at Pine Valley Sheriff's Department, get the information so quickly?

"Once I knew you were the person who found Mrs. Braxton and that she had ties to Pine Valley, I called your sheriff right away to request that we work together, pooling our resources."

"I see," she said. "Well, I have a lecture at four. I don't want to cancel at the last minute, so I'll do that and then I'm heading back to Pine Valley."

"I'll take care of some details here and then join you," said Evan. "It's going to take a bit before the autopsy results are in and the evidence is processed."

There was an awkward moment between the three detectives.

"I'll keep you informed of what I find out from the missing person's report. I'm heading back to my room," said McGaven. He gave his partner a look, indicating he had her back, before he left the scene.

"I obviously need to change," Katie said.

"What room are you in?" Evan asked.

"Four nineteen."

"I'll catch up with you before we leave," said Evan and he returned to the patrol officers, directing them to interview the security guards who'd had contact with Mrs. Braxton.

Katie took a breath and walked back to the elevator, heading to her room. When she pushed the button for the fourth floor, she looked at Mrs. Braxton's blood smeared across her fingers and palm. Katie had been under stress lately, and this situation made her feel anxious—even more than usual. Subtle symptoms from her post-traumatic stress began to surface.

Tingly hands and feet.

Shortness of breath.

Heaviness in her chest.

The trauma from her time in the Army would always be with her. It was up to Katie to work through it in every way possible. Her instincts told her this case wasn't going to be routine or straightforward; rather, it was going to be a case she couldn't prepare for.

Find the million-dollar man... you'll find my Anna...

THREE

Wednesday 1445 hours

Katie was relieved that a security guard had found her files and laptop computer in the parking garage, and had returned everything to her. Once inside the quiet solitude of her hotel room, she sat down and took slow even breaths. She began to feel better even though her mind raced with everything that happened—including seeing Evan again.

Luckily she had packed a backup change of clothes. Looking at herself in the mirror, she realized she couldn't just change her clothes and wash her hands and face; she needed to take a shower to make sure all Mrs. Braxton's blood was gone. Her faraway gaze and blood spatter across her face and hair made her appear to have walked in from a battlefield. A war she would have to fight again and again.

Katie took a quick shower and changed into fresh clothes. Her slacks and blouse were thrown into the trash. She had combed her hair and reapplied her makeup when there was a knock at the door.

It was McGaven.

"Hey, partner," he said and walked into the room. He put down his laptop and a small hotel notepad.

"What did you find out?" she said.

"More than I thought I would."

Katie pulled up a chair. "Share."

McGaven did the same as he opened the laptop. "Okay, Mrs. Stella Braxton filed a missing person's report for her daughter, Anna, eight days ago."

"Eight days?"

"Yes. And according to her, as well as Anna's best friend, Jasmine, Anna was going to the mall. When she didn't come home and no one had seen her, a few friends and Mrs. Braxton started their own search. Here's a recent school photo of Anna."

She was a pretty girl with long brown hair and bright blue eyes. Her smile was sincere and not forced.

"Is there a Mr. Braxton?" Katie asked.

"No, he is deceased. It's just been the two of them ever since Anna was two years old."

Katie thought about this. She was beginning to put together a picture that the two of them were most likely very close. It contributed to the urgency of Mrs. Braxton's behavior. She knew something was very wrong—and had wanted someone to listen to her.

"Now, their address is 217 Birch Drive. They have a small house. It's in a very quiet area."

"Did Detective Alvarez visit the house and mall?" she said.

"Yes, and did a preliminary canvass, but didn't turn up anything. He followed up as protocol. And no one has seen Anna since she left her house that day," he said. "The only family member Alvarez could find is Mrs. Braxton's sister, Lana, living in Nevada. And from that, it seems they are estranged."

"We need to start at their house," she said. "There should be all kinds of information we can glean that might help us."

"I was thinking the same thing."

Katie's cell phone rang.

"Scott," she said.

"Is McGaven with you?" said Sheriff Scott in a serious tone.

"Yes," she said and looked at her partner. "You're on speaker."

"Have you spoken with Detective Daniels?"

"Yes."

"You understand that you'll be working with SPD?"

"Yes. But that the homicide is their case jurisdiction and the missing person is ours."

"There will be overlap, of course, but I need you both on this right away."

"I'm leaving after my last presentation. We'll be back in Pine Valley before dark."

"Keep me updated."

"Copy that," she said.

"Katie?" said the sheriff with a softer tone, sounding more like her uncle than the county sheriff.

Katie waited.

"Be careful. Both of you."

"We will," she said.

"Yes, sir," said McGaven.

The call ended.

McGaven looked at his partner. "What's wrong?"

"Nothing." She glanced at her watch. "I've got to get back to the conference." She grabbed her notes and laptop.

"I'll keep digging," he said.

Katie nodded. "The last thing Mrs. Braxton said to me was 'find the million-dollar man and you'll find my Anna.' I'll see you back here in about an hour."

McGaven took quick notes. "See you in an hour."

. . .

Katie calmed her mind and focused on her presentation. She knew it backward and forward, but she was still finding it difficult to shake off the day's earlier events. On her way to the conference area, she saw it was filling up with people, huddled in groups. Making her way past them, Katie caught a few words: murder, stabbing, mother, and Katie's name. She wanted to say something to them, but it wouldn't do any good.

Katie began her presentation and it momentarily helped her to clear her mind of the attack on Stella Braxton. She needed her strength and focus to sharpen, which meant that she had to get a handle on her anxiety symptoms.

FOUR

Y

Thursday 0700 hours

Katie stood at the investigation board, which was usually filling up with information on a current case—but was now blank. She stood there wondering where the murder of Mrs. Braxton and her missing daughter Anna would take them. There were so many questions and she wasn't sure if anyone could answer them—yet. They would have to dig deep to try to find out.

"Katie?" said McGaven as he leaned inside the doorway.

The police department had limited space in the detective division, and the cold-case division was part of the forensic area downstairs, which made it quiet and conveniently close to evidence results. It worked well for Katie and McGaven.

She turned to her partner.

"Ready to go?" he said. "Detective Daniels will meet up with us later."

"Let's go." Katie followed her partner out to the parking lot.

McGaven drove, Katie remaining quiet next to him. They were headed to 217 Birch Drive, which was listed as the Braxtons' home on the report. Katie's body felt as if it was on pins and needles, and she found it difficult to relax. Hoping the Braxton home would reveal pertinent information and that they could get to the bottom of where Anna was as quickly as possible was the main objective. She wanted to get back to the cold cases.

"Okay, looks like it's..." said McGaven as he slowed the police sedan, "there." He pulled over and parked.

Katie unhooked the seat belt and readied to exit the car.

"Wait," said McGaven.

Katie looked at him.

"I know you're getting tired of hearing this... But is everything okay? Anything I need to know?"

Katie sighed. She wasn't in the mood to have an in-depth talk. "Yes. And no."

"Okay. I can live with that." He always respected his partner and her boundaries.

Katie stepped out and stood in front of the small two-bedroom home. It was one story, yellow with white trim, and shaped like a square. The front yard had freshly planted flowers that were drooping from the lack of water, but the colorful blooms in purple, white, and yellow still brightened the area. The weather was overcast and the wind nonexistent, making the home look even more deserted.

McGaven gestured to the next-door neighbor. There was a woman in an oversized denim shirt and beige pants, stooped over planting annual bulbs and ground cover during the fall so they would bloom in the spring. She looked to be in her sixties but moved like a much younger person. Katie decided to talk to her.

"Hello," she called as she made her way over to the woman's yard.

The woman stood up, watching Katie and McGaven approach. "Yes?"

"I'm Detective Scott and this is my partner, Detective McGaven. We're from Pine Valley Sheriff's Department."

"Detectives?" she said. Her face clouded as if bracing for bad news. "It's about the Braxtons, isn't it?"

"What makes you say that?" said Katie as she tried to gauge the woman's sincerity. She had a hunch the neighbor knew quite a bit about the mother and daughter.

"Anna went missing over a week ago."

Katie calmed her nerves. "I'm sorry to say Mrs. Braxton was attacked at a conference center in Sacramento yesterday—and she succumbed to her injuries."

"Oh," the woman said as she tried to catch her breath. "How? I mean why?" She fought back tears, clearly shaken.

"We're investigating the case. What's your name?"

"Clara Taylor."

"Mrs. Taylor, can we ask you a few questions?"

"Of course. But I don't know what I can tell you that I haven't already told the other detective. A Detective Alvarez."

"Sacramento PD is investigating Mrs. Braxton's murder and we're here to find Anna," Katie said. She proceeded gently. "When was the last time you saw Anna?"

"Eight days ago. I saw her leave with her backpack. I learned later she was heading to the mall."

"The mall is quite a ways to walk," said Katie.

"She was walking to Jasmine's house for a ride. It wasn't unusual. But Jasmine never saw Anna that day."

"When did Mrs. Braxton begin looking for her?" said McGaven.

"I don't remember the exact time, but it was before dark. I guess around five thirty or six."

"It was a Wednesday?"

The neighbor nodded. "I think so."

"Why wasn't Anna in school?"

"It was a parent-teachers' conference last week."

"So where was Mrs. Braxton?"

"She was working until four. At a small accounting office."

Katie glanced around and could imagine Anna wanting to get out with her friends. The area was very quiet and most likely boring to a teenager.

"Thank you, Mrs. Taylor," Katie said, handing the woman her business card. "I'm sure we will have more questions, but we need to get inside the home now. We don't want to damage anything, but since the death of the owner it's exigent circumstances."

"Oh, you'll find a key under the blue pot on the front porch," she said. "Please... whatever I can do to help."

"Thank you," said McGaven.

The detectives walked to the residence and Katie quickly spotted the blue pot. There was a single house key underneath. She took a moment to look around, but nothing seemed out of place or disturbed. The curtains and blinds were down, so they couldn't see inside the small dwelling.

Katie and McGaven pulled on their gloves to protect any potential evidence. Katie was just about to unlock the front door when she stopped. She looked to the neighbor's yard and Mrs. Taylor.

"What's wrong?" said McGaven.

"I don't know. Let's take a look around back first."

McGaven didn't hesitate to follow his partner. They had been through so much together—they trusted each other implicitly.

Katie felt something was off. Perhaps it was her own rising anxieties and feelings masking their investigation, but she always followed her instincts. The house was locked up tight and quiet. She would rather be overreacting than not paying attention to potential subtle clues or ruining potential evidence. This case was more than troubling, with a teenager who had gone missing and then her mother brutally murdered.

She knew they were only seeing a snippet of what was going on.

Fine gravel crunched under the detectives' footsteps as they made their way along a narrow pathway to the backyard. A tall wood-plank gate appeared to have been replaced recently with new wood and a latch, which was closed. Katie touched the handle release, pressing it slightly, and found it was secured. The small backyard had a little deck and more flowerpots. There was a four-foot-wide square patch of lawn in the corner. This area too appeared to be clean and well taken care of.

She walked up onto the deck looking for a doggie door but there wasn't one. The back entry was just a single door with a two-foot glass window at the top. Peering inside, Katie saw it led into the kitchen and dining area. Everything seemed fine upon first inspection.

Katie looked down and noticed that along the lower frame of the door was a red dried substance. There were claw marks consistent with a small dog wanting to come inside. She didn't know for sure, but the red areas did look like dried blood. When she turned to McGaven, he was scanning the backyard still.

"You feel it?" she said. Not quite knowing how to describe the unease she felt.

He nodded and spoke softly. "It's almost as if someone is watching us. Kinda creepy..."

Katie inserted the key and it fit into the back door lock. It was common for people to have all doors fitted for the same key. She looked at McGaven and then turned the knob and pushed open the door. Taking a step inside, the interior was cool, giving Katie a shiver. Across the linoleum, there were dark-red droplets leading to the other room.

McGaven tapped Katie on the shoulder, signaling for her to be cautious as they quickly searched the house. She nodded.

Katie followed the trail of blood toward the bedrooms, and McGaven took the other direction to the living room area.

Katie wanted to assess everything before they began searching for information. She could imagine Mrs. Braxton and her daughter living here, but now it felt as if they had simply vanished into thin air. She saw neatly folded laundry in a basket on top of the washer, and the first bedroom, which appeared to be Mrs. Braxton's, was neat and tidy like the rest of the house; the bed made, and the curtains pulled tightly shut. On the low dresser were photographs in silver frames of Mrs. Braxton, Anna, and what looked to be family and friends.

The next door before the second bedroom was closed. She figured it was the bathroom. She opened the door to find a small single bathroom with a sink, toilet, and a shower with a crazy cow-pattern curtain pulled across. Two rings were missing from the hooks, making it flop unevenly.

She could hear McGaven moving around in the living room as she stood there for a moment staring at the curtain. Down the side of the wall were small dark droplets. She slowly raised her hand and touched the shower curtain, gripped it, and pulled it across the bar.

Katie stepped back as her breath caught in her throat. She half expected something or someone to be present, but it was empty.

FIVE

Katie was staring at the shower and tub.

"I found an appointment book and dates that might—" said McGaven as he walked in.

Katie turned to her partner and snapped out of her trance. "Call in forensics ASAP," she said. "I want to search Anna's room to try and find out where she went or who she met—and we need to track Mrs. Braxton's last days. I know it's Daniel's case but..."

Katie was already headed to the girl's bedroom when her cell phone chimed with a text from Evan Daniels.

Just received cell phone records for Stella and Anna. Will catch up.

She shared it with McGaven.

"Okay," said McGaven as he coordinated with forensics to come to the house.

Katie entered Anna's room. She could still hear McGaven talking with John Blackburn, updating him on the situation.

Anna had a typical teenage girl's bedroom. There were posters of young cute actors and current bands on the walls. The twin bed had a rose-pink comforter that had been neatly made with two throw pillows. A soft teddy bear with a pink bow was tucked between them. There was a nightstand with a frilly lampshade, but the surface was clear. It was obvious Anna took after her mother when it came to keeping things neat and organized. A small desk had a bookshelf component above filled with trinkets, photos, and pink pens with feathers. There was a jewelry box with a decoupage photo of Anna and a blonde girl that Katie assumed to be her best friend, Jasmine. They would know soon enough when they questioned the girl.

Katie opened the box, but there were only earrings and necklaces that didn't seem to be significant. She continued around the room opening drawers, running her hands underneath surfaces, looking behind furniture, and then looking between the mattress and box spring. Her fingertips touched a small book. Pulling it out, she saw it was a journal with a colorful balloon design on the cover.

Katie remained standing as she thumbed through Anna's diary. There were large printed words, some in all caps while others were underlined. The entries were basically about the same things. It seemed that Anna was unhappy with her life: she didn't get to do what she wanted, her mom was too strict. Her dream was to become a model and actress, but it was clearly stated that no one supported her. She never wrote anything really negative about her mom, just that she felt her mother didn't understand her.

Katie kept reading and nothing seemed to catch her attention. It was the usual teenage complaints and pains that everyone went through. She was disappointed Anna hadn't referred to anything specific about the million-dollar man her mother had named, but there were mentions of "MDM." And there was nothing that indicated where she was going the day she disappeared. Katie read her last entry, two days before she was supposed to go to the mall with Jasmine.

> *I want to do MORE. Why won't <u>anyone</u> listen to me? T.S. and J. talk behind my back making <u>fun of me</u>. Why would they do that?*

McGaven stood at the doorway. "Anything?"

"Found Anna's journal. Nothing specific to where she might have been going—the usual teenage angst. But we need to document it as evidence. How far off are forensics?"

"John's ETA is about half an hour."

Katie nodded. "I'm going to keep searching here."

McGaven disappeared, and she heard him moving around in Mrs. Braxton's room.

Katie continued her systematic search around Anna's room, even checking if there were secret stash areas around the baseboards, rugs, clothing pockets, and every nook and cranny she could find.

Nothing.

She went to the kitchen. From previous searching experience, where there were secrets, she would often find notes and important paperwork in the kitchen. Whether the secret item was hidden in drawers or cookbooks, it was a place many women would hide things.

Katie opened drawers and was surprised that Mrs. Braxton hadn't organized them like she had the rest of the house. Everything was in disarray. But she then realized that they had already been searched. The counter had been left messy with things out of place; the small appliances, like the toaster, shoved back in a cockeyed position; the utility and knife holder seemed to be missing some items.

"Gav," she called. "I think someone has been here..."

Her partner joined her in the kitchen.

"I think someone was here searching... for something. The drawers are disorganized and things are shoved to the back. The rest of the house is so tidy," she said. "What were they looking for? A random burglar wouldn't have taken the time to push the drawers back in."

"I noticed the same with Mrs. Braxton's dresser drawers."

"Whoever was here made sure to be careful the house looked neat." Katie glanced around. "We need everything dusted for prints."

"And they seemed to take some time too while they were here," he said. "What's the motive?"

"A warning? Revenge?"

"Anna goes missing. Her mother is brutally killed. Someone must've been watching her to follow her all the way to the conference. Unless it was random... which I don't think it was."

"We have to go back to before Anna disappeared and see who they might've come in contact with," she said.

"The cell phone records should tell us something."

Katie looked around the kitchen once more. "Let's finish the preliminary search before John gets here."

"On it." He looked at his partner. "Do you think it might be someone close like a neighbor, since there's a hidden key? It wouldn't take someone very long to find it."

"Right now, we can't trust anyone surrounding this family... and can't rule anyone out."

SIX

Katie and McGaven were on their way back to the Pine Valley Sheriff's Department. The partners remained quiet, each rolling the events through their minds. Katie gazed out the car window as she tried to make sense of everything—attempting to begin to put pieces of the puzzle together.

Her thoughts were interrupted by her cell phone ringing.

"Scott," she said.

"I think we've found Anna Braxton," said Detective Alvarez.

Katie put her phone on speaker. "Where?"

The detective hesitated. "The body of a teenage girl matching her description was found in the basement of a house in a small town in Bright Valley that burned down."

Katie's energy sank. There had still been hope of finding the teen alive. "When was she found?"

McGaven's expression changed. He too was heavy-hearted.

"I received a call from the Pine Valley Fire Department about half an hour ago," Alvarez said.

"Who owns the house?" she said.

"I'm tracking that down, but it looks like some type of company."

"Did anything connect the Braxtons to it?"

"No. I'm here now. Can you and McGaven get here? I'm sending the address."

Katie nodded to McGaven. "We're on our way." She ended the call. The address came in and she relayed to her partner: "1133 Old Stagecoach Road."

McGaven thought for a moment. "I know the area." He found a safe place to turn the sedan around.

"I'm going to text Detective Daniels to let him know our plans have changed," Katie said.

It was difficult to concentrate. Now they were headed to Anna's final resting place.

"You okay?" said McGaven.

"I will be."

"This case..."

"Is going to be difficult to get through..."

After twenty minutes, the detectives drove up a steep windy driveway. As they climbed, the hillside was sharply vertical in places, as if someone had plowed through a mountain, and there were areas of erosion due to previous heavy rainfall.

"Looks like some serious acreage," said McGaven.

"And not a convenient location," Katie said.

They finally reached the top of the property, where the land leveled out. There were still fire rescue vehicles, patrol cars, and an unmarked police sedan. All the vehicles were fanned out around a moderate-size house, which was now almost completely reduced to rubble. There were some beams, interior walls with doors, as well as a brick fireplace still remaining. The smoke from the fire had dissipated, settling in the trees and leaving the area with a haze around the property. Some nearby branches had been scorched. The ground had deep divots from where equipment had been dragged and firefighter boots trampled. Water still dripped in places, causing a faint mist of steam to rise.

"Wow, complete loss," said McGaven.

"This seems like a very secluded place, perfect to hold someone hostage. No one would hear any noise or see anyone coming and going," said Katie. "There won't be much forensic evidence left. Except maybe about how the fire was started."

She was already putting together in her mind a checklist of everything they needed to know. The main question, if it was Anna Braxton's body in the basement, was how and why she crossed paths with the person who brought her there. They needed to follow the trail if it wasn't already too cold.

Katie stepped out of the police sedan and was immediately hit with the smell of burnt wood mixed with heavy forest odors. She could feel residual heat on her skin even though the initial fire had been extinguished. She scanned the area. It was quiet except for a conversation between two of the first responders. She didn't see Detective Alvarez yet.

Looking for the person who was in charge, Katie noticed a white SUV with "PVFD Arson Investigator K9 Unit" and she immediately thought of Chad. Her fiancé had left Pine Valley to pursue his career in arson investigation in Los Angeles. It pained her. There wasn't a day she didn't think about him. They were supposed to be married, but their differing life choices broke them apart.

Katie pushed her emotions aside; they had a job to do.

Detective Alvarez appeared with a small notebook. He worked missing persons. He was short and stocky, and sweating from the heat or out of stress. Hurrying toward the detectives, he paused a moment and spoke with a man who seemed to be the arson investigator.

There was a roar from the large fire truck as it revved into motion and slowly began to vacate the property, leaving a few vehicles behind. Katie had wanted to talk with the fire captain, but she would have to read a report or hear the details from Alvarez.

"Detectives," said Alvarez.

McGaven nodded.

"What do we have?" Katie asked.

"It appears the fire was set intentionally. The girl we believe to be Anna Braxton is in the basement, which is completely intact. We don't know how long she had been there or what was the cause of death, but the smoke inhalation would have killed her if she wasn't already deceased. The ME's office and John are en route."

Katie wanted to see the area immediately, so she started to head to the ruins. An arson investigator carrying a gun pushed his way to the group, stopping them.

"This isn't your investigation, Detectives. You're here as a courtesy due to your missing person case and to view the area with the body," said the man. He was tall and fit, with sandy hair and dark penetrating eyes. He didn't seem to mind staring intensely at the detectives and gave the impression he was used to giving orders.

"Detectives Scott and McGaven, this is Arson Investigator Luke Ames. He also heads the bomb squad K9 unit," said Alvarez.

"I didn't know Pine Valley Fire Department had a K9 bomb unit," said Katie. She glanced toward the SUV and saw a decal on the vehicle that read "K9 Blitz."

"I just transferred in from Red Bluff. Lateral," said Ames. He eyed the detectives curiously. "So is it true what I've been hearing about you?"

"Hearing what?" said Katie. She immediately didn't like the alpha-male attitude, but she kept her cool, wanting to access the crime scene. She had met many men like him when she was in the Army and knew the best way to handle them was to keep her wits and do her job.

The arson investigator smiled and kept her gaze. "Your perfect record of solved cold cases. Is that true?"

"That's correct," said McGaven. It was clear he didn't particularly like the investigator's attitude either and he took a step forward, closing the gap between them.

"Impressive. Just checking. You know how gossip can be." Ames matched McGaven's gentle challenge and stood his ground. "The truth always seems to get convoluted one way or another."

Katie didn't want to push the situation any further. They would have to work with the investigator, especially if they had questions about the fire, so she kept her comments to herself. She didn't want there to be any problems getting in the way of her work.

"What's your preliminary assessment of the fire?" she said, hoping to move things along.

"Follow me," said Ames, turning and heading directly to the site.

As the detectives and investigator headed to the burned-out house, there was a deep bark from Ames' vehicle.

"Is Blitz a German shepherd?" said Katie.

"Czech shepherd," said Ames. It was clear he didn't want to engage in any more chitchat or talk about his dog.

Katie kept quiet.

Tension filled the air.

As she stepped into what was once a home, she could see large dark circular areas. There were interior doors along one side that she assumed to be where the bedrooms were located. The doors had big holes in them, making Katie wonder if the fire had caused them or if they had been made intentionally.

"Here's the main area where the accelerant was used," said

Ames. "I photographed the areas and took samples. Final results will be forthcoming."

"What's with the doors?" she said.

"Good eye, Detective. Many arsonists break holes in doors and walls to cause the fire to spread quickly throughout the building—basically in hopes that it will completely destroy the structure," he said. "Which it never does... there's always something left behind."

"I don't see any furniture," said McGaven.

"Correct. The house seemed to be empty, with the exception of the built-in appliances." He directed the detectives' attention to a refrigerator and stove.

Katie thought it was unusual that whoever was holding the teen hadn't stayed here.

"Everything has already been documented in the house," said Ames. "Your department will receive our report when it's completed." He walked to an area where there was a perfect square opening approximately three-foot across. The investigator donned a pair of gloves as precaution and moved the door. "I caution you, be careful where you step. Even though we've briefly checked it, there still could be weak spots. Once we found the body we called you."

Katie and McGaven quickly pulled on gloves as well. Alvarez stayed behind making notes.

Katie glanced at the investigator, who seemed to watch her with curiosity. She cautiously stepped into the area, feeling the first and second steps. The air was stale and permeated with the stench of decomposition. She tried to breathe shallowly. She glanced behind her.

Investigator Ames, almost as if he'd read her mind, handed her a flashlight.

"Thanks," she said. Katie flipped on the light and it immediately lit up the cavern below. She turned to McGaven. "Let me

get down there first." She knew that the stairs might be weakened with the weight of both detectives.

He nodded. It was standard when they worked a crime
scene. Katie would enter first and then they would work the
areas together.

Slowly descending the squeaky staircase, Katie reached the
bottom of the nine steps. The temperature drastically dropped,
making her skin cold and clammy. Even though the environment was cool, the air stank and it was heavy and stagnant,
pressing against her chest. Her lungs worked harder to get
oxygen, causing her to move slower. She swung the beam of
light around the small basement. It looked to be a type of cold
storage with a brick liner. Most likely a root cellar that was once
used to store various canned and jarred items.

Katie's gaze then fell on the teenager lying on the dirt floor
on her back, her right arm above her head as if she were merely
sleeping. The girl's head was turned slightly to the right. The
contrast of the yellow dress she was wearing made her look
otherworldly. Long dark hair fanned above her head, accentuating her obviously broken neck. Vertebrae were visible, poking
through the skin. Her bare feet and lower legs were darkened
and bloody. Her body was already beginning the putrefaction
stage, with dark areas of purplish skin, and would soon expand
with bodily gases, making it highly probable she was dead
before the fire. It also made it difficult to see if there were any
other injuries, so they would have to wait until the autopsy was
performed.

Katie glanced up, expecting to see McGaven, but he wasn't
hovering at the opening. Rather, he was waiting for her a few
steps from the entrance, while she conducted a preliminary
search. It was very quiet. She didn't hear any voices from above
—not even the assertive investigator. No sounds from outside. It
was as if she was in a soundproof room underground—an
unnerving perception.

Katie moved from where she was standing, just after the last stair. She continued to sweep the flashlight around the walls, floor, and then up the stairs behind her. If she had to make a first quick theory it would be that the girl fell backward down the stairs, breaking her neck—and then she was left where she had landed. The fire was most likely after the fact—in hopes of getting rid of the evidence.

Katie saw what appeared to be claw marks around the walls and wondered if they were all from Anna—or were there others before her? They would need to bag her hands as well as take samples from the walls. What made the kidnapper decide to cut and run, eliminating Anna, and possibly her mother, as well as destroying the house? Forensics needed to document the area and gather any evidence of fingerprints or fluids connecting Anna or others.

Taking a slow deep breath and steadying her nerves, Katie moved forward, directing the flashlight closer to the body. She felt slightly lightheaded but she knew it would soon pass when she was outside again. She retrieved her cell phone and swiped to a photograph of Anna Braxton from the missing person's report. A beautiful sixteen-year-old girl with long brown hair and a beautiful smile was compared to the body lying in the underground basement of a burned-down house. It wasn't an official notification, but Katie knew. The body in the cellar was Anna Braxton.

After returning her phone to her pocket, Katie stood a moment, staring at Anna. It was difficult for her because she thought of the girl's mother dying in her arms only a day earlier.

She heard the sound of footsteps coming down the stairs. Katie turned, expecting to see McGaven, but it was Investigator Ames instead.

"You get everything you need?" he said. It seemed he was asking more out of curiosity than ordering her to move along. The flashlight illumination made the investigator appear different—almost macabre. His dark eyes appeared sunken and he seemed taller and larger in the weird lighting.

"Not yet," Katie said. She knelt down next to Anna. It was difficult, but she needed to take a closer look before the ME's office took the body.

She heard the investigator move closer.

"Please," she said. "This is a crime scene. The fewer people the better." She was surprised by how curt she sounded and hadn't meant for her tone to be that way.

"First, this is my crime scene—" he began.

"No, what the fire left behind is your crime scene," she said. "This... is the sheriff's department's crime scene—homicide or not."

Katie heard the investigator sigh and could almost feel the tension of his annoyance, but she had a job to do. He still didn't leave. Not wanting to say anything else, she scrutinized Anna's dress. There was something beneath Anna's left shoulder. Carefully uncovering something plastic, Katie revealed a small sandwich bag with what looked like parts of a sandwich. Leaning closer, she could see a small water bottle and more remnants of a sandwich. The kidnapper must've supplied Anna with some food—small amounts. It meant that they wanted to keep her alive. Why? For how long? Would he have eventually let her go?

Katie stood up, not wanting to disturb any more evidence. She faced the staircase. "Gav," she called. "We need John to document this entire area before they remove the body."

"He's leaving Eva to finish up at the Braxtons' house. He's about twenty minutes out," said McGaven from above.

It annoyed Katie that Ames was still standing in the same place. "We need to let forensics do their job," she said.

"Of course," said Ames.

"We need to go back up," she said. Her voice sounded strange to her. The air had been sucked out of the cellar. Katie was finding it difficult to breathe and she wondered how Anna could have stayed alive down here. There had to be some type of way for air to...

Katie wavered, falling forward, grabbing the stairs to try and steady herself.

"Whoa... slow down, Detective. Just take slow breaths," said Ames.

Katie was trying to, but it was as if her body had already taken up all the air. She was dizzy. The staircase warped in her vision. Her arms and legs felt as if she had been tethered to cement blocks. She fought the urge to faint. There was a slight movement of airflow coming from above, but it didn't seem to help or give her any relief.

"I..." she said. "It's just..."

"I gotcha," said Ames as he wrapped his arms around her waist, squeezing gently, and assisted her back up the stairs.

"Katie?" said McGaven. "Are you all right?"

"C'mon," said the investigator as he picked up Katie and carried her out of the burned-out house.

The outdoor air was still smoky, but it gave Katie some relief and gradually she began to feel better. "You can put me down." She was embarrassed and tried to brush it off.

McGaven was at his partner's side. He assisted Katie back to their police sedan and had her sit down in the passenger's side.

She felt better as her strength came back. "I felt like I couldn't breathe." Then she said, "It's her... no doubt... it's Anna. But I don't understand how she could survive down there if there wasn't air coming in from somewhere..."

"Maybe I can explain that," said Ames. He handed Katie a bottle of water. "Sometimes when there are fires like this anything outside like vents, plumbing, or outlets get blocked from debris and heat. I think that's what happened with the cellar—there will be some kind of vent or vents to the outside somewhere."

"I didn't see any," she said.

"They'll be there, no matter how small," said Ames. He watched her with curiosity.

Katie drank some water and it was the best feeling, helping to refresh her. She gestured to the bottle. "Thanks." She thought about what the investigator had said about the vents—it made sense. "John should be updated about this development for his search."

Detective Alvarez approached them with a serious look on his face. "I just got a call that Anna Braxton's best friend, Jasmine MacAfee... has gone missing."

SEVEN

Thursday 1445 hours

Katie and McGaven immediately left the fire location and headed to the MacAfee residence. There was nothing more they could do at the moment from the burned-out house. Forensics needed to do their job and Investigator Ames would be updating them about the fire accelerants' results when they became available.

The detectives had already planned to visit Jasmine's house to speak to her, but now it was imperative to see if they could catch the trail before it went cold—it could be the key to finding out what had happened to Anna and how she ended up in that cellar. This particular case was complex and there were other agencies that Katie and McGaven had to coordinate with. Was it going to hamper their investigation by slowing it down? Or was it going to strengthen it? Katie contemplated this as they hurried to Jasmine's home to get some answers.

Katie rode shotgun once again—she usually drove, but since she was still feeling a little bit weaker than normal, she was fine riding instead of driving.

"How are you feeling?" said McGaven as if he had read her thoughts.

"I'm fine, really."

"So Investigator Ames seems like an unusual guy."

Katie laughed. "If you mean arrogant, pushy, and a know-it-all, then yes, he's an unusual guy."

"I wasn't expecting an arson investigator like him. All the fire department guys are really cool... and... oh... I'm so sorry, Katie."

"It's okay, Gav. Our job is going to be connected with the fire department sometimes and it does makes me think of Chad... but I have to be okay with that," she said. It did bother her, but she was determined to work through it, and she didn't want McGaven to worry about her.

There were a few quiet moments between the detectives before McGaven chuckled and said, "I thought it was cute when Ames carried you out of the burned building..."

"I know, what was up with that?" Katie couldn't help but laugh. "I wasn't going to fight him."

"A detective being carried from a crime scene... now that's something new," he said.

Katie chose to stay optimistic about them solving the case, but it was difficult to stay that way after seeing Mrs. Braxton and Anna.

"Okay, this looks like the house," said McGaven. He parked in front of the modest home.

Katie got out and looked around. There were toys strewn across the front yard—bicycles lying on their sides along with various bats, balls, nets, and clothes. The air was fresh and she could smell the pine trees. She took a moment to take several deep breaths, hoping it would shake the memory of the stagnant cellar and the smell of death.

She followed McGaven to the front door, noticing that her strength had returned and her body felt recharged.

Before the detectives reached the front door, a large friendly brown-and-black dog met them. Katie pets the dog, thinking about her dog Cisco at home. She knew her uncle would check in on him. Cisco was a black German shepherd that came home with her from the military. They were both Army veterans and Katie didn't know what she would do without him.

McGaven knocked on the door. Within a minute, an attractive dark-haired woman answered. Her face was drawn and it was obvious she was worried about her daughter.

"Mrs. MacAfee?" said Katie.

The woman nodded.

"I'm Detective Scott and this is my partner, Detective McGaven, from the Pine Valley Sheriff's Department. We're here about your daughter, Jasmine. May we come in?"

"Of course," she said quietly.

The detectives entered the home and moved to the living room. It was quite different than the extremely tidy Braxtons' house. Three sofas had toys, books, and clothes scattered around them. There were plates and glasses pushed to the middle of the coffee table.

"I'm sorry," said Mrs. MacAfee as she quickly tidied up so the detectives could sit down.

"Where are your other children?" Katie asked. It was quiet in the house.

"I sent them over to the neighbor's. My husband is still at work." She had a difficult time holding the detectives' gaze.

Katie wondered if there was something else about the family that they needed to know. "Mrs. McAfee, I know you already gave Detective Alvarez information for the missing person's report. Can you please tell us what happened in your own words?" she said, wanting to gain a rapport with the upset mother.

"Jasmine was supposed to get ready for a dentist appointment this morning at eight thirty, and when she hadn't come downstairs, I went up to see what was taking her so long." The woman was clearly trying hard not to cry. "But... when I went upstairs, Jasmine was gone. Her backpack, keys, and I'm not sure what else. No note or anything."

"What do you mean, gone?" said McGaven.

"Gone... Her bed was made, but it was as if she hadn't slept in it. She's never done anything like this before."

"When was the last time you saw Jasmine?" said Katie.

"At dinner last night... around seven."

Katie asked, "Did she seem like her usual self or was something bothering her?"

"No, she can be quiet, but she seemed like she always does." Mrs. MacAfee stood up and began absently folding clothes.

Katie felt bad for the mother, but she still couldn't dismiss her sense that there was something more to this story. "Mrs. MacAfee, I know Jasmine was good friends with Anna Braxton."

"Oh yes, they've been friends since the first grade."

Katie didn't want to tell her that Anna was dead because it wasn't official nor was it her place to do so. Instead she asked, "They were close?"

"Closer than sisters."

"Did Jasmine ever tell you about Anna's life?" said Katie.

"What do you mean?"

"Like her hopes or dreams. Boyfriends. Things like that."

"It was no secret both girls wanted to be actresses. They had been in school plays for as long as I can remember."

Katie glanced to her partner and then shifted her weight. "Where do you think Jasmine might have gone?"

"I... don't know..."

"Where did she like to go? The park, mall, to get a burger? Anything that might help us."

"Well, the girls spent a lot of time at the mall. They liked to meet other friends there, eat, and hang out."

Katie watched Mrs. McAfee, who seemed more nervous than concerned.

"Would it be okay if we looked at Jasmine's room?" Katie asked.

"Oh. Yes, of course." She went to the stairs and waited for the detectives.

Jasmine's room was at the end of the hall. Katie and McGaven opened the door and stepped inside. Katie closed the door and could hear Mrs. MacAfee walk back down the stairs.

McGaven pulled gloves out of his pocket and handed a pair to Katie. "Just in case... I'll take the left side," he said.

Katie pulled on her gloves, noticing her partner's somber face.

Jasmine's room was different than Anna's. There were brightly colored bins stacked with stuffed animals, books, and other miscellany. The bed was made just as Mrs. MacAfee had stated, it had a pink and purple comforter and white ruffled pillows. There was a nightstand with a lamp that had a shade with stars cut out of it, to project onto the walls, as well as a box of Kleenex, a beaded necklace, and two pens. On a small bookcase in the corner there were some books, but mostly framed photographs. There was one of Anna and Jasmine smiling with what appeared to be an amusement park in the background. Katie used her cell phone to document the photo. She took note that Jasmine was blonde with long hair and bangs. The girls' appearances almost the direct opposite of one another.

McGaven was searching the closet and checking pockets of various articles of clothing.

"Anything?" said Katie.

"Nothing yet."

One thing that struck Katie was that there weren't any photos or posters of boys. There was no indication of boyfriends or other friends apart from Anna. She searched drawers, under the mattress, and various other cubbyholes. Nothing telling or unusual.

Katie suddenly felt a wave of anxiety wash over her. Looking down at her hands, she saw for a brief instant Mrs. Braxton's blood. The image shook her but disappeared as soon as it had appeared. She looked at her partner, but he was busy searching and didn't notice her brief episode. Continuing to shake off the ill feelings running through her body, she refocused, combing through the room.

"Have you seen a laptop or cell phone?" she said, aware her voice sounded different to usual.

"No."

"There wasn't one in Anna's room either. Seems strange," she said.

"It does. What are you thinking?" McGaven said.

"It's beginning to look like the rooms have been sanitized. You know, like certain items have been removed. Backpack, journal, phone, any electronic devices."

"Except for the journal you found in Anna's room. We don't know for sure if that was her main journal or just a venting one."

Katie nodded and continued to look around. "But why?" She looked at several photos of the girls, dressed up and wearing a lot of makeup.

"I noticed that you didn't ask Mrs. MacAfee about the 'million-dollar man,'" McGaven said.

"No. I doubt she would know—even if she did, I don't think she would say anything. Just my gut thinking. I want to do more research and see if that description pops up again."

Katie spotted a cute porcelain dog on the shelf. She picked it up and saw a folded piece of yellowish paper beneath. Carefully opening it, she saw the name "A-1 Talent Agency" and below it "auditions."

"Gav," she said, "I think we have our first clue." She showed the stub to her partner. "I can't quite make out the address. Maybe John can use some alternative light sources."

"I'm sure he can. Usually when people use 'A' or 'I' in the name of a business it's so that their name comes up first in searches."

"What about Anna's journal entry: 'Why won't anyone listen to me? T.S. and J. talk behind my back making fun of me. Why would they do that?' Is 'J' Jasmine?"

"It seems likely, but we can't know for sure without more proof."

"We have to tread carefully. And not make assumptions, even if it seems reasonable." Katie took more photos, panning around the room, using the doorway as a reference point. She didn't know if it might be useful later on. "We have a place to start."

"I'll check phone records and social media," McGaven said.

"And we need to do background checks on the parents. There has to be something we're not being told," she said.

It was typical that McGaven did the background computer work and Katie did interviews and profiles. That was why their partnership worked so well.

Both their phones received a text message at the same time.

"It's Daniels," she said.

"Yep."

"We need to get back and regroup." She made a sour face.

"You should be happy there's three of us working these cases. Not to mention Alvarez too."

"True. But things always seem to get more complicated with two jurisdictions."

"Is that the only reason?" he said, smiling at her.

"Really?" Katie didn't want to have a conversation with her partner about how she felt about Daniels.

"Just trying to keep things interesting."

EIGHT

Katie and McGaven arrived back at Pine Valley Sheriff's Department. They made their way to the forensic division, where they'd been told Detective Daniels was waiting for them. It was quiet when they entered, which seemed strange to Katie because whenever there was someone visiting they were usually talking with John. But the forensic supervisor and technician were busy with the two crime scenes, and they found the Sacramento detective in their investigation room instead.

"Detectives, I hope you don't mind, but I started to map out the investigation on your board," said Detective Daniels.

Katie was a little annoyed at that. "Who let you in here?" she said.

"The sergeant came down to let me in... since I've been here before and we're working together," he said.

"Okay," she managed to say. She silently berated herself as she noticed how handsome he was.

"Awesome," said McGaven. He went to the investigation board where they would lay out their working cases chronologically. There were already photographs up of Mrs. Braxton and the crime scene from the conference center parking garage. "How did you get the photos so quickly?"

"The crime scene tech at SPD sent them to my email," Daniels said. "I brought my laptop and borrowed your printer. I hope you don't mind." He looked at the detectives, but his gaze settled on Katie.

"No, of course not," Katie said.

"Whatever keeps the investigation moving," said McGaven.

Katie updated Daniels on what they had found at the Braxton home and their conversation with Mrs. MacAfee. "John and Eva are still working the scenes at the burned-down house as well as the Braxton residence," she said.

Daniels had made notes on the board. It showed the crime scene for Mrs. Braxton, which included an overall view, nearby areas, and then a rough outline of where she had fallen. Even though the body had been taken by ambulance, the vivid imagery left in Katie's mind was just as disturbing. There were also preliminary notes from the medical examiner's office stating it was a homicide and the victim died as the result of hypovolemic shock due to massive bleeding.

"What do you think?" said Daniels.

"I'm wondering what kind of weapon was used. What type of knife? How did the killer come and go? Did they wait? Were they stalking Mrs. Braxton?" she said. "I'm still waiting on the video from the garage, but after assessing where the cameras were located when I was there... there are definite blind areas." She continued to study everything on the board.

"Okay," said McGaven. He had been scanning the cell phone records that had been left on the desk. "There are many calls to Anna's cell phone from the same number."

"Who is it?" said Katie moving closer to see the report.

"Unfortunately, it's a burner phone. No ID. No way to trace. And I'm sure it's been discarded by now, so we won't be able to find out which cell tower it's pinging from," said McGaven.

"No, but it gives us a pattern of behavior. Look at how many times Anna was called. And they were long—twenty, thirty minutes each—and then closer to the time she had disappeared they got much shorter. One, two, and five minutes," she said.

"What do you make of it?" said Daniels.

"That whoever was calling and talking to Anna was friendly, or at least made her think they were a friend, because of the amount of time they chatted. The times were consistent, this one at 10:30 a.m. and then after 4 p.m. Most of the calls were around these times. And then with the short call, it might mean that they were finalizing something, where to meet, for example."

"Okay," said Daniels. He began to write notes to that effect on the board.

Katie thought about the calls. "What about Jasmine?"

"We should have her cell records in a day or so," said McGaven.

Katie was frustrated and concerned that Jasmine might be being held somewhere. "We also need to do a background into Mr. and Mrs. MacAfee. And"—she thought some more—"make sure to find out if there're any family issues."

"Like?" said McGaven.

"Any police calls, domestic, juvenile issues, anything that might raise a red flag. We need to know what's going on with the family. Mrs. MacAfee was hiding something."

"On it."

"I also want to know what Anna was doing her last few days before disappearing," she said. "And the significance of the house at 1133 Old Stagecoach Road where Anna was found."

Katie's cell phone rang.

"Detective Scott."

"It's Alvarez. We just canvassed Jasmine's neighborhood

and the mall. Nothing, except some of the vendors remember seeing both girls over the last month or so."

"Okay, thanks, Alvarez. We have a possible lead on a talent agency that might have some answers."

"Keep me posted."

The call ended.

Katie opened her laptop. She typed in *A-1 Talent Agency*. A few agencies came up across the US. She then made her search more specific: *A-1 Talent search models teens Pine Valley*. This time she got a result saying: *Pine Valley Mall models wanted. Begin your career.* "Looks like that talent agency Jasmine had written down did a model search at the mall. Could be a good place to start."

"Okay, since the forensics results are going to take a bit. We need to scour the mall and try to ascertain if Anna was there the day or day before she went missing. And see if cameras can place her there," said Katie.

"I'm going to keep digging," said McGaven.

"I'll go with you," said Daniels.

Katie still was hesitant about working with him, but the cases dictated they needed to spearhead it. Her nerves were on high alert, causing her to be anxious and short-tempered—that wasn't where she wanted to be so she pushed herself to move forward.

"Okay." She looked at the time. "We need to go to the mall before it gets too late. I don't want to wait until tomorrow."

NINE

The faded drapes were pulled tightly across the large windows, making the room dark and dingy. Along one side of the curtains a tiny stream of sunlight peeked through and shot across the room as a spear of brightness. Dust particles swirled around in the string of light.

The living room was cramped with an old antique sofa, which had been beautiful at one time, with an emerald velvet cover and intricately carved wooden arms and back. Now, it was grubby, dusty, and threadbare. Another antique chair sat in the corner near bags of garbage tied up neatly.

No carpet remained. A simple beige rug had been laid over the worn-out remnants of what was left of shag carpeting. Pushed against the interior wall was a wooden table that appeared to be an old schoolteacher's desk. The chair, which was the newest piece of furniture in the room, was an ergonomic design. On top of the desk were carefully organized containers with attached lids that upon first glance looked more like colorful fishing tackle boxes.

The man sighed; his body exhausted. He flexed his muscles, arms and legs, and then stretched his back. Even though he was still relatively young, middle aged, his joints had betrayed him on many occasions. Movement was the only activity that eased the pain. Most didn't notice his distress.

Deeply saddened by the recent chain of events—he was unable to fulfill his fantasy, yet again—he had to let her go and cover his tracks. There was nothing else he could do. The threat was too high. Anna had stumbled backward and fallen down the stairs, breaking her neck. She had died upon impact. Burning down the house was just cleaning up a miscalculation. He punished himself for such a blunder. It had happened several times before, but he was adamant about sharpening his skills and would do whatever it took to get it right. There was a fresh bandage wrapped around his left forearm where he had punished himself with a razor to make sure he wouldn't make the same mistake again.

Opening one of the plastic boxes revealed all types of movie makeup—different bases for whatever skin color he wanted to have. In other cases there were wigs, various types of facial hair, and everything he needed for scars, tattoos, and other identifiable human markings. Whatever character he wanted to become, he would transform himself. It took many years to perfect his skill, moving among people to make sure he could fool anyone—absolutely anyone. He was going out shortly to prove his skills once again. It was an attempt to make himself feel better.

In the closet, there were all types of articles of clothing from teenage to elderly outfits with everything in between. It was more than dress-up; he was a chameleon. He could walk among society as anyone—at any time. That gave him power; more than money, more than prestige, and more than any priceless artifact. It was a way to survive. He could control his circumstances and what he wanted people to see. Everything he had suffered he was now in control of. No more ridicule. No more punishment. He was in control now.

There were a million identities he could transform into. He was the only one true to the craft of make-believe and image. And to those girls who desperately wanted to become rising stars in the modeling and acting world—he had a rude awakening for them. Even if it took years or decades, he would spend the rest of his life training them. If and when they failed, and they always did, he would set them free...

TEN

Katie drove out to the Pine Valley Mall. She kept rolling through her mind everything they had learned so far and nothing seemed to fit. There were too many pieces and no matter how hard she tried to make them fit—nothing did.

"It's nice to see you," said Daniels.

His comment jarred Katie back to the present.

"It's been a while," he said.

Silence followed. It was a stilted pleasantness that made things more difficult.

"Yes, it's been a while," she echoed. "Where's Mac?" Katie referred to Daniel's retired military K9 German shepherd he usually had with him.

"I didn't know how long I would be in Pine Valley, and back and forth to Sacramento. He's staying with a buddy of mine. And I'm sure being spoiled."

Katie nodded. She remembered vividly the moment she'd first seen Evan Daniels when he had assisted with the missing person's case of her now ex-fiancé. That she'd been surprised had been an understatement. He had been her K9 training officer in the Army and they became close; seeing him again then—and now—brought up all kinds of feelings.

"Hey, I know this may not be appropriate, but I can tell there's something wrong," Daniels said. "Want to talk about it?"

"I'm fine," said Katie, glancing at him. "It's just this case. Whenever there's been a homicide with a teen missing, it gets to me. You know?"

He sighed, watching the landscape race by. "I do know... And it doesn't help with memories from the battlefield either." His voice was soft.

Katie knew he meant well and understood, not only the job, but what it was like in the Army and what many soldiers brought home emotionally.

They were approaching the Pine Valley Mall. Katie was going to enter via the south entrance, which was near the food court and was the least populated parking area. She parked and turned to Detective Daniels.

"Ready?"

He made eye contact with her and smiled. "I'll follow your lead."

"We need to find out who A-1 Talent Agency is and how often they recruit from the mall. And, of course, if anyone recognizes either Anna or Jasmine."

"And get the security footage."

She nodded.

The detectives exited the car. The covered parking garage instantly brought back memories of Mrs. Braxton's death. Katie shuddered.

Even though it was a Thursday, the mall seemed fairly busy. Katie pulled her jacket across to make it less obvious that she was a police detective. As soon as they stepped inside, a rush of clashing sights and sounds greeted them. The small merry-go-round with the high-pitched happy music collided with a few kids squealing with glee. The aroma of hot dogs, burgers, and all types of fare hit her senses. It made Katie's stomach growl and she realized she had skipped lunch.

"Which way?" Daniels said.

Katie didn't visit the mall often, but she knew where the kids liked to hang out. She pointed and they approached the nearest escalator going up. It dropped them on the second floor, in the middle of the food area. There were dozens of eating outlets and half-filled tables. The detectives walked by the eateries, and toward the laughter and the sounds of teenagers. As they neared, they could see several small groups talking and sharing videos on their phones, while others were making videos of each other. All the kids had phones. There were back-packs piled in the corner.

"What do you think? Should we just get to the point and ask about the girls?" Katie said.

Daniels studied the kids for a moment. He nodded. "Teens can be a wealth of information... when they want to be."

Katie scanned the groups and settled on two girls and a boy that seemed the quietest and were having a regular conversation. The detectives made themselves known as they neared the teenagers.

"Excuse me," said Katie. "Can we talk to you for a moment?"

They looked at Katie, eyes wide, and then to Daniels.

"Are you on a case?" said one of the girls.

"What gave us away?" Katie said smiling.

"Uh, the badges and guns," said the boy.

Katie laughed. "We're trying to find out some information about a couple of girls. We're not sure if you went to school together."

"Ask away," said the boy.

"I'm Detective Scott and this is Detective Daniels from Pine Valley Sheriff's Department."

"I'm Kayla, this is Deb and Trevor," said the first girl.

"Nice to meet you all," said Daniels.

"What are you investigating? Murder?" said Trevor.

Katie was careful not to mention the homicide of Anna. Her death hadn't been disclosed to the public yet. "We're looking for two missing girls."

"Who?" said the three teens in unison.

"Anna Braxton," Katie said.

Two of them shook their heads, but Kayla stared at Katie and said, "I know Anna. I have a couple of classes with her. She's really nice."

"When was the last time you saw her?"

"It's been a while. We had a school break, but I hadn't seen her in class for a couple of days before that."

Katie watched the girl as she spoke; she seemed to be speaking truthfully. "How well did you know her? Did you ever see her here?"

"Just from class. She hung out with another girl mostly... I think her name is Jasmine."

"What do you know about Anna? Did she seem like she always did before she went missing? Quiet? Stressed?" said Katie.

"Um... I don't know. The same as usual, I guess," said Kayla.

"You might want to look on her social media page," said Trevor. He quickly accessed his phone and began furiously thumbing through pages. "Here she is... Is that her?" He showed Katie his screen.

It was definitely her.

"May I see this?" said Katie.

Trevor handed his phone over to her.

Katie scrolled down Anna's page. There were the usual jokes and memes, selfies, and cute photos of dogs. Then she looked at Anna's bio where it said: "Not to try is to fail. Follow your dreams."

She gave the phone back. "Thank you."

"Sure, no prob. Did it help?" Trevor said.

"I think so." At the very least she knew she could get Jasmine's social media page through this account.

"Cool."

"What about Jasmine MacAfee?" said Daniels.

The three teens shook their heads.

"Is she blonde?" said Deb.

Katie nodded.

"I think she was in my calculus class, but she transferred out after a week."

"Are you sure neither of you have seen Anna Braxton or Jasmine MacAfee here at the mall?" said Katie.

They shook their heads again.

"Thank you for your help," said Katie. She pulled out a card and gave it to Trevor. "You can call me at this number if you see either of the girls or remember something. Okay?"

Trevor took the call. "Will do, Detective."

Katie and Daniels continued walking through the mall. There seemed to be more people filtering in.

Katie stopped at one of the store directories. She quickly scanned the list and noticed that two of the spaces were empty.

"I think we need to check out these," she said pointing to 214 and 216.

"Let's go," he said.

On their way they passed an area that read "Security."

"Wait," Daniels said.

"Go. I'll meet you in a few minutes. I want to see these spaces first," said Katie.

"I can go with you," he said.

"I'll text you if there's something," she said. "I'll be quick."

He hesitated but went to the security area.

Katie had a hunch these areas might be used for rented-out days for special things, like recruitments, business insurance, and even information about modeling assignments. The mall would be a perfect place to find girls, and no one would think anything wasn't valid. Katie observed that most people were too focused on buying, what they had to do next, and what to eat to pay attention to teenage girls waiting with the hopes and dreams of being a model.

Katie reached the area where spaces 214 and 216 were located. It was farther than she realized—around a corner toward the end of the section and near an exit. Interestingly, it was quiet and had little traffic. She began to think that maybe her instincts were wrong.

A large wooden board painted yellow with one white stripe was placed in front of the space. A roll-down shutter security gate closed off the opening. Katie peered inside. It looked to have been some type of clothing shop. There were racks along the outer edge and a few hangers were on the floor in the back. She thought it would have been cleaned up better. A long counter with shelving was situated in the middle. Two sets of what used to be dressing rooms were on opposite sides of the store.

Absently, Katie put her hand on the security gate and it gave way. It hadn't been locked. The side was not attached and there was enough room to slip inside. She looked back and there was no one around. The security camera wasn't facing the section.

Katie slipped through.

Behind the long counter there were two desks that seemed to have been set up for a temporary meeting space. She opened the drawers and looked around. Nothing.

To be thorough, she walked the space and spotted a small torn piece of paper on the floor. It caught her eye because it was the same color as the paper they had found in Jasmine's room advertising A-1 Talent Agency. She picked it up. It was too small to know for sure if it had been the same, but it was interesting. She slipped it into her pocket. Still taking a few moments to look around, she didn't see anything else of interest.

She was just about to leave when she saw a back door leading to the employee entrance. There was usually a long enclosed hallway that led out to the parking lot, a way for workers to enter and leave without going through the mall. The door was painted a slate blue and the hardware was silver, making it blend into the background.

Curiosity tugged at Katie, so she decided to check it out. Then it wouldn't be nagging at her that she hadn't completely followed through her search. It was going to take some time for security to pull up footage they wanted to see. She flipped the silver top deadbolt latch and turned the knob. It opened. She pulled the door inward and glanced out. Automatic lighting came on. It was a long hallway, no windows, and a cement floor. She could see a few doors along the corridor. It was quiet. She made sure the access door into the empty space didn't close all the way just in case it might lock behind her, then she stepped into the hallway. All other noises drifted away. It was like being in a tunnel or a soundproofed room.

Even though the two spaces were close to the exit inside the mall, there was no exit door from inside the hallway. It meant that employees were directed to one or two specific exits for security and safety purposes. Once inside, the doors opened manually when leaving. Entering from the outside, the locks took keys or swiped ID badges.

Katie wanted to see how far the exit was and if someone could have been smuggled out without being seen. She looked up and didn't see any cameras. She assumed they were at the exterior doors, both inside and out, to the parking lot.

As she walked along the corridor, she imagined all the employees who entered and exited every day. The long walkway was clean. There were no posters or trash or anything. It was spotless. She glanced back, and it was pitch dark. It made it difficult to see how far she had walked. Once she reached the end where an exterior door was, she decided to go back and meet up with Daniels.

Katie briskly walked back to the section that said "214" and hoped the door was still ajar. As she walked into each section of lights, the last one didn't illuminate. She walked back and forth, but it was darkened in the section she had come from.

It was a malfunction, she thought. But then her police detective mind prompted another angle. Was it turned off on purpose?

Katie hurried through the darkness and stopped at the door she had originally exited. The door was shut and locked. Her first thought was that she was at the wrong door. She moved back and forth in the hallway and knew she was at the correct one.

She retrieved her cell phone, which lit up the immediate area around her. She was going to send a text to Daniels to let him know where she was, but there was no signal. Of course, she thought. The cement hallway was like a bunker, cell phone signals couldn't penetrate.

She used her hands to lightly touch the wall as she moved cautiously toward the outdoor exit. When she was about ten feet away, she heard a soft click coming from where she had originally started.

Katie swung around, holding her meager cell phone light out in front of her. Standing in the shadows was a dark figure—frozen.

"Who's there?" she said.

No response. No movement.

Katie blinked, trying to clear her vision, but the figure was still unmoving. She dared to move closer.

"Identify yourself."

Was it an employee playing games?

All lights went out.

She dropped her phone.

ELEVEN

Katie's heart pounded, causing her head to throb. If there was ever a time that she felt trapped like a rat in a maze—this was it. She listened intently. Nothing.

Katie spun around and moved as quickly as she could to the outdoor exit. It seemed longer than she had remembered and there wasn't a light indicating the exit anymore. What had happened to it? She was running down a long dark void.

Without warning, Katie was slammed from behind. There was no sound of footsteps, breathing, or any other noise to indicate someone was there. The impact thrust her forward and she hit the ground hard. Strong hands grabbed her, holding her down, pressing hard against her waist and torso. She could tell the perpetrator was male, average height, lean, and strong.

Instinctively, she worked to flip onto her back and begin to fight. Using her knees and elbows, Katie managed to stun the man. She clawed her way to the exit, seeing cracks of light around the framework, but it still didn't illuminate the area.

Before she could get the door open, the man shoved her aside, slammed open the outside door, and ran into the parking lot.

Light filled the hall and was momentarily blinding. Katie scrambled to her feet and took off after the assailant. She briefly saw that he was wearing gray sweats and a hoodie. As quickly as he had appeared in the dark, he was gone. No trace or indication of where he had gone. She went one way across the parking lot and then the other, but there was no sign of the culprit. She searched systematically around each car. There was no way he could have vanished that quickly without her seeing where he went. Frustration took over.

"Katie?"

She turned and saw Daniels had joined her.

"Are you okay? What's going on?" His face was deeply concerned.

"There was a guy in the corridor exit that came from one of the empty stores," she said, winded. "He attacked me. Why are you here?"

"I was at the security station and there was a breach of a door. We saw you run out here."

Katie still surveyed the area, trying to figure out how the man had made his escape. Was it just a random attack or was it someone who had something to do with the investigation? Turning to Daniels, she said, "Did you find anything from the security footage?"

"We were just about to look at the timeline when Anna went missing. Katie? Tell me what's going on."

"I want to quickly go into each store on this wing and see if anyone fits the man's description," she said.

Daniels nodded and followed Katie. After recovering her phone, they spent about twenty minutes talking to employees and describing the man Katie had encountered. No one seemed to have seen him. Katie decided the person must've followed her into the empty spaces or had another way of entering the mall.

"Let's get back to security," she said to Daniels, walking to the main entrance.

"Hey," he said, gently touching her arm. His dark eyes seemed to see deep inside her mind when he looked at her. "I'm here to help, remember? We're working this double homicide together. And whatever is going on here, we need to get to the bottom of it."

"It's..." Katie stopped herself from getting personal. He was right, they were working two homicides and that's where her head needed to be. "We need to find a solid lead."

Daniels looked as if he was going to say something else, but seemed to decide not to. He and Katie went back into the mall to the security area.

Katie was surprised by the technology in the security offices of the mall. It reminded her of surveillance she'd seen in police and federal buildings. There was a long console in a half-moon shape with several screens showing various areas of the mall— including entrances. They were told there were two security officers at all times during mall hours viewing the camera feeds.

"This is Detective Scott," said Daniels. "And that's Tom and Patrick." He gestured to the two men seated at the console.

Tom nodded. "I've managed to pull up the footage from eight and nine days ago." He clicked a keyboard and several different camera views appeared on the screens.

"I'm sorry, but could you check something first?" Katie said.

"Sure."

"Can you check if someone entered the exit route from the stores on the east side in the past half hour?"

"Give me a sec," he said.

Within less than a minute, they were watching the mall entrances and exits.

"What are you looking for?" Patrick asked.

"A guy in gray sweats and a hoodie. Thin. Tall," she said.

They watched, but no one matched that description. They looked closer at men in their twenties and thirties who were of average height, thin, and wearing different clothes, but no one seemed to fit.

They started watching the footage from around the time Anna Braxton had left home on the day she went missing.

"There," said Katie.

They watched Anna walk into the mall dressed in jeans and a T-shirt and then she went to the food court area and sat down. She had a backpack and cell phone. The teenager didn't talk to anyone or get anything to eat, but she kept checking her phone. She didn't watch patrons or anyone around her—she seemed oblivious to everything else.

After the video footage ran for almost nine minutes, Anna picked up her phone and was talking to someone. It seemed she had been waiting for the call.

"Can you zoom in closer? And go back to when she answered the call," said Katie. It was difficult to see the girl alive and talking; thinking of her broken dead body splayed out in the cellar.

"Will do," said Tom. "And I can do one better and slow it down."

Katie and Daniels leaned in closer. They watched Anna smile and nod, which made it appear to be a friendly conversation.

Daniels shook his head. "Not enough information."

Katie pulled out her cell phone and brought up a photo of Jasmine MacAfee. "We're looking for this girl too. She went missing late yesterday. Can you see if she entered the mall this morning or before closing last night?"

"It's going to take a while," said Tom as he pulled up the footage. "Wait, let me take a photo of her." He took out his cell phone and took a quick picture of Katie's screen. "I'll text you when I find something."

"Better yet, please send it to this email," said Katie. She handed him her card after she jotted down McGaven's email address. "And could you also send that video of Anna Braxton too?"

"Got it," he said as he took the card.

TWELVE

Katie finally pulled into her driveway after an extremely long day. She parked, turned off the engine, and then stayed in the Jeep, sitting behind the wheel staring out the windshield. She recalled everything that had happened that day. It seemed more like a week rather than one work shift. Her body ached, and her energy was dangerously low and close to crashing.

She opened her car door, still reeling from events. Vivid images flowed through her mind of the bodies, the burned-down house, the attack at the mall, and seeing Anna alive on video in the food court. The thought of Evan Daniels working alongside her also wasn't too far from her mind. All these mental pictures flipped through her brain, over and over, making her anxious and unsure of what was going to happen next.

Katie stepped out of the Jeep. She leaned in and grabbed her briefcase, laptop, and jacket. And that's when she heard the deep baritone bark coming from inside the house. She had received a text message earlier from her uncle, letting her know he had come by to feed Cisco. He loved the dog almost as much as she did. They always worked out ways of making sure Cisco was taken care of, no matter what Katie's work schedule was. Sometimes she would even bring Cisco to work and have him stay in the police K9 kennels.

"I'm coming, Cisco," she called as she walked up to her porch, fumbling for her keys. She could hear the big dog sniffing the perimeter of the door and the faint sound of his nails along the bottom of it.

Stepping inside, Katie was greeted by a large black German shepherd with yellow wolf eyes. Cisco ran from the living room to the kitchen and back again. He was so happy she was home. Even though he was a retired military working dog, he still acted like a puppy at times. He had been her military K9 and she was able to bring him home with a little help from her uncle when she left the Army. Katie put down her things and took a few moments to give Cisco some attention.

As she did, she saw a note on the kitchen counter that read: *Your favorite takeout is in the fridge. Love Uncle Wayne.*

She was extremely lucky to have had her uncle in her life after her parents were killed in a car crash when she was just a teen. He was her only family. He was Pine Valley's sheriff and though sometimes there was a sticky line between family and police officer, at the end of the day he was still her uncle.

"Did you have fun today?" she said to the dog that now sat at attention wondering if there were any food scraps.

Katie opened the refrigerator and found a white bag from Bella Italia. She took the bag and grabbed a plate and utensils. Katie retrieved the Caesar salad and raviolis. Quickly putting the pasta in the microwave to warm, she poured herself a half glass of red wine. She didn't realize how hungry she was until she sat down at the counter.

Her stress had been too high today and she needed to unwind and reflect on everything they had found out. She knew from past cases that the most important thing to accomplish was to not make things personal—but it was difficult when it involved children.

Her phone alerted her to a text. It was from McGaven.

You better be relaxing and eating something healthy... see ya in the morning, partner.

Katie smiled. She knew her incident at the house had made Gav concerned, but he acted like everything was fine. They had been through more than most police partners, but they always had each other's back. She replied.

Bright and early.

The microwave chimed. She opened the door and the amazing aroma of cheese spinach ravioli in marinara sauce greeted her. As much as she wanted to do some snooping on social media pages for Anna and Jasmine, she needed to make sure she ate first.

Katie savored her meal as Cisco patiently waited for anything that might hit the floor. She sent a quick text to her uncle to thank him. She was relieved he didn't pressure her for daily details, since there was quite a bit to report. It had been procedure to send him updates ever since she headed up the cold-case unit.

The evening was mild and Katie decided to take her laptop outside so Cisco could get some exercise. Being out on her deck allowed her to relax and she loved any opportunity to be outside.

The outside light flickered a few times, before burning brightly. She went straight to the porch swing. It was old but was still her favorite place to be ever since she was a child. It evoked wonderful memories with her parents that she kept close to her heart.

After they were gone, she'd inherited the farmhouse. Many suggested to her that she should sell, but that was never on her mind. Even with her ex-fiancé, they had discussed buying a new home together after they were married. She never wanted to. Maybe she knew all along things weren't going to work out with Chad—the love of her life.

Cisco took off running on the property, enjoying stretching his legs. It took only moments before he returned with his favorite ball, dropping it at Katie's feet. She took about ten minutes to play with him. Her recent schedule wasn't what the dog needed. Thinking about the cases, she thought she would probably use Cisco to do some rural searches, especially around the burned-down house. She would have to work with the arson investigator and knew that there would be responsibility issues that would arise.

Katie sighed, trying to put potential problems out of her mind. She took her seat again as Cisco seemed happy to lie down on the deck within view of her.

Katie knew she needed to go to bed as work would be particularly busy tomorrow, but first she wanted to take a look at Anna's and Jasmine's social media. It would keep her awake thinking about it if she didn't do it.

She also decided to try to find anything about A-1 Talent Agency, but it was just a generic name that seemed to be part of many talent and acting businesses. She hoped McGaven could find out more information on his search.

Seeing Anna on the security surveillance at the mall drew Katie closer to the teen. She knew the image of the girl's body at the bottom of the basement stairs would never leave her mind—it would become less and less of a strong memory, but it would never leave her.

Katie realized after her first case. of searching for eight-year-old Chelsea Compton, none of these cases would ever be forgotten. That case revealed itself to be much bigger and more shocking than she feared. Deep in the forest, she had unearthed a makeshift cemetery: a row of graves, each with a brightly colored teddy bear in the victim's arms. They were now a part of her, and she feared every additional case would be too. She was sure that even if Chad had stayed, he would have become resentful of her and the baggage she carried. That was the last thing she ever wanted.

If it was truly meant to be, they would find their way back to one another.

After spending a few moments scrolling through social media accounts, she found Anna Braxton's profile. There was nothing for her mother, Stella Braxton, that she could find. She slowly read the postings and enlarged the photos to see if there was anything that might help the investigation. The last post was from the day before she disappeared.

Katie scrolled back from then. She stopped on a selfie photo of Anna that looked like she was walking home, from three days prior to her disappearance. Her expression was serious, even concerned. The comment was: *How did I get here? I won't be here long.*

What surprised Katie even more was that the hashtag wording included #MDM. She recognized those three letters from Anna's journal. Could it be "million-dollar man"? Anna's mom had said, "Find the million-dollar man and you'll find my Anna."

Katie checked a few results from when she searched "million-dollar man." Responses including slang came back with everything from sport's titles to the perfect man, and references to old television shows and movies. But one description in particular caught her attention. It said on the outside a man may seem perfect, but he's far from it in reality; a man with a million faces.

With her energy fading, Katie decided to go to bed and start fresh in the morning. Cisco followed her inside and waited as she cleaned up the kitchen and put her laptop away. She double-checked the security cameras, noting everything seemed to be in place with no activity.

"C'mon, Cisco," she said.

The big dog padded behind her as she readied to go to bed. As Katie was at her dresser, she glanced at the one framed photograph that was turned down while all others were face up.

She paused for a moment.

Picking up the wooden frame, Katie stared at a photograph of her and Chad from about a year ago when they had gone camping. Both were smiling, suntanned, and appeared to be a happy couple. Sadness overwhelmed her, but she fought the urge to cry. There had been too many tears in the past couple of months. She put the photo in one of her drawers and shut it.

Grief caused many different emotions and you never knew when they would hit—usually at the worst possible times. Katie took a quick shower and was in bed before eleven. Cisco snoozed in his overstuffed chair in the corner of the bedroom. She watched him for a few minutes; his breathing relaxed. Finally her own exhaustion pushed her into a deep sleep.

THIRTEEN

Friday 0610 hours

Katie was awakened by her cell phone ringing from her nightstand. It was still dark outside, which made it seem more like a dream environment than her bedroom.

The phone stopped. Within a few seconds, it began ringing again.

Cisco grumbled.

Katie pushed off her covers and sat up. Grabbing her phone, she said, "Detective Scott."

"Katie, you awake?" said McGaven.

"I am now... kinda early?" she said, glancing at the clock that read a little after six in the morning.

"We have another one," he said.

"Another one?" Katie's was still groggy.

"I just received a call that there is another body in a burned-out house."

Katie stood up, completely awake now. "A teen?"

"Preliminary assessment is yes."

"What about..." Katie thought about Jasmine.

"All I know is that we've been called to the scene."

"Where?"

"Lost Falls."

"Okay. I'll meet you at the department and we can head there together."

"See ya soon."

"Oh, Gav?"

"Yeah."

"When you said you'd see me early in the morning. I didn't mean this early."

"Ten-four."

Katie moved through her house as quickly as possible and made her way to the department. McGaven was already waiting. They jumped into the police sedan to make their way to Lost Falls.

"There are some great hiking trails and camping spots here," said McGaven. "I haven't been in a while, but there are a lot of places I used to visit... I need to get back to that."

"Me too."

McGaven looked at his partner. "You do. All the things you love to do are still there."

Katie looked at him, but didn't say anything. She knew what he meant. Just because her life had changed without Chad in it, didn't mean she couldn't still enjoy all the wonderful things she had in the past.

A fire truck passed them heading back into town.

"Looks like the fire is out," she said.

It was fortunate as this was a heavily wooded area and a house fire could have taken a good portion of the forest down.

"What's on your mind?" said McGaven after a few minutes of quiet in the sedan.

"Just thinking that this is piling more on top of what we

already have... and we haven't even been able to build a firm timeline for Anna or her mother yet."

McGaven drove through a narrow area, weaving around several groups of pine trees. It was a miracle the fire truck had been able to get through.

The forest area opened wide into a beautiful clearing in the sunshine. They must've had to clear out many trees to create this type of oasis... well, what she imagined was an oasis until the fire that had clearly devastated the house.

"Wow," said McGaven.

Katie thought the same thing. The large black spot that had once most likely been a nice home was now a few pieces of structure resembling a skeleton.

There were several emergency vehicles present, including unmarked ones. The PVFD K9 unit was also parked to the side.

"Again, who owns this property?" she asked.

"I don't know, but there's Hamilton now. I'm sure he'll have some answers."

Detective Hamilton's usual sour expression was no different under the circumstances. Most of the past tension between the detectives had dissipated as they had worked more cases together. What began as a tense working relationship had slowly cooled down—they all had a job to do.

Katie and McGaven got out of the car.

"What do we have?" said McGaven.

"Body. Juvenile female. She barricaded herself in the closet," said Hamilton.

"Why did you call us?" said Katie.

"Come with me," he said. "We've determined the owner, which is a vacation rental company for a family trust that we're running down now."

"Was the victim related to the owners?" she said.

"It's unclear."

They followed Hamilton into the house. Just like the day

before, what was left of the structure was still hot, and dripping with water, giving off a steam that made the area appear cloudy. There was a smell of burnt wood that was difficult to ignore. The heat seemed to grow in intensity as they walked inside. This house seemed different from the other. It clearly had been furnished and most likely lived in or regularly rented out.

"Over here," said Hamilton. He handed Katie and McGaven gloves.

Katie watched him move part of what looked like a wall, but in fact was a closet door in what had been a bedroom. Preparing for the worst and not wanting to see a completely burned body, she looked slowly down. Inside was the limp form of a young female. The body was slumped to one side, with her arms down and her head cocked at a peculiar angle. Her feet were bare and dirty. She had medium-length light-brown hair with short bangs matching slight features, and her fingernails looked to be some type of press-on acrylic in bright pink. All ten nails were amazingly still intact. Katie was able to determine that it wasn't Jasmine based on her basic features.

But what immediately caught Katie's eye and stopped her cold was the dress the girl was wearing. It was yellow and similar to the one Anna wore, if not the exact duplicate.

Katie couldn't determine why the body was so undamaged in the closet and why there were no indications of the girl trying to escape. It was as if she was tossed there as an afterthought, like a rag doll. Was she unconscious?

"Was there anything identifying on her, like a purse or personal item?" she said.

"There was nothing," said Hamilton.

Katie took several photos with her phone. She wanted to have something documenting the scene before receiving the ones following John's collection of the evidence. She knelt, taking a closer look at the girl's dress and hands. There was something clutched in her left hand. It was a thin beige scrap of something, and it seemed to be slightly rolled on the corners.

"What is this?" she said, carefully moving the girl's fingers. "It almost looks like it could be skin, but it couldn't be because it has a rubber quality to it." She looked at McGaven and Hamilton.

They too took a closer look.

"It looks like putty or some type of silicone?" said McGaven.

Katie stood up. "Her hands need to be bagged and anything on her dress and body needs to be handled carefully so as not to lose any potential evidence." She studied what was left of the walls in the closet. It was difficult to see what had been caused from the fire and smoke, and what might have been there before.

"Detectives," said a voice behind them. "I didn't expect to see you again this soon."

Katie turned to see Arson Investigator Ames. He looked at her closely, never averting his gaze. It felt as if he was challenging her—about what, Katie didn't really know. She stood her ground and didn't shy away from his stare.

"Investigator Ames," she said, acknowledging his presence.

"Luke is fine," he said, referring to a first-name basis.

McGaven and Hamilton nodded their introductions.

"Can you give us an overview?" she said.

Ames looked at Katie and then turned to look toward the crime scene. "This is a typical attempt at arson. I'm assuming the fire-setter wanted to burn any evidence. But it appears random. You can see where the fire was started," he said, referring to the living room. "And here in the kitchen."

Katie wondered why the arsonist didn't begin the fire closer to the victim.

"Accelerants? Does this show a more complex technique?" she said.

The arson investigator smiled. "I like the fact that you get to the point, Detective. And the answer is: gasoline was used. If you move closer to these areas, you can still smell a little bit of it. I took several samples along with documenting the areas."

"And you'll forward the report to us?" said McGaven.

"That's how it works."

"We don't know if this victim is connected to Anna Braxton or our investigation. Upon first inspection, I would say yes, but we're going to have to run our own search and recovery of evidence at this point," said Katie.

"And you'll forward the report to us?" said Ames.

"That's how it works," said Katie.

"It's going to be a bit before John can get here," said Hamilton as he coordinated things from his phone.

"Thanks," said Katie. She walked out of the house followed by McGaven.

"What do you think?" he said.

Katie sighed and stared at the burned-out structure. "It's a bit of a waiting game now... waiting to see what reports say— forensics, autopsies, fire, victim ID. And Hamilton is running down the owner." She looked around the area and realized it seemed to be cultivated, with grass, flowers, ground cover, and not just the usual forest of trees.

"So, Hamilton is going to take point on this case?" McGaven said.

"Looks like, but we have plenty to do."

Katie decided to take a look around the property. Before being trampled by fire crews and vehicle tires digging holes in the ground, it appeared to have had nice landscaping and there were sprinkler heads dotted about.

McGaven seemed to read her mind. "Looks like the property has been taken care of... maybe there's a landscape company involved."

"Where we can get more information about the owners," she said.

McGaven made notes.

Katie saw there was a trail leading down from the main area of the landscaping. There was a small garden gate that intrigued her, so she went through it. Moving farther away from the fire area, the air began to clear, making it easier to breathe. The morning sun began to lighten everything too.

Katie stood facing the east and enjoyed the moment. There was no view of neighbors, and she estimated that the nearest house was more than a few acres away.

Suddenly she saw movement down below. It was a tall figure moving away from the property.

"Gav," said Katie. She opened the gate and took off after the unknown person.

"Katie!" said McGaven.

Katie heard her partner calling her, but she wasn't going to let the person get away. It could be nothing... or it could be something.

The trail was narrow and surrounding foliage pushed small branches and leaves closer, making it even narrower. As Katie tried to catch up with the person, she felt the low-lying branches brush past her. She silently berated herself that she wasn't wearing the shoes to run for any length of time.

Up ahead, she saw the back of a man wearing a gray hoodie pulled up over his head. It made her think of the person in the mall entryway who'd attacked her.

"Stop! Pine Valley Sheriff's Department!"

The figure hesitated and slowed down, but Katie kept her speed and gained on him.

"Stop!"

To Katie's surprise, the person stopped. She eased up on her pursuit.

The person slowly turned around to face her. He was tall,

thin, and appeared to be in his forties or fifties. His face was gaunt and eyes sunken. He patiently waited for her.

"Why didn't you stop when I called?" she said.

He put his hand up to his ear. "I had my hearing aid turned down and I didn't hear you."

"I see," said Katie as she took a moment to catch her breath. "What are you doing here?"

He paused a moment. "Just being a nosy neighbor. I saw the smoke and heard the fire trucks, so I wanted to see what it was all about."

"What's your name?" she said.

"Kip. Kip Johnson."

"You said you're a neighbor?" she said.

"Well, actually, I'm house-sitting for a friend."

Katie watched the man. She couldn't ignore her instincts. "Do you always run this trail?"

"I have a few times—sometimes the longer one on the north side."

"Have you seen anything out of the ordinary over the last few days?"

"Like what?"

"People? Cars? Anyone that might be scoping out the place?"

"No... it's pretty quiet here."

"Have you seen any teenagers?" She watched him with curiosity.

"No. I don't think so."

"Hey," said McGaven as he came near, scrutinizing the situation. "Everything okay?"

"Mr. Johnson, this is my partner, Detective McGaven... and I'm Detective Scott from the Pine Valley Sheriff's Department."

"Detectives? Wow."

"We're just here checking out the area," she said, not wanting to talk about the body they'd found.

"Oh, I see."

"You said you were house-sitting? For how long?"

"For another week," he said. "Is there anything else I can help you with?"

"No, thank you, Mr. Johnson, for your time," said Katie.

"Nice meeting you, Detectives," he said and jogged away.

McGaven stood next to Katie. "Anything?"

She shook her head. "No."

"He was a bit weird."

"Definitely."

FOURTEEN

Hamilton was in charge of the homicide until further notice. Katie and McGaven had places to visit and people to talk to while they waited for forensics and autopsy.

Katie was behind the wheel driving to Mrs. Braxton's workplace as McGaven searched from his phone and iPad. She watched the road, trying to piece together the events they were investigating and what everything meant.

"Okay, since we were summoned so early this morning," said McGaven, "we didn't have a morning meeting."

Katie nodded, ready to hear any new information.

"First things, Anna's cell phone pinged off the tower that was closest to the mall around three thirty on the day she disappeared. There has been nothing after that and no GPS trace. Most likely the phone was turned off."

"Or destroyed," she said, still thinking about Anna's body at the bottom of the basement stairs.

"Now Mrs. Braxton's phone shows something different.

Her phone pinged off areas around Pine Valley the day Anna went missing, *including* near the mall."

"Interesting. Could she have been looking for Anna?"

"Staying to one area? Why wouldn't she keep looking? And then on Wednesday, you can see that she was coming to Sacramento by the towers."

"To find me," she said. "But why me?"

"It's not clear yet."

"Maybe we'll learn more at her place of employment."

"From her credit report, finances seemed to have been strained. Past-due bills, et cetera. It seems she was barely making ends meet."

"What about the house?"

"Payments have been on time, it looks like... but she made a larger deposit than normal last month for twenty thousand dollars. Definitely more than her regular employment deposit."

"That seems like a lot for a single mother. Was it an investment? Inheritance maybe?" She thought it unlikely, but it raised more questions to answer.

"There's no indication of what the amount was for. It was a cashier's check with no other identifiers," said McGaven.

Katie thought about it. "Were there any big purchases since? Like something for the house, a new car, or maybe opening a new bank account for Anna's college?"

"Nope."

"Usually people put that kind of money in a savings or another type of interest-earning account." Katie recalled Jasmine's household as well. "What about the MacAfee family?"

"I've just started on them. And there's a ton of stuff. Mostly not good," he said.

"What do you mean?"

"Bad credit. Creditors practically at their doorstep. There were two instances child services were called."

She frowned. "What about?"

"The school had called saying the younger children weren't being taken care of..." he said, reading. "No clean clothes, no lunches, or money for lunch. They hadn't been turning in homework. Stuff like that."

"That's terrible. And now Jasmine is missing."

McGaven looked at his partner. "What a mess. We don't know if it has anything to do with Jasmine running away or if she was somehow lured away like her best friend."

"Well, we're here to find out more about Mrs. Braxton. Maybe from a coworker or her boss?"

Katie pulled into the parking lot of a small navy-blue building with a sign that read: "Armstrong Accounting Firm." Nothing seemed unusual. The parking lot had been recently upgraded with new asphalt and the building painted. There were flowers along the front of the property.

"Nice little place," said McGaven.

Inside, there was a young woman at the front desk with a pile of files. She appeared to be entering the information into the computer.

"Hi," said Katie. "Detectives Scott and McGaven here to see..."

"Mr. Chris Booker," said McGaven.

"We're from the Pine Valley Sheriff's Department."

The woman looked at the detectives wide-eyed. "Okay." She got up and went into another room. It was only a couple of minutes when the woman and a large man came back.

"Detectives," the man said. His voice was shaky and he seemed nervous. "I'm Chris, the manager."

Katie and McGaven shook his hand, which was clammy.

"Please, let's talk in my office."

The detectives followed Mr. Booker toward the back where there was an enclosed office with a glass window. They passed three desks where two women and a man worked diligently—

there were no other offices or cubicles for privacy or to separate desks. There was one empty desk. It was quiet and no one gave them any eye contact.

Katie noticed immediately that the office environment seemed stressed and the workers weren't happy. Having a big window giving the boss a view of every move the employees made seemed unnerving.

"Please, sit down," said the manager.

Katie and McGaven each took a chair. The manager then closed the door and flipped the blinds for privacy. The office was neat with perfectly stacked folders and files. The bookcase and filing cabinets were completely filled. It smelled like stale coffee and some type of Danish. The remnants of food had been tossed in the trash.

"I have to say that when I received your call I was concerned," he said.

"Mr. Booker, we are here to inform you that Stella Braxton has passed away," said Katie.

He gasped. "What? What happened? She hadn't showed up for work the last few days..."

"When was the last day she was at work?" said Katie.

"Uh, it was Tuesday," he said. He took a notepad with handwritten notes. "Yeah, Tuesday. It's been three days now."

Katie noticed that he was sweating—more than just from the stuffy office—and his forehead was shiny. He seemed extremely nervous and was fidgeting.

"How well did you know her?" Katie asked.

"I dunno. Just from work."

"Did you ever socialize with her or with the others here?" said Katie.

"I don't like what you're insinuating, but we're a professional group."

"Did you know anything personal about Mrs. Braxton?"

"I know she has, or had, a daughter. I heard she ran away."

Katie wasn't going to discuss anything about Anna. "How long has Mrs. Braxton worked here?"

"About four years now. She's one of my best bookkeepers." He looked down, saddened by the loss of an employee.

"Mr. Booker, did you see any changes in her behavior lately? Or did anyone visit her here? Anything out of the ordinary?" said Katie.

McGaven stood up and casually gazed around the office. It was a tactic he used to keep people who were being questioned off balance. He seemed to sense that the manager could be hiding something.

Booker shook his head. "No, I don't think so."

"So where is Armstrong?" said McGaven, looking at binders.

"Armstrong?"

"Yes, the name on your sign? Is that the owner?"

"No. I made it up. It sounded better than Booker."

Katie stood. "Can we see Mrs. Braxton's desk?"

"What is it you're looking for?" he said.

"Anything that might give us some idea what had been going on in her life," she said.

Booker turned and picked up a banker's box and set it on the desk. "Here are her things. Since I didn't hear from her, I packed up her desk." He pushed the box forward. "Since she's gone and I have no one to give it to, take it."

Katie studied the man and wondered if this nervous squirmy person could commit such heinous crimes. Her instinct said no, but her observations made her suspicious of what he might know.

"Thank you," she said and picked up the box.

"Are we done?" said Booker.

"Yes. If we have any other questions, we'll be in touch," she said.

"Thank you for your time, Mr. Booker," said McGaven.

Outside, Katie put the box in the back seat before getting behind the wheel.

"What do you make of Booker?" said McGaven.

"I think he knows something he doesn't want us to know, but I don't think it has to do with Mrs. Braxton."

"Meaning?"

"He seems to be cagey, no eye contact, sweaty, nervous, and he never asked how Mrs. Braxton died. Strange?" she said.

"Weird."

Katie chuckled. "Okay, weird."

"And he had packed her things up very quickly."

"Can you get a list of employees?"

"I think so."

"Then we can go through Mrs. Braxton's phone contacts."

"On it." McGaven scrolled through his phone. "I had sent John a quick text and he said he'd have some information for us soon." He looked at Katie. "Have you heard from Detective Daniels?"

"Nope."

"So what do we have, really, so far?" said McGaven.

"Well... we have two teenage girls found dead in burned-down houses—houses we haven't been able to track down owners for. A mother who was brutally stabbed to death in Sacramento in broad daylight. The home of mother and daughter has been searched—and we don't know why."

"When you state it like that... we don't have much."

"I want to know what Mrs. Braxton had been up to—or what she had been involved in." Katie turned to McGaven. "Could she have been tracking down Anna's connection in the modeling agency?"

"Maybe she found something?"

"She definitely found something—she was killed for it," said Katie. "But we don't know if her death had to do with Anna or something else."

"Twenty thousand dollars of something else."

"Since we know Anna was seeking out A-1 Talent Agency and then she ended up at 1133 Old Stagecoach Road..."

"I see where you're going with this," said McGaven.

"I want to search the surrounding areas on Old Stagecoach Road with Cisco."

"We'd better get in contact with the arson investigator to clear the channels and not step on anyone's toes," said McGaven. "I'll give him a call."

Katie nodded. Her gut told her this killer was sloppy and trying to not leave evidence behind but likely failing. She wasn't looking forward to asking for permission from Arson Investigator Ames to search the scene, but that was just the way it was going to be.

FIFTEEN

The man sat in front of a vanity, with the bright rounded lights surrounding the mirror giving him the feeling of being a star on center stage—he took after his mother. He stared at his reflection, moving his head slightly from side to side. He paused. Not moving or blinking. His eyes seemed to morph into another person, staring back. The longer he remained still, the more someone else was trying to come through. It didn't matter. He would win anyway.

He snapped back into reality. Expertly he removed the pieces of latex around his face that gave him the gaunt look—including some patches on his hands and arms. He popped out his blue contacts and gently put them in an antique dish. He pulled off his gray toupee pieces. He carefully washed his skin until his face, head, and arms were clean and he was back to his normal self.

Still sitting in his chair, he studied himself in the mirror. Slowly taking his clothes off, he remained naked. It was the only time he felt like an individual. Free. He was just an ordinary man who could transform himself into extraordinary characters. No one would suspect him—he could be nice, he could be mean, and he could be the most ruthless killer society had ever known. He had played so many personas and roles that he had lost count, but it didn't matter, because he knew that he was king of impersonations.

No matter how hard he tried, he still couldn't hold a candle to his mother. She had been beautiful, talented, a model and an up-and-coming actress who was going to grace the movie screen. She would always talk to him about what his life would be like and that he would earn millions. Everything he learned was from his beautiful mother—he truly loved her. That was why that fateful day has never left him. The image, the feelings, and the reality of that event would always be burned into his mind.

He pushed away those thoughts.

After a rigorous workout of calisthenics and weight training, he ate more than enough food for two people in a single meal. All perfectly balanced with protein, vegetables, and fruits—he ate until he couldn't anymore. It was important to gain his strength and endurance.

He stood in the middle of the outdated kitchen drinking four glasses of water. He could feel the liquid slide down his throat and enter his stomach.

His relaxation turned angry as he looked for his jacket. Thrashing around the house. Swearing. He had to find it. Once he did, he pulled out a photocopied article from a year ago.

"You," he sneered. "You think you're going to win? You think you're going to find me when I'm right under your nose?"

The well-worn piece of paper had been folded many times, leaving the creases almost bare. He unfolded it again to reveal an article about a solved cold case and the headshot photo of Detective Katie Scott along with another photo of Detectives Scott and McGaven.

"You will never find me."

He felt a rush of adrenalin.

He left the room and dropped the article onto the floor. He made his way into the kitchen, where there was a pantry door. Opening it, there was another door.

He stopped, grabbed a sandwich bag, and stuffed a peanut butter sandwich into it. There were two twelve-ounce water bottles on the counter. He took everything and then walked to the interior door.

Balancing the food and water, he managed to unlock the door. He pushed it open and switched on a single light. The bulb swung on a long wire, casting the light around the stairs and across the walls.

He dropped the food and water, and could hear it hit the basement floor.

Standing at the top of the stairs, he wasn't worried about an ambush or even any type of confrontation because he was in control. It was a matter of time before the fate of his guest would depend upon if they were worthy of being true to the craft of acting and modeling.

He looked down at the teenage girl with long blonde hair and bangs wearing a flowing yellow dress. Her terrified stare was something he would keep with him. She didn't say a word or move toward the food and water.

Jasmine MacAfee remained perfectly still, terrified, and awaiting her fate.

SIXTEEN

After returning to the Pine Valley Sheriff's Department, Katie and McGaven agreed to meet in about an hour. McGaven would dig for more information back at the office, and Katie was on her way home to get her gear and get Cisco ready for the search.

She hurried home, pressing the accelerator harder. She was anxious to investigate the outdoors at Old Stagecoach Road. She had listened to McGaven talk to the arson investigator, and it took some convincing, but he had finally relented, although they had some rules that applied to their search. It wasn't that Katie didn't believe in protocol, but she didn't like being told how to conduct her searches. She was very experienced.

It was early for Katie to be home and Cisco was ecstatic as he ran the length of the house.

"Calm down. You're going to wear yourself out," she said, smiling. Katie loved working with Cisco and she didn't get the opportunity as much as she would have liked. Just recently he had been sworn in with the Pine Valley Sheriff's Department as an honorary deputy, which basically meant that Katie could take Cisco officially on searches.

She quickly changed into clothing that would be better suited to the outdoors and uneven terrain. After she put on her tactical boots and made sure that she had enough outer gear, she readied Cisco with his search vest and sent a text message to McGaven.

When she and Cisco arrived back at the department, her partner was already waiting in the parking lot with a duffel bag from his truck. He too had changed clothes and resembled more of a SWAT officer than a detective. Katie knew McGaven loved to be part of the searches, even though he'd never said so specifically.

McGaven opened the passenger door, put his duffel in the back seat, and made himself comfortable. "Hey."

"Looks like you're ready to take on some bears," she said smiling.

"You never know... especially being your partner."

Katie laughed.

McGaven turned to Cisco. "Hey, buddy, I've missed you." He petted the shepherd as the dog whined with happiness.

"You haven't visited lately," said Katie.

"I know... things are just..." He didn't finish his sentence.

Katie drove out of the parking lot and she realized for the first time that her partner sounded like he had something on his mind. She glanced at him. "Gav, everything okay?"

"Yeah." He looked out the side window. "Just everyday stuff."

Katie could tell there was something wrong, but she didn't want to overstep their boundaries. She cared about those around her, but her life had been extremely difficult recently, and sometimes the things going on with her stole her focus from what was going on with the people she cared about.

After twenty minutes, they were back at Old Stagecoach

Road and the location of the first house fire. No longer smoldering, the house remnants looked forgotten and almost eerie. What was left was partially boarded up and there was still crime scene tape stretched across. The open landscape around the home appeared more spread out and larger than it did the other day too.

Katie looked in the rearview mirror. "You didn't tell me he was coming out."

McGaven turned and saw the fire service's large white SUV with Arson Investigator Ames behind the wheel. "It was the only way to officially get clearance. I didn't want any hiccup with the case by sneaking out here."

"Okay." Katie wasn't pleased, to say the least, but she was determined to make this investigation work in order to find the killer.

Cisco barked twice, watching the investigator approach.

"It's okay, Cisco," she said and exited her Jeep.

"Detectives. This makes three times now," said Ames. He was dressed in more tactical clothes with a long-sleeved shirt including the fire department logo and heavy boots. His gun, which was an issued Glock, was obvious on his hip. At first glance he looked like a police officer rather than an arson investigator.

Katie nodded and opened the back door where Cisco was ready.

"Ames," said McGaven as he readied himself to be Katie's backup and spotter on the search. He secured his clothing and weapons.

"My superiors aren't happy," said Ames.

"Why is that?" Katie said.

"Cases can get convoluted and evidence can get compromised. They don't want any mistakes."

"Noted," said Katie. She shut the back door, leaving Cisco in the car. "We don't need a babysitter."

Ames laughed. "I have better things to do than babysit two Pine Valley detectives."

"Good to know," she said.

It was the first time she'd actually seen a personality emerge from the investigator.

"Then why are you here?" said McGaven. "We know how to handle forensics and searches. And I think our record speaks for itself."

"Call it part curiosity and part duty. I want to make sure my arson crime scene stays intact," Ames said. "And when am I ever going to get the chance to see Detective Scott in action?" His words seemed to hang in the air.

For the first time, Katie wanted to get the search over with quickly. She had always looked forward to searching with Cisco, but now she was annoyed at having someone scrutinizing her skills and being a third wheel.

She decided to take a look at where they were going to be searching before taking Cisco out. She remained quiet as she slowly looked at what was left of the house and the new boards. They had been attached with large nails and screws with a border of two-by-four beams for extra strength.

Carefully stepping, she saw mostly work and police-issue bootprints. She took a few moments to survey the areas around the building before moving on. Glancing back, she saw McGaven and Ames keeping some distance. She knew her partner had instructed the investigator to wait. She shook off her irritation and began to focus on the surrounding areas.

The house and detached garage were positioned on level ground. It was the most appealing situation, with views of the trees and peeks of the valleys below. Behind the house were three large pine trees with thick branches nearly the size of most tree trunks. The owners must have left these beautiful giants while clearing other areas. One of the trees still had what was left of a massive swing. The heavy rope hung precariously, moving slightly in the mild wind.

Katie saw two trails leading down to the valley. The paths meandered slightly to keep the steepness to a minimum, which allowed for easy access. She scanned from left to right and then back again. It wasn't immediately clear if they would meet another road or lead to the nearest neighbor's property. It didn't matter, they were going to begin at the house and do a slight circling search, fanning out. Then they would begin to descend and see if anything seemed unusual or alerted their attention.

She paused a moment, closing her eyes, facing the vast acreage away from the house. She knew that McGaven and Ames couldn't see her face, so she took a deep breath. This was part of her routine. The potent aromas of the trees along with the accompaniment of the forest steadied her pulse and calmed her nerves, which would lead her to conduct a productive search with Cisco. The wind was light. The temperature was mild and comfortable. Overall, the area was quiet without any type of nearby road noise. She wondered if the killer, the arsonist, left by the main road or made some other escape, mindful not to give anything away about them.

Once satisfied, Katie turned and walked back to the Jeep, where Cisco waited patiently. She shed her heavy jacket; it made it easier for mobility. Not only did she check her Glock and an extra magazine, but she secured a modest-size knife in her boot sheath. She put in her earpiece and attached a small micro walkie-talkie to her shirt.

She looked up at her partner attaching his earpiece. "You ready?" She double-checked Cisco's vest and long lead.

"Ten-four," said McGaven.

"I'm going to shadow. Is that acceptable?" said Ames.

"I just ask that you don't interfere with the search," she said.

"Wouldn't dream of it."

Katie guided Cisco out of her Jeep. He was amped up with energy, so she took a moment to calm him and direct his focus.

"What's his name?" said Ames.

"Cisco."

"He's a hero, Army veteran, and just plain amazing," said McGaven.

Ames remained quiet and watched as Katie and Cisco took lead.

When Katie got in search mode with Cisco, nothing distracted her. She took a few minutes to let Cisco check out around the house and foundation. Nothing seemed to be of interest to the dog.

Walking to the main trailhead, Katie paused before she said, "*Such,*" a German command for Cisco to search.

Cisco took the command with seriousness. His body became rigid, ears perfectly straight up and slightly forward, tail relaxed and trailing the body. He moved forward with assertiveness, but no faster than the long leash. His large paws padded along the path. He changed between keeping his nose up and down at the ground—picking up scent along the land and any still wafting in the air.

Katie watched the dog to see if there were any indications or change of behavior. She glanced back and could see McGaven.

"Hear me?" she said, testing their communication. They always used the high-tech walkie-talkies in case something happened or if they became separated.

"Loud and clear," said her partner. He chose to climb down with her, keeping an eye on anything that might be dangerous or pose a problem.

She didn't know where Ames was, but it didn't matter. He might be back at the house keeping a distance.

The trail was difficult in a few areas, with loose rock and odd divots from erosion, but it was clear it had been used recently. Katie could see footprints, some made by animals, but there were others indicating an adult-size shoe. It didn't have the tread of a running shoe with complex lines and zigzags, but rather the pattern of a hiking boot, with a deeper print at the heel making it more pronounced.

The sun disappeared behind cloud cover making it seem as if it was late in the evening. Katie slowed her pace, which Cisco didn't seem to mind as he navigated easily the terrain ten feet away. There was nothing of interest for him at the moment. The pine and earthy smell changed to more of a damp-earth odor as shadows emerged within the trees.

Katie didn't hear any footsteps approaching, but she had the distinct impression that someone was watching. She had developed a sixth sense when she would take point on an Army maneuver. Her skin prickled and she actually felt a chill run down her spine. It was something you didn't want to ignore. It could mean the difference between life—or death.

Cisco slowed, becoming agitated: low whines, nose pointed in the direction they were moving. Then he stopped, standing completely still like a statue. It was difficult to see if he was breathing; his body was firm. The dog had definitely caught wind of something... or someone.

"Gav, come back," she whispered.

She waited. No response

Again, she said quietly, "Gav, location, come back?"

Everything told Katie to turn around and retrace their steps. Something was wrong. It may have sounded irrational to most, but she had been on many searches and guided her Army team through dangerous situations. She had an instinct for these things.

Katie's forehead perspired, causing a slight sweat to trickle down. Her hands and arms felt peculiar. She flashed back to some of the maneuvers she and Cisco had endured. It brought back memories—many weren't what she wanted to think about.

"Gav, location?" she repeated.

Nothing.

Katie kept moving forward, making sure her footing was solid. She realized McGaven knew where she was heading and hoped that he was most likely having some technical difficulties with their communication gear. She looked at the terrain next to the makeshift path and noticed some slight changes. Weeds were bent over and a few small twigs had been snapped recently. These were things she would mark for her partner, the experienced tracker, to be able to follow or find her.

Reeling in Cisco to about three to four feet, she kept him close. He still hadn't changed his behavior to indicate that he was tracking a scent.

Katie stopped. There was a rustle coming from an area just ahead.

She knew there were bears in the vicinity, but usually they were at higher elevations.

The sound repeated.

Cisco growled. It was low and made his black fur spike down his backside.

Katie pulled him closer. The leash was taught, but she knew the dog wouldn't bolt.

After a few tense minutes, two gray squirrels scampered out of the bushes chattering, one chasing the other as they ran up a nearby tree.

Relief filled Katie and she couldn't help but chuckle. She had been on hikes and camped most of the areas in the county her entire life. Her hesitation and anxieties were elevated more than usual.

"Katie?" said McGaven. His voice crackled.

"Here. Over."

"You okay? I lost you for a bit. Over."

"Affirmative. Over."

"I'm right behind you checking out some unstable ground. All good. Over."

"I'll leave you some signs where Cisco and I are headed," she said. She kept moving in the direction that paralleled the house and property. It was precisely where she wanted to be so she could double back.

There was nothing indicating that the killer and arsonist had used this path to escape after setting the fire. There wasn't anything visible on the trail like trash, something from the killer, or anything that might have been inside the house before it was set on fire.

Taking another ten minutes, Katie decided they should end the search and continue with the rest of the investigation. She looked above the main part of the property; thought she saw something. There was no audible sound, but something seemed to be moving, well hidden in the forest.

Cisco snapped his head in that direction too. He took several deep breaths as if he was fighting the urge to bark.

Katie didn't take another second to contemplate the situation; she made the instant decision to move downward, cutting across the trail into the wild vegetation while pushing Cisco ahead, just as two bullets whizzed by them.

SEVENTEEN

Friday 1445 hours

Three more gunshots echoed around the forest, making it difficult to pinpoint the exact location they had come from, except it was near the house. Katie and Cisco huddled together in a partially hollowed-out tree stump. Her view was that of the trail in both directions. She waited, hoping to see or hear the shooter coming toward them.

Katie had drawn her weapon, readied a bullet into the chamber, and remained at a steady alert in case she had to protect them. She didn't want to start shooting in the direction of the shots and take the chance of hitting McGaven or Ames. It also would give away her location to the shooter.

"Gav? We're okay," she whispered. Not wanting to repeat herself and give away their exact location, but she wanted her partner to know they were safe.

Katie counted a total of five gunshots had been fired. The first two were extremely close. She scratched her arm and realized it was sore and her hand was bloody. The bullet had grazed her, taking some of the flesh from her right arm, but the bleeding had already stopped. With concern, she checked Cisco and he was fine. The dog had been ahead of her and protected by her body and the trees. Her breathing accelerated, making her feel weak and woozy. Cisco pushed his body closer to her side and Katie could feel the heat from his body against her. He remained quiet as he did on those maneuvers in the Army. The dog's instincts had kicked in and he knew when to be quiet and when to support his partner.

Katie quietly leaned forward and listened intently for movement, footsteps, or anything that wasn't the typical sounds of the forest. The only thing she heard was the wind blowing through the trees.

She assumed the bullets had been aimed at just her and Cisco, but what if there were a couple of bullets aimed at McGaven and Ames? What if they were in trouble and she was just sitting and waiting? What if they needed medical attention?

Her breathing began to accelerate again. She shifted her sitting position to a kneeling one, stretching her body toward the trail. Turning her head from left to right, she didn't see or hear anything. The forest wildlife knew when there was a predator nearby and remained silent until they knew the threat was over.

Katie retreated into her perfect hiding place, contemplating what to do.

Who was shooting?

Why?

It wasn't random. The bullets were aimed directly at her—that much she knew.

Katie rolled everything through her mind. She still didn't know if the shots were made to kill or if they were to scare them away. Her throbbing outer right arm said it was the first option. It was too close for just getting them off the property. That made her think there was evidence the killer and arsonist didn't want the detectives to find.

Cisco's tail began to move as if he was happy to see someone.

Katie moved cautiously to a lower area and heard slight movement.

Cisco moved with Katie and she knew it was a friendly visitor.

"Gav?" she whispered. Her voice sounded strange as if she had just regained her hearing.

The bushes moved and she saw her partner emerge. He was crouched with his weapon in hand. His eyes were wide and filled with relief when he saw her.

"Gav," she breathed. It amazed her how such a tall man could move so stealthily.

"I think whoever it was shooting is gone now," said McGaven. There hadn't been any shots for more than fifteen minutes.

"What about Ames?" she said.

"I don't know, can't find him. Hopefully he can handle himself."

"Do you have your phone?" Katie had left hers in the Jeep.

"Yes."

"Call him."

McGaven pressed Ames's number. They waited. Katie grew more concerned until...

"Ames," said McGaven. "You okay?" He nodded to Katie. "Okay, we're on our way back." He ended the call.

"Is he okay? Did he see anything?" she said.

"Yes. He heard the shots and tried to find where they were coming from."

Katie let out a sigh. "What do you think?"

McGaven saw her bloody sleeve. "I think you should have told me you were hurt."

"I'm fine. It barely grazed me."

"Grazed? That was from a bullet?"

"Gav, it's okay."

"That means they were aiming at you."

"It means they got lucky or were just trying to scare us off."

"Don't downplay this," he said. "Why is it that every time we chase a killer, they get nervous and want you out of the picture?"

"I'm lucky, I guess."

"Seriously, Katie?"

"Let's get out of here." She wanted to change the subject and get back to the Jeep.

"Ames said he would come down to meet up, making sure things were clear."

"Okay."

She crawled out of her hiding place with Cisco as McGaven covered her with his weapon. He kept vigilant, watching from every direction as they made their way back to the top, where they finally met up with Ames.

"You guys okay?" the inspector asked.

"Yeah, we're fine," said McGaven.

Ames saw Katie's bloody sleeve. "You hit?"

"Just a scratch."

"I've got my first aid kit. You need that taken care of immediately," he said.

Katie didn't want to argue, so she politely nodded.

The three of them tracked back to the cars in front of the house without a confrontation. McGaven called in the incident and their location while Katie gave Cisco water and settled him back into the Jeep, rolling down the windows.

"Okay," said Ames. "Let's take a look at your arm."

"Really, I'm fine," she said.

"I'll decide if you are." Ames opened the back of Katie's Jeep and put down a first aid kit. "C'mon." The investigator seemed to have genuine concern for her well-being.

"Fine." She sat in the cargo area as Cisco pushed his nose over the back seat, making sure she was okay.

Ames opened the case and took out a small pair of scissors. Before Katie could protest, he cut her sleeve away from the wound. He proceeded to wash, sterilize, and take a good look at it.

"Well?" she said as she grimaced from the pain of the disinfectant.

"You're right, the bullet did only graze you."

"See, I told you."

"I was hoping to practice my stitching skills." His serious expression turned into a smile.

Katie couldn't help but laugh.

"Do you always have someone shooting at you during your investigations?" he said.

"It's happened before," said McGaven. "Actually, a few times..."

"Interesting," said Ames as he bandaged Katie's arm. "Just be sure to change the bandage every couple of hours. Okay?"

She nodded.

"I mean it. If it gets infected, then you'll really have a problem."

Katie watched Ames put the first aid supplies away and noticed burn scars three to four inches wide on his right forearm. She wondered if he had been in a fire during his job or at another time.

The investigator saw her looking. He casually pulled down his sleeves. "I can't wait to read this report." He walked back to his vehicle.

It wasn't long before two patrol cars showed up, along with a police sedan and the sheriff.

"Uh-oh," said McGaven.

Katie turned to see what he was looking at. Sheriff Scott stepped from his SUV and headed straight to the detectives.

Katie knew she had some explaining to do, but at least they now knew the killer and arsonist was watching them closely. It meant their police presence didn't spook him and he wasn't leaving anytime soon.

Detective Hamilton pulled McGaven aside to get details, and the sheriff approached the Jeep.

"You okay?" he asked.

"Yes, I'm fine. Ames bandaged it," she said.

"I see," he said, keeping his eyes on his niece. "What are you doing here?"

"We wanted to find out more about this property. We can't find the owners' names and the house was empty. There could be some evidence around the house and property. That's why I brought Cisco."

The sheriff didn't immediately respond. He looked around, contemplating. "I'm debating taking you off the cases."

"What? No, please don't do that," she said.

Another SUV entered the property. Detective Daniels got out and took a moment to look around.

"If I do, it'll be an order," the sheriff continued.

"We're in the middle of working a timeline for Mrs. Braxton and Anna. There are some strange things in this case."

"I can see that."

"Please don't take me off," she said. Katie knew that when the sheriff made up his mind there was no way of changing it. She tried to plead her case and hoped for the best. "Besides, Detective Daniels needs our cooperation. And both these murders are connected. With the three of us, we will be able to cover more ground."

"You know what it's like every time you take these cases," he said quietly, not wanting anyone to hear him. "You've put yourself right in the middle of the bull's-eye."

Katie knew that, but they were beginning to make headway

and they hadn't even seen the autopsy and forensics yet. She remained silent.

"As your boss, you're on the cases with McGaven and Daniels," he said. "As your uncle, please think twice before you run into the fire."

Katie thought that was an appropriate use of words considering they stood in front of a burned-down house.

"Thank you, sir."

"I suggest you call it a day and start again early in the morning."

"I will." It was difficult for Katie sometimes working with her uncle, who was her only living family, and who she was close to. There was a fine line between detective and niece. "We need to find the spent shell casings—unless the shooter picked them up," she said.

Everyone worked the area: the patrol officers scoured for shell casings, which they eventually found, giving them the location of the shooter when he fired at Katie and Cisco; Katie, McGaven, and Ames recounted their stories to Detective Hamilton; and Detective Daniels walked around the area and the house to get up to speed on where Anna Braxton was found.

As the group began leaving, McGaven approached Katie.

"The sheriff gave me direct orders," said McGaven.

"What's that?" she said.

"He doesn't want you to be alone. So it looks like I'm bunking in your guest room."

"Gav, you don't have to do that. Why doesn't anyone realize I can take care of myself? I'm a cop, ex-military. I have Cisco *and* security at my house."

McGaven stared at her.

She sighed. "Fine. Cisco is going to love it."

Daniels joined the detectives. "I'll see you both at o600 tomorrow."

"Of course," she said.

"We have quite a bit of information to cover." He looked at Katie before he left.

"See you tomorrow," said McGaven.

Katie and McGaven walked to her Jeep and got inside.

"Why do I get the feeling that he has a thing for you?" McGaven said.

"Why do I get the feeling that you're not telling me something?" she replied, raising her eyebrows.

"Okay then... I guess we both have feelings about stuff."

"I'm hungry," said Katie.

"You got my attention," he said.

EIGHTEEN

Katie and McGaven headed to her house after picking up food and stopping at the department so McGaven could pick up some things. The police sedan was still parked in her driveway and they would take it to the department in the morning.

Once inside, McGaven put the bags down on the counter and was followed closely by Cisco. "I don't know, Cisco, there might be some scraps after we finish." He had the dog's undivided attention.

"Please don't give him anything. He'll be a forever beggar if you do," she said as she went to her bedroom to change her clothes.

Katie could hear McGaven talking to the dog. "Did you hear that? Maybe when we're cleaning up I can sneak you something."

She smiled listening to her partner talking to Cisco. She peeled off her shirt and tossed it in the garbage. Her arm was still tender. The bandage was fine; in fact, it was well wrapped and secure. She wasn't sure what to think of the arson investigator, but it didn't matter. Her hope was that they would get some pieces of the puzzle fitted together with the fire forensics reports.

After cleaning up and changing into comfortable sweats, Katie began to feel better and her stomach growled as her appetite vied for her attention. When she returned to the kitchen McGaven had already unpacked the food and had portions of chicken, vegetables, fries, and salad divvied onto plates. He had scavenged for cold beers from her refrigerator and was in the middle of bringing them to the bar counter.

"Thanks, Gav," she said, taking a chair. "This looks so great."

They both dug into their meals and were quiet for a few minutes, enjoying their food.

"Okay," said Katie. "I know something is wrong."

McGaven kept eating and didn't make eye contact.

Katie was worried that something had gone bad between McGaven and his girlfriend, Denise, the supervisor for the records division at the sheriff's department. Katie loved seeing them together. They had been in a relationship almost as long as she and McGaven had been partners.

McGaven stopped eating and stared at his partner. Katie remained patient, letting McGaven gather his thoughts.

"It's Denise and me," he began. "We've been together for a while, living together. I love her more than anyone ever before. And Lizzie. She's like my daughter."

Katie smiled. "Sounds wonderful."

"It is."

"What's wrong?"

"Denise wants to get married so that I can adopt Lizzie."

"Gav, that's great. What's the downside?"

He took several sips of his beer. "Why can't things stay the way they are?"

"Nothing ever stays the same. Situations evolve. Love grows."

McGaven leaned back. "My parents couldn't make it work. Most of my friend's parents, siblings, and friends can't seem to make it work after getting married."

"So you're dooming your relationship because of other people's experiences? Gav, you have something wonderful. When I see the three of you together, you're the ones everyone else should want to be like."

"What about you and Chad? You were sweethearts forever."

His words stung Katie.

"Oh Katie, I'm sorry. I didn't mean..." He squeezed her hand.

"No, it's okay. Really," she said. "You're right. Things can happen. But... you have built such a strong foundation to your relationship. Your situation is different than mine was... One thing I have learned is to cherish what you have, reach out and love even if it's scary... because in the end you never want to have any regrets for not loving someone—no matter how it turns out."

McGaven looked down. It was clear he had difficulty meeting Katie's gaze.

"Gav, I know you and I've seen you two together."

"I love Denise, there's no doubt."

"I won't tell you what to do, but I'm always here for you," she said.

"You're right. Thanks, partner."

Katie got up from her chair and moved to McGaven. She hugged him tight. "I'm always here for you."

After cleaning up the kitchen and checking the security cameras—twice—the detectives worked the cases by seeing what they could dig up before their big meeting with Detective Daniels in the morning.

NINETEEN

Katie and McGaven rode in together to meet with Detective Daniels. They had spent time the night before tracing the timelines of where Mrs. Braxton and Anna had been before their deaths. Anna was off school for the week due to parent-teacher meetings, though there was no record of Mrs. Braxton ever attending the scheduled meeting. She had been going to work until the day after Anna went missing. According to neighbors, Anna was seen at home playing with her dog and doing chores. The last time anyone saw the teen, she had been heading to the mall. Nothing seemed to deviate from their usual routines.

In addition, McGaven had spoken with all of Mrs. Braxton's work colleagues, but it seemed that none of them knew her well. It was another dead end.

Katie ran her security card at the entrance to the forensic division. She was well rested, but her concerns about the cases were front and center.

As the detectives walked through the secure entrance and down the long hallway, they heard voices. Two distinct voices, to be exact. The conversation sounded cordial, but the volume was higher than usual.

Katie walked up to the main forensic examination room and pushed open the door. She leaned inside and saw John and Daniels looking at something on a computer screen.

"Morning," she said.

"Good morning," said Daniels.

"Hey," said John, looking at his watch. "You're early."

"Wanted to get started as soon as possible," she said.

"What's going on in here?" said McGaven.

"I have some preliminary things when you get settled," said John.

"Okay, we'll be back," she said.

Katie went into their office and put her things down. She stared at the investigative board. She walked up to it and began filling in information they knew so far. Daniels would have to update everything from Sacramento and Mrs. Braxton's murder at the conference garage. As she wrote, she could still hear the guys talking from the forensic area but she wanted to get her focus and preliminary theories together to build a strong investigation and to move with the most efficient use of their time.

She had to write out the timelines for Anna and her best friend, Jasmine. There were holes and undetermined times they needed to fill in; the blanks of their last days and hours before their disappearances. They still didn't know if Jasmine was still alive—and that made their next moves that much more important.

Anna Braxton

Fifteen years old (sixteen in three months) 5'7" tall, long brown hair, hazel eyes, good student, shy, few friends.

*Anna left her home **217 Birch Drive** to go to the mall late morning.*

1005 hours *she arrived at the mall, seen (via security cameras) in the food court area talking on her cell phone.*

Cell phone call received *10:30 a.m. was from a burner phone/not traceable except the call pinged from nearby cell towers.*

Anna then seen walking into the parking lot. The cameras didn't capture her getting into a car or what direction she would have walked.

9 days later she was found in the basement of a burned-down house.

Wanted to become a model/actress. Per her journal, she wanted "To be seen and important," "more," and asked, "why won't they believe me?"

She had been seen at the mall on several occasions by some of her classmates.

Seemed to have been in contact with A-1 Talent Agency —can't find definite connection but meeting instructions may have been given during multiple calls from burner phone.

From single-mother household. No siblings. Aunt, Lana, from Las Vegas.

Found wearing fancy yellow dress. Given food/water rations (peanut butter sandwiches).

Forensics/autopsy pending.

Stella Braxton (Anna's mother)

Forty-one years old. 5'8" inches tall, brown hair, brown eyes, healthy, bookkeeping job at Armstrong Accounting Firm for four years, Supervisor Chris Booker.

In debt, having trouble paying bills.

Came to the law enforcement conference in Sacramento to ask Katie for help.

How did she know Katie was going to be there? Why Katie?

Why didn't she ask for help from Detective Alvarez in

missing persons—only just filed a report? Why didn't she come
to the police department?

She was angry/scared.

Stabbed and murdered in parking garage.

"Find my daughter. Find the million-dollar
man... you'll find my Anna." MDM?

Home was extremely neat/organized.

"Hi, Katie," said Daniels.

She didn't know how long he'd been standing at the doorway.

Looking at him for a couple of moments, she said, "I'm trying to get some things down to see if I can see any patterns or inconsistencies."

"I can fill in what we know about Mrs. Braxton," he said.

"What do we have?" said McGaven, entering the room. He put down his laptop and took a seat.

Daniels opened his laptop. "Okay, I have forensics and the autopsy."

Katie stayed near the board to update it.

"First, I'll give you the bad news," Daniels said. "We couldn't get an ID on the person who attacked Stella Braxton. If you see here... and here..." He played the video on the screen.

There were only two places that showed what appeared to be a man, average height and build, wearing sweats and hoodies. He also wore a baseball cap and dark glasses. The man seemed to know where the cameras were placed to turn his head at the right time.

Katie leaned in closer. "You can see blood on his hoodie."

Daniels zoomed in on the image. It was clear there were large blood stains. "We found the discarded hoodie in a trash can and it tested positive for Stella Braxton's blood."

"It shows that the killer planned the attack and knew about the garage's surveillance," said Katie, adding to the board. "The big question is... was Mrs. Braxton's killer part of Anna's disappearance and death or was there something else going on?"

Daniels left the best view of the killer paused on the screen, a brief moment where he had glanced at the camera.

Katie studied every part of his face. "Can you print that?"

"Of course."

The printer buzzed.

"Other bad news," continued Daniels.

"There's no such thing as bad news... everything means something," said McGaven, smiling at Katie. "That's what my partner says."

"She's right," said Daniels. "Everything means something. We just have to figure out what."

"So what else?" said Katie.

"We also found the weapon used in the trash can."

"Let me guess: wiped clean," she said.

"Yes. But what was interesting was it was an ordinary knife, like from the average kitchen."

The room became quiet. Katie's mind raced to the Braxtons' residence, recollecting the kitchen drawers and counter. There had been utensils missing. Could the murder weapon have been one of the Braxtons' knives?

"The autopsy was what we expected," said Daniels. "Mrs. Braxton died from her injuries. Otherwise, she was in good health. There was nothing under her nails. I believe the attack was so sudden and violent she didn't have time to fight with the killer."

Katie added a few remarks to the board.

Daniels brought up the image of a photo that appeared to have been printed from a website. It was the advertisement for the law enforcement seminar. "This was found folded in her pocket. That's how she knew where to find you... and when."

"But it still doesn't answer why me?"

"Well, we found several web searches for murder, kidnapping, and cold cases in Pine Valley. It was clear she researched you."

Katie didn't know what to think. There were other investigators.

"Maybe she felt more comfortable contacting a woman?" said McGaven.

"Maybe," she said.

"Let's face it, you've been in the news a lot over the past year," said Daniels.

Katie added to Mrs. Braxton's profile that she researched her and found her at the conference. "She was so desperate to find Anna. I'm glad she didn't know her daughter had been taken hostage and died." She reread her lists. "What did she know about this million-dollar man?"

"I've been digging," said McGaven. "Did you know having the net worth of a million dollars doesn't necessarily make you a millionaire? I guess now you'd have to have a net worth of 2.5 million dollars."

"Inflation," said Daniels.

"We use the word 'million' for a lot of things. It doesn't really have much meaning anymore," Katie said. "However, I read a case once that referred to a serial killer who proclaimed 'he was more than a million.' His found victims were forty-two, but they knew there had to be many, many more. They were all young women between the age of eighteen and twenty-five—and all of them were wearing fancy prom dresses."

"I don't get it," said McGaven. "Is it a number or a description?"

"You're forgetting this is the mind of a serial killer. He's working from his fantasies, perceptions, and experiences. Namely childhood experiences. Million-dollar man could mean something very specific to him—and make sense from his perspective only. It's up to us to figure out what it means, in his mind, and how to use that to find him before we find another body," said Katie. "It will make sense. Just not to us."

"That's creepy," said Daniels. "How do we find him besides following the clues he's left for us?"

"Well, our victim, Anna, wanted to be an actress or model so that people would really see her. She put herself in the killer's path without even realizing it," she said.

"We're talking about a teenage girl," said Daniels.

"Yes, but we all have a need to be seen, heard, loved, respected, and so forth. This killer has honed his skills to find the right victims based on their wanting to be an actress or model. Seen by millions and making millions. The killer sees himself as the person to provide that."

"What about Mrs. Braxton?" said McGaven.

"She was going to find out what happened to her daughter no matter what," Katie said. "And it's my theory she possibly stumbled on something much bigger than she was anticipating."

"Which got her killed," said McGaven.

Katie nodded. She walked to the board and wrote:

Clara Taylor (next-door neighbor of Braxtons)

    Chris Booker (manager at Armstrong Accounting Firm, Braxton's boss)

    Kip Johnson (neighbor, house sitter next to the Old Stagecoach Road)

    Teens at Mall (Kayla, Deb, and Trevor)

    Mrs. MacAfee (Jasmine's mother)

    MDM Million-dollar Man

Katie stepped back, reading the list.

"What are you thinking?" said McGaven.

"We haven't talked with enough people about the Braxtons."

"There's been a canvass."

"Somebody *knows* something..." she said. "I guarantee it." Katie thought about Mrs. Braxton's boss. He'd seemed cagey and too quickly packed up his employee's things.

She went out and came back in with the box they had from the accounting firm, making room for it on the table. She flipped the lid and began digging through. There were two photographs similar to the ones in Anna's room, a novel, pens, pencils, a notebook, a small empty wooden box, a scarf, gloves, and receipts.

Katie looked through the notebook, but it had been used to write down expenses' due dates, payroll, and some notes on various clients. "Here's a notation of two clients. Looks like Pane Construction and Delilah's Spa."

"And you think they might know something?" said Daniels.

"After visiting that office, where no one looked up from what they were doing and the boss definitely seemed like a jerk to work for? Yes. I think her clients might know something about her—like if she was upset, anything about the workplace, and if she ever came to them for help."

"I could see that," said McGaven.

"I don't think going to Anna's school will help much, or speaking to other kids, but someone has to know something about the Braxtons."

"How do you want to do this?" said Daniels. "I can check out these places."

"Hey, sorry to interrupt," said John at the door. "I have some time and there are some forensics you should see."

"Oh sorry, I forgot," said Katie.

McGaven looked up from his phone. "Dr. Dean at the medical examiner's office has information about Anna too."

Katie thought a moment. "Gav, you and Evan go to the medical examiner's office, and I'll talk to John."

McGaven hesitated. "You sure you don't want to wait for the autopsy results?"

"I think we've been waiting too long on these cases," she said. "Let's go."

TWENTY

Katie stood over the forensic examination table waiting to hear what John had found out. The forensic items were impeccably organized as usual. She waited for John as he pulled up reports and images on one of the computers.

"You okay?" he said.

"Fine. Except for this case."

"That's not what I mean. I know you were shot yesterday and that the sheriff is worried about your safety."

"He's my uncle. He's always worried about my safety." Katie knew what John was getting at, but she didn't want to talk about it.

John seemed to pick up on her wishes and didn't push her any further. "Okay. We had a lot of things to cover, but I've streamlined it. You and Gav will have my reports, but I wanted to talk to you in person first. First, the Braxton residence. It was difficult to search because everything was incredibly neat. Does that make sense? And many areas appeared to be wiped down."

"Wouldn't it be easier if it was neat? Where things were messy would be an indicator of the perpetrator."

"True. But Eva and I noticed that some of the neat areas had had their items carefully moved and then put back. The laundry area and the bathroom."

"We documented the house and dusted for prints. The area was mostly wiped down, but there were some smudged areas."

Katie began rubbing her arm where the bandage was. She realized she hadn't changed it in a while.

"Is that bothering you?" John said.

"What?"

"Your arm?"

"No. Well a little. I need to change the bandage."

John turned and went into the next room. He came back with a first aid kit. "No time like the present."

"No, really, I'll do it when we're done."

John ignored her and pulled out the bandages and gauze. Katie sometimes forgot he'd been a Navy Seal and he knew more than most about first aid. She watched as the forensic supervisor expertly and quickly changed her bandage.

He paused a moment to look at the wound. "Yep, you've been grazed by a bullet. A nine millimeter."

"How do you know that?"

"I can tell," he said. He finished securing the bandage.

"Thank you."

"We found five nine-millimeter shell casings at the Old Stagecoach Road location." He looked at a report. "But until we find the gun to compare them with, they're going to sit and wait."

"What about prints?" she said.

"Getting prints off shell casings is tricky, and generally when you do find prints, they're smudged." He watched Katie. "But I did find something unusual that I don't think I've ever found on a shell casing before."

"What's that?"

"Well, I found a small deposit of plastic."

"Plastic? From gloves or something?"

"That's what I first thought, but the composite was an inorganic synthetic polymer, which is more like latex with some inorganic minerals."

"Interesting."

"You're going to love this..."

Katie watched John as he keyed up two magnified photographs. "They look identical."

"They are. This is the latex material found on the nine-millimeter shell casing and the other was that material found in the second victim's hand."

Katie flashed on an image of the unidentified girl lying in the closet wearing the yellow dress. "Are you sure?"

John laughed. "Of course. This doesn't lie," he said referring to the images.

"That connects the person who held the unidentified girl in the closet and the person who took shots at me."

"I would say they are one and the same."

Katie thought about what a huge clue this was, but she wasn't sure what it meant—at least not yet.

"And Arson Investigator Ames hasn't sent reports yet," John said.

"Okay."

John moved to the large examination table where there was Anna's yellow dress, the plastic sandwich bag, and the water bottle. "We did a thorough search of the basement. There were about three different blood types on the brick wall that we were able to retrieve. Type O, O positive, and AB. Type O is consistent with Anna's blood type. Haven't finished the DNA tests. It'll take a bit—always does."

Katie looked at the food bag and water bottle, but the dress really caught her attention. She'd never forget seeing Anna's lifeless body at the bottom of the cellar stairs. "What about the dress?"

"Eva meticulously combed through everything and used different light sources to see if there were any foreign fluids or trace evidence."

"And?" she said.

"There were foreign hairs and what appeared to be carpet fibers."

Katie thought that sounded encouraging.

"The foreign hairs were not human. It was some type of domestic animal. The carpet fiber appears to be from wool carpeting, not typical of most carpets, which are made of polyester or nylon these days. That's not to say that no one has wool carpets, but this particular piece of wool is older, dated back to say the 1940s or 1950s. It's not only wool; it's extremely worn and the actual fiber was difficult to pinpoint."

Katie looked at the dress and imagined where Anna would have picked up this carpet fiber. "It wouldn't be from a vehicle?"

"No. They use different types of carpeting."

"So... where would Anna pick up a fiber from antique carpeting?" She looked at the rest of the forensic evidence. "It would have to be from an older home. The residence on Old Stagecoach Road seemed newer."

"Maybe the fire report might have some answers?" he said.

"True." She thought about that for a moment. "What about the Jane Doe's dress?"

"We didn't find much. The fabric is clean with the exception of the smoke damage. It's a dress that's mass-produced on the lower-end spectrum—the same quality as Anna's. It's unclear if they are identical, but they definitely resemble each other." He watched Katie closely and seemed to want to say something, but decided against it. "When I find out anything else, I'll let you know immediately."

Katie nodded. "John, thank you. You've given us a lot to think about," she said.

"I wish I had more, but there are other tests that will take a bit of time. I hope the autopsy report will help."

She turned to leave.

"Katie?"

"Yes."

"Be careful."

Katie smiled and nodded. She appreciated John's sentiment. He never overstepped professional boundaries, but he clearly valued their friendship and still let her know that he cared.

Katie left the forensic exam room and quickly updated the investigative board. She added under the column of forensics:

Same latex found on nine-millimeter shell casing at shooting scene and in the hand of victim Jane Doe.

Antique, worn carpet fibers on Anna's yellow dress.

Katie stared at the notes of the evidence and timeline. Things were falling into place. They just had to figure out the correct order of the investigation that would lead them to the killer.

Every time it was quiet or she closed her eyes, she saw Stella Braxton's body in the parking garage bleeding and holding on to life; Anna's body at the bottom of the basement stairs; Jane Doe's in the closet. More vivid thoughts were about Jasmine and where she could be. They all deserved someone fighting for them and closure to their cases. The killer needed to be found and put in jail before there was another victim.

Find the million-dollar man... you'll find my Anna...

TWENTY-ONE

Saturday 1050 hours

The medical examiner's office was unusually quiet due to the fact it was a Saturday. Most of the sounds and voices were muted, but the distinct noise of wheels turning on gurneys was still audible. The floor was extremely clean and the disinfectant was much more pungent than normal. It was strange for McGaven to be going to the ME's office without Katie. He liked Detective Daniels, and he had proven dedicated and helpful in one of their past cases, but it still felt like he was more of an observer than a colleague. Katie's connection to him was still vague, but McGaven sensed they definitely had been more than police colleagues, and military K9 trainer and subordinate, in the Army.

"Where is everybody?" said Daniels.

"It's Saturday."

"Still... It's so quiet." Daniels looked around and it was clear he was uncomfortable.

McGaven suppressed a smile. He knew exactly how the detective felt. It had taken him a long time to be able to relax somewhat at the medical examiner's. He remembered the first time he and Katie had gone together.

"Detectives," said Dr. Dean as he appeared from an office. It wasn't difficult to recognize him due to his unusual and casual attire of a very bright Hawaiian shirt with red and yellow native flowers, brown khakis, and sandals. The soles of his shoes made a slight squeaking noise on the clean floors. "This way," he said and slipped into one of the exam rooms.

The detectives followed.

Dr. Dean put on his lab coat and grabbed two files from a side table—quickly skimming the information. There were two occupied gurneys, each with a white sheet covering the bodies.

The ME looked up at the two men. "Where's Katie?"

"She's with John," said McGaven.

"Ah, and you are?" he said to Daniels.

"Dr. Dean, this is Detective Evan Daniels from Sacramento PD," McGaven said.

"Nice to meet you. I assume there must be some type of a crossover case?" He raised his eyebrows in question.

"Something like that," said Daniels.

"All right then." The doctor walked over to the first gurney. He sighed, pulling the sheet back halfway, revealing Anna Braxton's body. "Anna Braxton, fifteen years old, healthy, a little underweight, no signs of sexual assault."

Her long dark-brown hair was combed and her body scrubbed. Looking at her in the bright fluorescent lighting, her features were very striking, even though her neck wasn't in the correct position due to the trauma.

"Did her aunt identify her body?" said McGaven.

"Yes, and then she left to go home to Las Vegas to make arrangements. I understand her sister, Anna's mother, was murdered in Sacramento. The poor woman lost two close family members." Dr. Dean sighed again. "Anna's neck was broken in two places, consistent with falling from a height and not strangulation. Two of her cervical vertebrae bones were severed, the C_2 and C_3."

"Could this be considered an accident?" said Daniels.

"Based on where she was found and the position she was in, it's more likely it was an accident. She was also severely dehydrated and well on her way to being malnourished. She had some bruising on her arms and hands." The doctor showed the detectives the locations. "The condition of her body, her environment—having been locked in a dark basement—lack of adequate food and water were signs of abuse rather than homicide."

"Does that mean you're not ruling it a homicide?" said McGaven.

"At this point I'm ruling manner of death accidental, and cause of death trauma to the cervical vertebrae... a broken neck."

McGaven wasn't pleased with the outcome of Dr. Dean's assessment.

"I can see you're disappointed," the ME said. "At this point, she accidentally fell. I don't see anything that indicates she was pushed. No bruising that would suggest that action."

"But due to her confinement and obvious abuse, someone could be charged with manslaughter, false imprisonment, and abuse," said Daniels. He stated that more to him and McGaven.

"That's for you and the courts to determine," said the doctor. "I'm sorry I don't have something you wanted to hear."

"What about toxicology?"

"There was nothing in her system from either illegal or pharmaceutical drugs. Her last meal was peanut butter and bread in a small quantity."

"Nothing under her nails?" said Daniels.

"We did scrapings, but it was dirt and brick, I'm assuming from the walls in the basement. John will have to confirm from what he excavated from the basement." He skimmed the reports. "She was basically clean from anything that would be considered foreign. She did have fine dog hair on her and that was the only other trace evidence we found."

McGaven sighed. "Okay."

"Now the Jane Doe was another story," said Dr. Dean. He covered Anna's body and moved around to uncover the other young girl. "We're still working on identifying her."

The Jane Doe was petite in build with shoulder-length brown hair and bangs. Her bright-pink fingernails were noticeable. Her expression bothered McGaven. He had trouble viewing most bodies, especially children. Her gaze was as if she was lost in an abyss. There didn't seem to be any indication of trauma to the body.

"She succumbed to the heat from the fire," said the medical examiner. "She had been burned and damaged due to the excessive head. There was not smoke inhalation, which indicates that she was already dead before she was put in the closet."

McGaven knew what was coming in the medical examiner's findings and it would be a first for them.

"As with Anna Braxton, the young woman didn't show any injuries to suggest she was murdered. There were no visible signs of sexual assault. No defense wounds indicating that she struggled with her assailant. There was nothing in her toxicology report. She had very little in her stomach, which signified that she was in borderline starvation mode and was also dehydrated."

"There were no other injuries or anything that would mean she was murdered?" said McGaven.

"She died from the fire—manner of death accidental and cause of death asphyxiation due to smoke inhalation depriving the body of oxygen. I did not find anything else to suggest homicide at this point," he said. "There were no restraints, other injuries, or wounds for me to rule it homicide. I'm sorry, Detectives. I know you didn't want to hear that from these two cases."

"I have to say I'm surprised," said McGaven.

"But that doesn't mean there aren't extenuating circumstances surrounding each incident and then fires intentionally set," said Daniels.

"Of course. But I have to rule within my legal and expert classifications of the body," said Dr. Dean.

The detectives remained silent.

"I'm sure Katie will fill you in more from John's findings, but I can tell you that Jane Doe had a small amount of substance in her hand that was latex in origin. Not under her nails, but in her hand."

"I see," said McGaven. He wondered about that and knew Katie was most likely working that angle as well. He was disappointed in the official findings, but that didn't change their need to find the perpetrator who lured, kidnapped, and held these teen girls hostage until their deaths.

"If anything new comes up, I will let you know," said the doctor. "I've emailed you the reports as usual. Please don't hesitate to reach out with any questions. I know these manners of deaths are unusual for your investigations."

"Thank you, Dr. Dean," said McGaven. He looked at Daniels, who didn't seem to have any questions.

"My pleasure. And say hello to Katie," the ME said before leaving the examination room.

McGaven and Daniels remained standing next to the bodies.

"I don't think Katie's going to be happy about the medical examiner's conclusions about the manner of death," said McGaven.

"No, she isn't," said Daniels.

TWENTY-TWO

Saturday 1230 hours

He pulled the car into the large three-car garage, closing the door behind him and cutting the engine. The owners of the oversized five-bedroom home wouldn't be back for some time due to their month long cruise.

It used to amaze him how most people were open books and revealed so much about their personal lives.

When they would be gone on vacation.

Where their children go to school.

Where they hide their money and valuables.

People were also careless with their cell phones, written notes, and casual conversations.

They never thought anyone was watching, waiting, and listening to everything they said and did.

When he'd heard the Jordans were going to be leaving their house without someone staying there while they were gone, he thought it the perfect backdrop to his plan.

He thought he would be disappointed at another failure from his casting call, but in fact he was amped up about it. He would put up a temporary casting call on social media asking for a photo and background. After a few days, he would choose the one that spoke to him. It proved his theory about people wanting to be a star but being unable to fulfill the obligation and promise of being a true actor of the people. He hadn't met anyone close to having the million faces. He knew he was special, but there was still hope he would find someone as he cleared the path to find the right one.

The man got out of the car. He went around to the trunk and opened it. Standing a moment to watch, he cocked his head, studying and waiting for something of interest to happen. But nothing did. Pity. His power was growing. He realized when the detectives came back to the property that he had them right where he wanted.

Soon.

Looking down, the previously chatty sixteen-year-old-girl, Cindy, who would not follow his simple instructions for her once-in-a-lifetime casting call, was being left to her last moments. She wasn't the one he was looking for—no lovely blonde hair and a walk that made others notice. Her acting ability was dreadful. She would always revert to her perky and annoying personality of being a know-it-all. She couldn't move smoothly enough for a model even though she had the tall lanky build of one. There was nothing trainable or natural about her.

Cindy's eyes, wide with terror, stared at him. He'd had to tape her mouth, bind her wrists and ankles. It was the first time for this and he thought it was quite useful and convenient. As he moved slightly, removing his prosthetics on his face and neck, her eyes watched him. He dropped the pieces on the floor—they soon would be melted from the heat.

He was curious watching the girl. His emotions were in the moment. Not angry. Not happy. Neutral.

He left her momentarily and opened the car's back door. On the seat were several containers of gasoline along with two small suitcases. *The fuel was primitive but effective. Nothing that would stump an arson investigator, but enough power to do the job. It wasn't messy, and an effective way to cleanse what was left behind. He put the containers on the garage floor where he would return to them later.*

He lifted Cindy out of the trunk and put her on the ground. She cried and squirmed, but it didn't make a difference to her fate.

Where to stage her?

The usual?

Or perhaps something new for the investigators to try to figure out.

He had plenty of time to prepare for Cindy's last performance.

TWENTY-THREE

Saturday 1315 hours

Katie had been scouring background checks of anyone who had been in the Braxtons' lives. The printer hummed with pages deemed important to the cases. She began putting together a history of the people who surrounded Stella and Anna Braxton, but they weren't close family or best friends, more like regular interactions.

Katie hadn't moved from her laptop and relished the quiet time in the office. After feeling somewhat discouraged listening to John's forensic findings, she plunged right back into the case. There were things they hadn't covered yet, but she knew Jasmine's time was limited and hoped that at any moment she would receive a call from Detective Alvarez that the teen had come home—that everything had been a big misunderstanding. Katie's gut told her the girl was out there somewhere, and they had to find her—in time.

The door opened as McGaven and Daniels walked in. It startled Katie because she hadn't heard any of the usual conversations echoing throughout the forensic division.

"What's happening?" she said. She saw the expressions on their faces and knew it wasn't going to be good news.

Both detectives read the new forensic additions to the board.

"Be glad you weren't there," said McGaven as he pulled out a chair and sat across from his partner.

"What do you mean?"

"Both Anna and the Jane Doe are... well, the medical examiner's official statement of the manner of death is considered accidental... for both victims." He exhaled loudly.

"Is this true?" she said, barely comprehending what she had just heard.

"Afraid so," said Daniels. "He couldn't find anything that would contribute to the direct evidence of homicide. Anna Braxton fell and broke her neck. There was no evidence she had been pushed and her body didn't show any defensive wounds. And Jane Doe didn't have any injuries and died from smoke inhalation."

"I don't understand."

"Well, there are extenuating circumstances that led to their deaths, which would be considered manslaughter. They were starved and kept against their will, but there wasn't a direct cause, like stabbing or shooting, causing their deaths. It's a strange judgment under these conditions that I think should be reviewed again."

"Why would Dr. Dean give that as his official statement? Wouldn't it be 'undetermined' at best?" she said.

"Good point. And no," said Daniels.

"This doesn't sound like Dr. Dean," she said, concerned.

"He did say if circumstances changed, he would consider changing the manner of death," said McGaven.

If Katie didn't feel disappointed from the lack of forensic evidence, this new addition to the investigation definitely frustrated her. "Well, we're going to have to dig deeper and spread a wider net."

"What did you have in mind?" said Daniels.

"I've been thinking about the people we've questioned so far. We're not getting an accurate account of the victims' movements before their deaths with such a small pool of people to talk to."

"I see your point," said McGaven.

"I did a little background search," she said. "I know this is your expertise, Gav, but I wanted to know. And my hunch paid off."

Daniels pulled up another chair, the three detectives now seated.

"I checked into Chris Booker," said Katie.

"Mrs. Braxton's boss?" said McGaven.

"And... he has been in trouble with the law before. Two breaking and entering charges, several trespasses, and there was even a restraining order against him in Arizona from an ex-girlfriend. He apparently broke into her home and tore up the place, explaining he was getting his stuff she wouldn't give him."

"Mr. Booker, you've been busy," said McGaven.

"Breaking in and tearing up stuff. Sound familiar?" she said. "I know it's a stretch, but it's a pattern of behavior that could match what we found at the Braxtons' house."

"Interesting."

"There was something about his behavior at the office and the way the employees were acting as well," she said.

"What do you mean?" said Daniels.

"It was like they were being kept in line," said McGaven. "So no one knows what he's been up to."

"It's well worth keeping an eye on Booker," said Katie. "I also did a basic background check on the owners of Pane Construction and Delilah's Spa, which were clients of Mrs.

Braxton—Stan Pane and Briana Nest-Smith. They seemed significant enough that she wrote them down in her notes. Could just be reminders or maybe something she was investigating."

"And?" said McGaven.

"Stan Pane has some minor offenses from his early twenties. But get this: he did some amateur modeling and a commercial."

"Now that's interesting," said Daniels.

"He has no connection to Anna apart from working with her mother, but I thought it was something to put on the list."

"What about the spa owner?" said Daniels.

"Briana Nest-Smith has been in business for about two years and the money to start the spa came from an ex-husband, Ed Smith, who mysteriously disappeared."

"What do you mean, disappeared?" said Daniels.

"I mean he apparently packed his bags, left the house, and has never been seen from again," she said. "I don't know all the details, but it's unusual."

"So he gave his ex some money and then skipped out?"

"Looks like it."

"I can honestly say that this case just keeps getting stranger —nothing like any previous case I can think of," said McGaven.

Katie leaned back in her chair. "This is the first time I'm not completely certain of a killer profile. Too many things seem odd and out of place. It's as if his traits and behavioral evidence conflict."

"Like?"

"Like, upon first glance it would seem that the crime scenes are staged—which is usually done for our benefit. But I think the killer sets up the scenes for his own benefit. He doesn't care about law enforcement's opinion. It appears fire might have a special meaning for him, but he doesn't stay consistent. One crime scene used fire as a means of covering up Anna's death. But Jane Doe's body seemed more like an afterthought," she said. "I'm beginning to think his moods play a big role in his murder scenes. And it's like he's desperate to find something... whatever it is... he keeps replicating the victim in the same dress and then a fire scene."

"A previous experience?" McGaven said.

"Maybe. I think it's something that was so traumatic that his fantasies will never make it right again." She hesitated, thinking things through. "I don't know at this point. We need to dig deeper."

"We can only go by what we have right now and move forward," said Daniels.

Katie and McGaven nodded.

"I had a thought about the two properties with the arson fires. We need to check on any of those live trail or game cameras. Maybe they might have caught something, if we're lucky," she said. "I wasn't sure how to access them."

"On it," said McGaven.

Katie looked at Daniels. She still didn't feel one hundred percent comfortable with him, but they needed to talk to the owners of those businesses Mrs. Braxton had jotted down in her notebook. "You up for checking out Stan Pane at Pane Construction?"

He stood up. "Let's go."

"I'll just be here," said McGaven as he keyed up several sites. "Don't worry about me."

Katie laughed.

"Bring me some food on your way back," said McGaven.

"On it."

TWENTY-FOUR

Saturday 1430 hours

Katie drove to Pane Construction, which was located in a more rural part of town where there were businesses that needed more space—automotive, industrial, and farming. Daniels rode shotgun and seemed more quiet than usual to Katie. She glanced at the detective and oftentimes it was difficult not thinking about their close moments when he'd made her feel secure and heard.

"Is everything okay with you?" Daniels said after a while.

"Sure. I mean, besides these cases." She tried to keep her voice on a positive note.

"Why don't I believe you?"

"You're a cop."

"Besides that."

"We all have ups and downs. Right now I'm concentrating on these cases."

Daniels seemed to study her for a few moments. He didn't press her for more information.

Katie really didn't want to talk about personal things with

Daniels. She didn't want to feel vulnerable with him as she had during the time Chad had gone missing.

"I think we're close," she said, glancing at the GPS. "I've never been to this part of town before, so bear with me."

"How do you want to handle Stan Pane?"

"I need to see how he reacts to our visit and go from there."

"If he's relaxed and cooperative, then it's easy... but..."

"If he's combative and rude, yeah, we'll push him to see if he's hiding anything," she said. "It will be interesting to see what he says about Mrs. Braxton and the manager, Booker."

Katie slowed and turned down a long gravel driveway. Tall pine trees arced over them, creating a natural canopy. It was dense and a country landscape, making it difficult to see the facility and buildings. She wasn't sure of the size of Pane Construction.

"Where is this place?" Daniels said.

"This is the correct address and it seems to be going somewhere."

Daniels frowned. Katie didn't know if he was annoyed or being extra security conscious.

Just when the tree line seemed to go on forever, Katie drove out of the forest tunnel and into a cleared area. There were two manufactured home structures and one extremely large metal two-story barn. New and old trucks were parked along the side of the area. Backhoes, a dump truck, and a wood chipper were lined up along the barn structure. An enclosed area with chain-link fencing held discarded house items such as cabinets, sinks, flooring, windows, and bathroom and kitchen fixtures.

"Looks like a fairly large business," said Daniels. "But it looks quiet."

Katie nodded. "Where is everybody?"

"It's Saturday. Workers must have the weekend off."

Two yellow-striped cats darted across in front of them and disappeared into the woods. Katie pulled the sedan to the side in the shaded area and cut the engine. She didn't immediately get out, surveying the area first.

"Where do you think Stan Pane is?" Daniels said.

"He's here." She pulled up a photo of Pane and showed it to Daniels.

"What makes you so sure?"

Katie got out of the sedan and moved toward the newest truck and touched the hood. It was cool. She glanced inside and saw mail with his name on it. Looking around, she said, "He's here somewhere."

"Maybe we should've made an appointment?" he said.

"I like to catch people unannounced. You get more of the real side of things."

"You mean they don't have time to prepare or not be around?"

"Exactly." She stayed in the same place, taking everything in.

"What are you waiting for?"

"I'm not sure, but it does seem unusually quiet. I'd expect to at least see a dog or two running around, but there's nothing but two cats."

Daniels scanned the area too, looking from the buildings to the barn, and around the trucks and equipment. He took his steps with thought, remaining aware of the surroundings.

Katie strained to hear some type of noise like machinery, voices, animals, or movement of some kind. Nothing. There was no indication someone was around. She looked to the structures, searching for some type of security, such as video cameras. If there were some, they weren't visible.

A slight breeze kicked up, which was the only noise through the trees. Dust whirled around in front of the trucks—and stopped as quickly as it had started.

Daniels moved closer to Katie. He leaned in and whispered, "It feels like someone is watching."

Katie stayed quiet and slightly nodded. She felt the uneasiness. Something was out of kilter.

"What do you want to do?" he said breaking the quiet.

"Let's look around." Her hand brushed against her weapon, a usual reflex when going into unknown territory.

Daniels' expression remained neutral as he seemed to ready himself. "Let's go."

Katie began her search of the area, looking for Pane. She decided the manufactured homes were the best place to begin. Daniels followed, carefully keeping watch around them.

The first structure on the farthest side of the area appeared to be the office. She stepped up to the door, which was closed, and knocked. She patiently waited, listening carefully for any movement or other sounds. When there was no response she decided to move on to the second housing structure. Knocking twice, she waited just as before. She glanced behind her and saw that Daniels was ten feet away, watching all directions.

The longer Katie waited the more frustrated she became. She knocked again. This time she tried the door. It was locked. Giving up on anyone being around, she walked into the middle of the property, looking at absolutely everything as she turned three hundred sixty degrees. Nothing seemed to be out of place, but that was what bothered her. There were no indications the business was closed: the property didn't have a gate, there were no no-trespassing or keep-out signs. She searched again for any cameras, but didn't find any.

"What do you want to do?" said Daniels.

Katie snapped out of her pondering. She searched for Pane Construction's phone number on her cell and dialed. Within seconds, they heard a phone ringing.

"Where is that coming from?" Daniels said.

Katie looked around. "Over here," she said and headed to the large metal barn.

There could have been many reasons Pane's cell phone was

ringing nearby. He could have put it down somewhere while he went and did something else. He could have forgotten it when he left. But... Katie didn't think so as she entered the barn.

"What's that?" whispered Daniels.

Inside they could hear a soft scraping sound they weren't able to hear before.

Katie moved farther into the barn. Due to the size of the two-story metal structure, sounds echoed strangely. The branches, the wind, and any movement made things seem bigger and louder. Maybe the sound was nothing at all—or maybe it was.

Katie saw an office, workbench, and some smaller equipment pieces along the wall. There were boxes with file folders spilled around. And there was one neat pile that stood out on the side.

She kept moving.

Stan Pane's cell phone rang once more and then suddenly stopped, leaving an unnerving quiet. Except for the dull scraping noise.

Katie walked past a wheeled stainless-steel table used to put tools on and roll around. On top was the cell phone. She picked it up and could see the missed call from her number. There was only fifteen percent battery left.

"Katie," said Daniels.

She turned to see that the detective had walked past her and was standing with his back to her. He looked round.

Joining the detective, she saw what he was staring at.

Hanging from a noose was the lifeless body of Stan Pane. His body gently swung back and forth, the sound of the rope moving against the steel support beam the noise they had heard. Heavy bags attached to thick chains had been used to offset the weight of his body to hoist him eight feet in the air. He was wearing jeans, a black T-shirt, and heavy work boots. His face, neck, and hands were swollen, indicating that decomposition had set in a while back—maybe a couple of days. The bluish-black coloring was disturbing, changing the shape of his face.

That wasn't the worst of it. The shocking part was the fact that his hands had been cut off, leaving behind bloody stumps. The hands weren't anywhere visible. There were two full gasoline cans sitting below the body.

As one, Katie and Daniels pulled their weapons as the shock wore off. They were preparing for anything.

That was when Katie saw it. She nudged Daniels to get his attention.

Spray-painted along the wall in bright red were the words:

I'm sorry for what I have done. Please forgive me.

TWENTY-FIVE

Saturday 1530 hours

There was a sudden crash from outside the metal barn, thrusting Katie back into the moment and the reason why there were at Pane Construction. Without hesitation, she ran toward the noise with her Glock directing her path.

"Katie!" yelled Daniels.

Katie knew the sound came from someone who had been just outside and she was going to get to the bottom of who it was. She hated feeling she was being manipulated—someone was playing her and the sheriff's department.

There were side doors to the barn, but they were closed, locked down, so she had to run out the main entrance from where they had entered. She heard Daniels continue to yell for her, but she couldn't stop her momentum if they were going to find out who was there. It could be the killer or it could be someone who had stumbled on the horrific scene and might know something that could help them.

Katie kept running as fast as she dared. She could hear

Daniels' footsteps behind her, but she had a good start on him. To her dismay, when she reached the storage areas, she saw beyond them was the dense forest, where the person she was chasing would have the advantage—and even could ambush her. Her heart pounded and a loud noise hammered in her head, causing her to feel off balance and dizzy. Taking deep breaths and finding her running stride helped to steady her wits and body. As she ran, the images of Anna and her mother flashed through her mind, making her energy soar.

Katie quickly cleared the storage yard and passed into the wooded area. As soon as she ran into it, the environment became cooler and quiet. The only thing she could hear was her heavy breathing; she fought to keep her presence discreet.

She slowed her pace, surveying the area and the ground. There were footprints with emphasis on the toe areas. It was clear the unknown person was running, and that Katie was in the right area, so she picked up speed again.

The forest's path continued to narrow, making Katie slow her pace until she couldn't go any farther. How could this be? She'd followed the footprints, but they seemed to disappear. She stopped and turned three hundred sixty degrees, looking in every possible direction. Nothing. The forest seemed to close in on her.

Katie heard running footsteps behind her and realized Daniels must be close. Remembering that he was an avid runner, there was no doubt that he could have caught up with her so fast. She began walking back to meet him. When she saw him approaching, his expression was worried.

"Anything?" he said, winded.

Katie shook her head. "Footprints, but they seemed to vanish into thin air."

"Katie," he said moving closer to her, "don't ever do that again. We're in unknown territory here... you can't run off. You have no idea what you could have been running into."

"But—"

"There's no excuse. You don't run off from your partner."

Katie knew she'd acted impulsively, but it had been an opportunity to catch either who committed the crime or someone who knew something about it.

"I'm sorry," she said, genuinely.

Daniels still looked concerned and even a bit mad, but he relaxed his demeanor. "What would Pine Valley do without their best detective?"

"Ha," she said.

"Did you notice anything else?"

"No, just the footprints. I didn't hear anything at all. I don't know how they escaped so fast."

"We don't know if this has anything to do with the Braxtons or our other cases."

"No, but it does seem strange. Mrs. Braxton had this company and Stan Pane's name in a personal notebook. Why? Did they know one another outside of the accounting firm? Or—"

"Or was it something she had been investigating?"

"Don't know—yet."

"Let's get back and call this in."

Katie took another look around before she followed Daniels.

Three patrol vehicles, forensics, medical examiner's van, and McGaven all showed up at Pane Construction. Katie and Daniels had secured the area and made sure no one else was on the property. Daniels spoke with the patrol deputies, instructing a canvass and securing of the area.

McGaven walked up to Katie. "Okay, did another deep dive on Stan Pane. It seems his business was going under or actually went under. He tried to get another loan, that was denied, and so he had let his five employees go. There were three construction workers, one yard maintenance guy, and a bookkeeper. He'd dug a hole of debt for two hundred thousand dollars plus change."

"Wife? Family?" she said.

"No kids. An ex who lives in Phoenix."

"What about Briana Nest-Smith at Delilah's Spa?"

"Nothing, it was also closed and looked like it had been for a while," he said.

"Interesting, but it may not have anything to do with Mrs. Braxton and the cases," she said.

John interrupted. "I think you need to see this," he said.

Katie and McGaven followed John into the barn. At a desk area there were boxes and file folders, three files were open.

"What is it?" Katie said, pulling on gloves.

The first file had Stella Braxton's name, photo, and preliminary background information, including details of her bank accounts, what her mortgage was on the house, and information about Anna—where she went to school and details about her friend Jasmine.

McGaven read over her shoulder. "Why would he have this information?"

"It looks like a report from a private investigator," she said. "I don't know who these people in the other files are."

"Look at these handwritten notes," said McGaven. "Was Pane doing some private investigation on the side?"

"Maybe to earn extra income."

"This is a nice setup," he said, referring to the barn.

"Times are tough, things are slowing down here, and there's a lot of competition in construction," she said thinking about the crime scene. "But it doesn't match with the statement on the wall: 'I'm sorry for what I have done. Please forgive me.'"

"Forgive him for what?" said McGaven.

Katie remained quiet as she thought about the message. "I

don't think the message is from Pane—I think it's from the killer."

"Obviously, the killer wrote it," said McGaven.

"No, I mean... the killer is apologizing and asking for forgiveness."

"That's a first."

Katie looked around. "There are a lot of things to document and go through here. And we need to take a good look at the storage areas and two house structures. We're going to need some help."

"Eva and I will process the area with the body so the ME's office can remove it, while you guys search everything else," said John. "We'll get there."

"Sounds good. We'll mark potential evidence areas with your markers for documentation," she said.

John nodded and left.

Katie sighed. "This is going to take a while."

"I have an idea," said McGaven.

"What?"

"Deputy Brandon Hansen is here. Maybe he can document everything out here and in the storage areas."

"Great idea."

"Hey, Hansen," said McGaven.

The deputy jogged up to the detectives. "What's up?"

"Do you have a camera?"

"Yeah, I have my digital camera in the cruiser."

"Great. We need you to make a list of everything outside and take photos of it—including the vehicles. Don't move or touch anything. If you see anything that requires examination, get us or John. Can you do that?" said McGaven.

"Absolutely. On it." He hurried to his cruiser to get his camera, notebooks, and gloves.

"I like him," said McGaven.

"Me too." Katie smiled. "I think you have your first protégé."

"Cool."

Daniels joined the detectives. "How do you want to work this?"

"Gav and I are going to take a look around the houses. John and Eva are working the murder scene. We also have a deputy documenting everything outside," she said.

"Okay," he said. "Do you need me?"

"What are you thinking?" she said.

"I can go and check out Delilah's Spa and talk with Briana Nest-Smith."

"That would great. Thank you. I can get a ride with Gav." She tossed Daniels the keys to the police sedan.

"Catch up with you later," he said.

Katie watched him leave. She was relieved Daniels didn't have a problem helping out. Many officers or detectives might not have been as chill with it.

"C'mon, partner," said McGaven.

The detectives went to the first house. The door was locked, but Katie searched around and found a key under a rock. She thought it was interesting that Pane would lock the door. Maybe he was on his own when the unknown person showed up. There were too many questions. It was time for some answers.

Katie unlocked the door and pushed it open. The interior surprised them.

"Wow, this is really nice," said McGaven.

"That's an understatement. Pane seemed to like nice things. Really expensive things."

"That most likely contributed to his debt."

Even though it was a manufactured home and was plain on the outside, the interior was where the money had been spent. The kitchen had expensive cabinets, granite countertops, beautiful glass fixtures hanging over the island. High-end pots and pans hung on the wall. Crystal glasses and stemware were visible in the clean glass cabinets. There was a special refrigerator for wines. The main refrigerator was huge and would hold enough groceries for three large families.

"Was he the only person living here?" said Katie, looking at the décor.

"All I could find. Maybe he had a friend or girlfriend who lived here?"

"I don't see any indication of someone else living here. Everything is so neat. There are no personal items like photos, knick-knacks, dirty plates... nothing. Everything is pristine and new looking."

"It reminds me of those spec houses showing buyers what their new homes could look like," he said.

"That's it. This must've been one of his model homes or showrooms."

Katie looked around at the three-bedroom, two-bath home. Every room resembled something you would see in a store, giving shoppers ideas for remodels or new construction. She looked in drawers and closets, which were empty. It confirmed their theory that it was more of a show home.

"Pane liked nice things. It looks like his vehicles and equipment were high-end," she said.

"Not to mention that metal barn. I priced a small one and it was out of my budget."

"I just want to make sure he didn't hide anything in this place."

The detectives took another fifteen minutes looking underneath things, inside cupboards, and anything else they could think of.

"What are you looking for?" he said.

"I'm not entirely sure. Paperwork, something personal, or maybe a safe?" she said.

Katie and McGaven double-checked the kitchen and bedrooms, but didn't find anything.

"I know what you say about an area with no evidence or clues," said McGaven.

"What's that?" She looked at her partner.

"That when you can't find anything, that *is* the evidence."

"You were listening," she teased.

The detectives went to the next manufactured home, which was unlocked. Katie examined the door, noticing the lock appeared to be broken.

"Someone pushed in?" McGaven offered.

"Not sure."

Stepping inside, the home appeared to be more like a place where someone would be living—especially a single man. The layout of the residence was exactly the same as the other home. The difference was the older furniture and the messiness. There were food containers all over the kitchen counters. The dishwasher was open and there were dishes inside—it wasn't clear if they were clean or not.

There was no indication that anyone lived with him. Checking the main bedroom and bathroom, there weren't any items that would belong to a woman, like toiletries or clothing. The other two bedrooms seemed to be used for storage, with boxes piled high and large plastic bags filled with various items.

"His office was in the barn," she said. "I don't see anything business-related in here. No bank statements, credit cards, wallet, or anything else. What about you? Find anything?"

"No," McGaven said.

"Nothing looks suspicious or out of place besides the mess."

There was a knock at the door.

"Detectives?" said Deputy Hansen.

Katie met him at the entrance. "Find something?"

"Yes," he said. "It's horrible." His face was pale and sweaty. Something had clearly spooked him.

"What?" said McGaven.

"It's better to show you."

The detectives followed the deputy to the storage area closest to the barn.

Inside a large flip-up toolbox were two severed hands. They were posed in a macabre thumbs-up sign.

TWENTY-SIX

Saturday 1730 hours

The detectives and deputy stared at the severed hands. It was so disturbing and completely unnerving that it made it difficult for them to turn away from the gruesome display.

"Get John or Eva here to document this," said Katie. She looked around but didn't see anything that would have been used to sever the hands. There were no blood drops or spatter against the side of the metal barn.

Deputy Hansen hurried to find the forensic technicians.

"We need to back up," said Katie. "There might be something the killer left."

The detectives carefully moved, trying not to disturb anything. It was difficult when the location was a working area in a rural setting—discovering anything that shouldn't be at the location could be tricky.

Katie and McGaven looked around, but didn't see anything out of the ordinary. They would let John secure the area and document and collect evidence—including the hands.

As Katie walked back to Pane's primary residence, she

couldn't get rid of the vision of the man hanging in the barn missing his hands, not to mention the hands in the toolbox. She wavered back and forth between the spray-painted sentiment of being sorry and the hands posed in a positive "yes" way. Was the killer trying to say that he was sorry and it's okay? That seemed very odd.

"You didn't hear anything I was saying, did you?" McGaven said.

"I'm sorry, it's just difficult to get Pane's hanging body and severed hands out of my mind," she replied.

"You and me both. I'm probably going to have nightmares about finding severed hands everywhere."

Katie and McGaven continued with their search of Pane's home, but didn't find anything unusual or helpful.

"Do you get the feeling someone might have already taken some things?" she said.

"There's so much stuff here—not to mention it's messy. Wouldn't it be difficult to search for what they were looking for?"

"I don't know, Gav," she said. "I get the impression the killer has been playing out their fantasies for everyone to see. If at this point we're to assume it's the same killer," she said. "Beginning with Anna's body in the fire. The casting call for young teenage girls. Jane Doe's body." Katie thought more about it. "And now Pane. There's some theatrics to this... the killer is trying desperately to show us a part of him, almost pleading with us. It's made me rethink everything. Could there be another killer? What are the odds?"

"You mean you think he's reaching out to us? Why?"

"Whatever the reason it means something to *him*. It's what drives him. It's caused by what he's experienced in his life—not just childhood—but life."

"So where do we go from here?" he said.

"Mrs. Braxton and Pane are connected by the accounting

firm. And Booker was cagey, as if he was hiding something, and the speed at which he packed up Mrs. Braxton's things makes him suspicious."

"And?"

"We should take a closer look at him. And..."

"What else?"

"I want to bring Cisco back here to search the woods. Specifically the trail where the killer escaped. I want to know how he got away from us. It was like he vanished into thin air." Katie thought about it. "If he didn't have a car... where did he come from? Did he already have his quick escape ready? There was no way of knowing that Daniels and I would be making an unannounced visit."

"Maybe Daniels will have something interesting to share about Delilah's Spa?"

"Hopefully."

"Well, let's go get Cisco and get back here before it starts to get dark," he said. "This time, I strongly suggest that you have two cover officers. We're not taking any chances of anyone taking shots at us. Understood?"

She nodded. "There's also something else," she said. It was what weighed heaviest on her.

"What's that?"

"No one has heard anything about Jasmine's whereabouts. We need to find her."

TWENTY-SEVEN

Saturday 1900 hours

It didn't take long for Katie to get changed into more appropriate clothing and boots and Cisco geared up. They were soon on their way back to Pane Construction.

Besides Cisco's energetic whines, the detectives remained quiet, each thinking about the case. Katie always felt they were taking a step back with their investigations, but they'd managed to figure things out on the previous cases. She berated herself quietly. She was known to push herself hard and when things didn't work out as planned she was her worst critic, and that's when her anxiety symptoms would rise up. She felt them now but determinedly pushed them away.

"What do you think Cisco will find?" said McGaven.

"The person I chased wasn't that far ahead of me, and they seemed to just disappear. I didn't hear any sound of a vehicle or footsteps or even movement in the forest."

McGaven thought about it. "Maybe they didn't leave."

"Meaning?"

"Maybe they hid."

"Like they already had a plan," she said.

"That's why you didn't hear anything, making it appear they had vanished."

Katie looked to her partner. "That's why I love brainstorming with you. You make me see other angles."

"Well most of the time they aren't correct, but at least I try." He smiled.

Katie laughed.

At Pane Construction there only remained one patrol cruiser and the forensic van. Everyone else had already left, including the technicians from the morgue.

McGaven looked up at the sky; the sunlight was waning. "We need to get you and Cisco out there."

Katie agreed. The woods were already going to be darker than the rest of the vicinity due to the tall trees and dense forest.

"Let's bring flashlights," she said.

As she readied herself and Cisco, McGaven jogged over to the barn and returned soon after with Deputy Hansen.

"All good?" he said to his partner.

"Great."

"How do you want to proceed?" said McGaven.

"Daniels and I pursued someone and it took us through there," she said and gestured to the opening of the trail. "We didn't see who it was, but there were fresh footprints. I was right on his tail and then he seemed to vanish into thin air."

Deputy Hansen nodded as he scrutinized the area.

"Gav, you cover me and Cisco. And, Hansen, I need you to make sure there isn't anything unsafe, like holes, booby traps, or anything else that doesn't seem right. Okay?" she said.

"Ten-four," said McGaven.

"Yes, ma'am," said Hansen.

Almost on cue, a breeze picked up, causing loose leaves to swirl around them. Katie pushed the horrible images of Pane and his hands from her mind. She wanted more than anything to find out who was on the property when she and Daniels had arrived. Were they waiting and watching? Was it the killer? The person who severed Pane's hands?

Katie took another moment after attaching Cisco's tracking leash. She wanted to get her wits and have complete concentration. Having McGaven and Hansen spotting and supporting her and Cisco lowered her anxious energy. She'd been noticing that her energy and symptoms had been elevated, but she didn't want to worry anymore about it. Right now she had a mission.

Cisco spun around with high-pitched whines, clearly ready to get to work. The dog looked proud with his newest Pine Valley Sheriff's Department badge attached to his vest.

"Ready?" she whispered to the dog.

Katie and Cisco began at the opening to the trail. It wasn't actually an official trail but appeared to be a pass-through to get to another part of the property.

"Cisco, *such*," she said with authority.

Cisco immediately switched to full search and tracking mode. He didn't take off at full speed but rather picked up the pace to find what he needed to.

Katie let the leash length out past six feet, watching Cisco's behavior as he searched. She would know when the dog showed a change at anything out of the ordinary.

It was getting later in the day and the shadows were prominent in the heavily wooded areas as they moved deeper into the forest. It looked different to Katie than it had a couple of hours before; it seemed darker, denser, and had a hint of foreboding that was difficult for her to shake.

She walked the same trail as she had done earlier in the day watching Cisco intently. Glancing to her left, she saw McGaven behind her. He was vigilant, no chitchat, just keeping his eye on the K9 team. A bit farther ahead and to the left, where it was darker and thicker, Hansen kept his focus on the terrain and in between every tree. His expression was somber; it was clear he took his assignment seriously. Both McGaven and Hansen had flashlights, which helped to see in the depths between trees.

Katie focused on Cisco as the dog weaved slightly from side to side and on occasion lifted his head to take in the air. The breeze was coming at them, keeping the temperature cool and any scent centralized. Her footing seemed stable on the dirt and compressed forest foliage—so her trek was uneventful.

They were almost to the end of the trail where she had been before. Katie was discouraged, causing her to doubt herself. Did they really hear someone? Were they chasing them into the woods?

Her berating thoughts were interrupted by Cisco's low growl. The jet-black dog bristled and kept his body low, still directed straight ahead.

Katie instinctively slowed her pace. She allowed Cisco to move farther until she could see what his instincts and scent had caught. It was uncommon for the dog to act this way on a track, but it was important to see what had caught his awareness.

McGaven and Hansen were silent. They too slowed their pace and waited for the dog.

Cisco barked. It wasn't just a couple of alerting barks, but rapid "there's a serious problem" barks, which usually indicated a bad guy in the area.

Katie tensed, glancing back and forth, expecting the worst. She stopped and held the leash firm. Her own instinct and senses were prickly at best.

Cisco finally stopped his barking and pushed his nose around a tree, where he then sat down, keeping his focus on something. He was in the shadows, which made it challenging to see the outline of his head and paws. The dog now panted, but didn't change his intensity.

Katie held up her hand to indicate that she was going to check out what Cisco had alerted to in between the trees.

The wind vanished, leaving the area still and quiet. Katie cautiously moved forward, gently patting Cisco as she stepped toward the dark area. Pulling a flashlight from her belt, she switched it on. At first she didn't see anything except the usual things you would see in the forest: tree trunks, undergrowth, low-lying bushes. She moved even farther into what was a narrow crawlspace.

Cisco growled.

Katie half expected to find something terrible—comparable to finding Pane's amputated hands—but as she moved even closer she saw something flat and light-colored.

"What *is* that?" she whispered. She took some gloves out of her pocket. Whatever it was, she didn't want to contaminate anything that might prove to have evidentiary value.

She heard the men's footsteps move in behind her, but remained quiet, carefully taking the beige piece of evidence that had adhered to one of the tree trunks between her fingers, before she slowly backed out.

"What is that?" said McGaven, moving closer to his partner.

"It looks like another piece of latex," she said. "It definitely doesn't belong here and it seems to have not been here long."

McGaven held open a bag so Katie could put the evidence inside. She took a photo with her cell phone of the area and marked it with coordinates.

"Did you see this?" said Hansen. He moved to where Katie had found the piece of latex and then took a sharp left turn. The deputy seemed to disappear.

"Hansen?" said Katie.

Within a couple of seconds, the deputy came back out.

"How did you do that?" said McGaven.

"It's easy. I just moved to the left where it looks like there are more dense woods, but there's like a hiding spot."

Katie looked closely. "That's how he did it. Of course. When we chased whoever it was, they tucked in and hid. We couldn't see them. And then when we left, he came out of the hiding place."

"Then where did he go?" said McGaven.

"Let's find out," she said, readying Cisco once again. Guiding the dog away from the find, she made sure he was turned in the direction of their hike. "Cisco, *such*."

Cisco instantly went into his search mode. He was about to turn back but then righted himself and continued on the trek. Katie kept moving forward through an area they didn't search earlier. It only took Cisco about six minutes to lead the group to another clearing as they emerged from the dense groupings of trees.

"This is where the person escaped without our knowing," said Katie. She was mad at herself for having missed it earlier, but they hadn't known what kind of dangers, including an ambush, they were up against.

"Over here," said McGaven. "Looks like there are fresh tire tracks. Maybe from a truck or a van."

"We need John and Eva out here right away," said Katie. She looked around at the wide-open area that dropped out to the main road. The light was dimming and it soon would be dark.

The detectives and deputy hurried back toward the crime scene.

"We need lights set up all around the area," she said.

"On it," said Hansen.

Katie put Cisco back in the Jeep.

"What do you think?" said McGaven.

"I think we need to get this to John," said Katie. "And..." She looked at the piece in the evidence bag.

McGaven looked at his partner questionably.

"I think I know what this is… or was used for…"

"What?"

"I think it's from a prosthetic mask."

"You mean the killer is changing himself and making disguises? Or one disguise?"

"Remember, this type of latex can be used for all types of disguises, not just facial features, but body features as well."

"You'd have to be extremely proficient with working with this type of disguise technique to get away with it."

"That's right. But that's not what worries me," she said.

"What does?"

"I don't know who they were, but I think it means we've already met the killer."

TWENTY-EIGHT

Saturday 2230 hours

Katie and McGaven headed back to Katie's house after a long day. She'd thought about asking him about Denise and if he had reached any type of resolution yet, but decided not to push him. McGaven seemed to have a ton of energy and wanted to blow off some steam with a beer and some food. He managed to convince a reluctant Katie to go to the Night Owl, which was a bar mostly frequented by law enforcement and first responders. It wasn't that anyone else wasn't welcomed, but it was a place where cops felt relaxed and among their own. She quickly changed and fed Cisco.

Katie drove into the parking lot of the Night Owl and wasn't too surprised that it was full on a Saturday night.

She received a text message.

Had to go back to SPD but will return soon. I'll keep you posted. Daniels.

"Who is it?" he said.

"Daniels had to go back to SPD for a bit."

"Okay. Good to know."

"You sure you want to go in there?" said Katie, nodding toward the bar.

"Why not? I need a break. You need a break."

She laughed. "I guess you're right, we do need a break."

The detectives exited the Jeep and headed to the front door. Voices and music could be heard even before they got inside.

As Katie got closer, she realized firefighters would be at the bar too and that made her think about Chad. She wondered what he had told his previous coworkers and if it would be awkward.

McGaven opened the door and upbeat noise escaped. "C'mon, partner."

It had been a while since Katie had been to the bar. With so much going on in her personal life and with investigations, there was little time for anything else. The interior had changed a bit with some new décor and more tables. The bar was busy and there were many lively upbeat conversations going on. Katie recognized the patrons, some of the deputies, two detectives, and some of the guys from the firehouse.

There was a free table in the corner, so she walked over and took a seat. She noticed a few of the patrons gave her a look, not knowing if they were casual looks or a look of discomfort because Chad had left Pine Valley, opting for a big city in Southern California.

"Hey, I'll get us a couple of beers," said McGaven as he headed to the bar to order them directly. He stopped and chatted with a few people on his way.

Katie guessed he needed to get out and socialize in between personal issues and these difficult cases. She didn't blame him.

Katie patiently waited for McGaven to get back with their drinks. She casually observed the energy around her. The jukebox was playing and there were two couples dancing nearby. She spotted Investigator Ames walking toward her carrying a beer. He smiled, which made him appear more relaxed than he was at the crime scenes.

"You alone?" he said. His sandy hair contrasted with his dark-brown eyes. His stare could be considered intense or just curious.

"My partner just went to get us beers," she said.

He nodded.

Katie could tell he felt awkward.

"I thought you might be here tonight. It seems everyone had the same idea."

"It's been a tough week," she said. Small talk wasn't her favorite pastime, but she wanted to be polite. She glanced to McGaven, who still hadn't been served.

Ames glanced to where Katie was looking. "Looks like he's going to be a little bit."

Katie sighed. "Have a seat," she said and hoped she wouldn't regret offering it out of courtesy.

Ames took a seat next to her instead of across. "I know who you are," he said.

"Meaning?" Katie wasn't amused, but she'd play along.

"You were top in your military K9 training. You love this town where you grew up; otherwise, you could go anywhere you wanted."

"You're either a stalker or you've been talking to Daniels, Hamilton, or Alvarez."

He smiled. "I just wanted to know if all the hype is true or some kind of department fiction."

"Why do you care?" She watched the investigator, still trying to figure out if she could trust him, or even like him.

"Since being transferred I like to know about where I'm working and the people I could be working with."

"Really?"

"Yep, that pretty much sums it up."

"Nothing else?"

"Nope. That's it."

Katie leaned back, feeling slightly uncomfortable being so close to him. She glanced at his right forearm, with the thick scarring. He wore a T-shirt with the long sleeves pushed up slightly on his forearms where it was noticeable.

"I heard about the scene at Pane Construction."

"Everybody probably has by now," she said.

"Are all your cases like something out of a horror movie?"

She stared at him, not answering right away.

"Just sayin', these are horrible cases. I'm beginning to wonder if moving to Pine Valley was a mistake with all the crime."

"Crime is usually committed by newcomers."

Ames took a drink of his beer and smiled. "I see."

"I don't think you do." She was about to ask him to leave so she could have some peace as she waited for her drink.

Ames seemed to ignore her comment. "So it must be hard having your fiancé move away."

Katie stopped cold. She stared at the investigator, decided to get up from the table.

"I'm sorry, that didn't come out right," he said quickly. "I just heard some of the guys talking about Chad Ferguson, that's all. I didn't mean anything by it."

"Of course you didn't." Katie didn't like being pushed into a corner and had had just about enough. She saw that McGaven was ordering the beers at the bar and thankfully would return at any moment.

"Detective, I thought we might've gotten off on the wrong foot, but I seem to be making it worse."

"You think?"

Ames stood up. "I'm sorry if I caused you any more grief."

"Don't worry about it," she said flatly. She wasn't entirely sure if he was being sincere or not.

He turned to leave. "Oh," he said and turned toward her again. He reached into his pocket and retrieved a flash drive, setting it on the table. "Here's the forensics and reports from both fire scenes. If you and your partner need anything else, please don't hesitate to reach out." He turned and walked away.

Katie let out a sigh, annoyed. Who did he think he was? What was all that about?

McGaven returned to the table, sat down, and handed Katie a beer. "There you are, ma'am." He noticed her expression of irritation. "What's wrong?"

"Investigator Ames gave me this," she said, holding up the flash drive before putting it back in her pocket.

"Which is?"

"The reports for the two fire scenes."

"And he just happened to be carrying that around?"

"I guess. I don't like him much, but I'm glad he gave us this."

"Is it going to be a problem when we work with him?" McGaven watched his partner.

"No." She wasn't completely sure, but the cases took priority.

"That didn't sound very convincing."

"It seems he's been researching me."

"About?"

"He knew about Chad and our cases."

"That's not a reach. He is working at the same firehouse that Chad used to work at."

"I know... it's just... I don't know, he's pushy, kind of know-it-all, maybe trying too hard."

McGaven laughed.

"What?"

"Have you ever thought that maybe he likes you? You're a legend around Pine Valley..."

"Shut up," she said playfully. "He does not."

"And you're a veteran, dog handler, cold-case maven..."

"Gav," she said. "I just said I really don't like him much, that's all."

"Why is that?"

"I get the feeling he's here under false pretenses."

McGaven took her beer. "You have to turn off that criminal profiler brain of yours—at least for an hour. I think you need a shot. C'mon..." he said, pulling her to her feet. "Let's go, partner."

"Okay. Just one."

Katie and McGaven returned to her house a couple of hours later. She pulled the Jeep into the driveway.

"Well, I have to admit that was more fun than I thought it would be. Thanks, Gav."

"It doesn't go unrecognized that these cases are brutal for us and the days are long and exhausting," he said. "We need time to blow off steam."

"And it got even better when Investigator Ames left the bar," she said.

"We're back to Ames again?" he joked.

The detectives got out of the Jeep, disengaged the security alarm, and entered the house to a very happy Cisco. Katie laughed as the dog zoomed around, tail wildly wagging.

"Wow, go, Cisco," said McGaven.

Katie opened the back sliding door and the dog instantly ran out. She followed and stood on the back deck as Cisco made his usual rounds in the large fenced area. She loved to watch Cisco run and play since the beginning of his life was trained for combat conditions and finding explosives. Cisco ran up and dropped a yellow ball. Katie picked it up and threw it.

"You okay?" said McGaven. He stood at the doorway.

"I'm fine. It was just a long day," she said. "I want to look at the reports Ames gave me, but I'll wait until tomorrow."

"Sounds good." He turned to leave but came back. "Thanks, Katie, for not pushing me about Denise."

Katie faced her partner. "I'm always here to talk whenever you're ready."

"Night."

"Goodnight," she said.

Katie decided to spend a few more minutes outside with Cisco. She still felt as if she was decompressing. The evening was cool but comfortable and it was quiet, in contrast from the day. She sat down on her favorite old swing and enjoyed the moment. Her life felt different. She wasn't sure if it was evolving the way it was supposed to be or if she was somehow being punished for something she did or didn't do.

Cisco decided he was done exploring and chasing the ball, so he sat down at Katie's feet.

All the images from the past few days filed through Katie's mind: the crime scenes, bodies, fire remnants, and the people they'd questioned. There had to be some type of order to all the events that would point directly at the killer. She just had to work out what.

TWENTY-NINE

Sunday 0605 hours

"Katie, wake up!"

Katie heard the voice, but she was enjoying a wonderful dream and didn't want to leave just yet.

"C'mon, we got to go!"

Katie sat up in bed to a dark bedroom. She could tell it wasn't daylight yet by the clock on her nightstand. Everything seemed okay. Cisco was gone.

Had she heard the voice or not? She was groggy and it was difficult for her to fully awaken, but she swung her legs over the side of the bed.

McGaven appeared in her doorway dressed in a T-shirt and pajama pants. He had turned on the hall light and he looked like an apparition with the light shining from behind him. "Get up," he said.

Cisco ran into the room and onto the bed.

"Okay, where's the fire?" she said.

"Interesting choice of words. I just got a call from dispatch alerting us that there's another house fire and—"

"A body?"

"Yes."

"I'm up." Katie got out of bed and began readying herself. Thoughts buzzing through her head at warp speed.

Within fifteen minutes, Katie and McGaven were headed to the address at 214 Oak Lane. They'd barely had enough time to drink a cup of coffee, brush their teeth, and get dressed. Katie hated to leave Cisco, but she didn't know what they were going to encounter at the scene and there wasn't any reason for him to be there.

"This address is in an affluent neighborhood," said McGaven. "I know it from my patrol days. These are rich people."

"Well it must be something important to the killer to have staged the fire there," she said. "What, I don't know, but we're going to find out."

Katie had set the GPS in her Jeep to 214 Oak Lane. She drove fast but had to slow in areas where people were heading to work. Taking the turnoff for the freeway, Katie drove toward a developed area of Pine Valley laid out with expensive homes. She had only ever driven through before and had never known anyone personally who lived there.

"There," said McGaven indicating a sign that said Oak Lane.

Katie didn't need to look for the address. There were two fire trucks, two unmarked vehicles, and three police patrol cars. Several firefighters were getting ready to leave and putting away hoses and equipment.

The visible flames had been extinguished, but smoke still lingered around the area. Neighbors weren't close together—each residence had a two- to five-acre parcel. There were two people dressed in robes watching the scenario play out, probably keeping a watchful eye making sure nothing got too close to their homes.

Katie parked a little distance away. She wasn't looking forward to what they were going to find. Once again, the killer was several steps ahead of them. It made her heart heavy and her frustration was simmering at the surface.

The detectives approached the property, walking past a fire truck. The captain met with them. The name on his jacket read "Cross."

"Detective Scott and Detective McGaven?" he said.

"Yes," said Katie.

"Dispatch called us," said McGaven.

"I had them do that," said the captain. "There's a body been found and it seems to be similar to the other two recently. Investigator Ames is working the fire scene right now. Let him know you're here and he'll escort you to the area."

"Captain, where are the owners or occupants?"

"Luckily, no one was home. The police were able to locate them. They were on a month cruise in the Caribbean and are on their way back."

"Thank you," said Katie. She knew the owners' information would be in the police reports and they didn't need to worry about that now.

Katie and McGaven left the captain and walked to where the house had been set alight. Unlike the other two homes, half of this house was still standing.

McGaven stopped two of the deputies. "Can you do a canvass of the area? That includes vehicles too."

They nodded and left.

Katie walked through a wrought-iron gate that was bracketed by brick and stone fencing. There were several groupings of oak and pine trees for privacy and to highlight the natural beauty of the location. A walkway made of flagstone pavers meandered from the gate to what had been the front door. It appeared as if there had been planted flowers and various ground covers, which were now trampled and burned.

There were two deputies securing the area with crime scene tape. Katie wasn't sure if it was clear for her and McGaven to enter the house yet, so the detectives waited in the front yard.

"Are we the only detectives called to this scene?" she said.

"Yes, that was what I was told from dispatch."

"We're going to need everyone we can. These cases are stacking up against us," she said.

"I'll text Hamilton and Alvarez," he said and immediately took out his phone. "And John."

"Detectives..." said Ames as he exited the building with a beautiful sable shepherd. "I'll be right back." He turned away from them and went to his SUV, where he put up his K9.

McGaven gave Katie a look that generally meant he was not really impressed.

Ames returned and looked at the detectives. "Didn't think I would be seeing you both so soon—just hours."

"Where's the body?" said Katie not wanting to waste any time.

"Hold on," he said. "We've collected some evidence of where the accelerants were used."

"We were called out here," said McGaven.

"Yes, by my request."

Katie looked at the investigator. "Are you going to tell us anything?"

He pointed to the structure as another investigator vacated carrying small metal containers.

"Just waiting for him to finish," said Ames.

"It looks like the arsonist wasn't as thorough as the previous two times," said McGaven.

Katie knew her partner was trying to change the conversation because it was becoming almost weird.

"You may think that, but it was strategic. From everything we've found, it appears the arsonist wanted to burn something specific and not the entire structure," said Ames. He turned and walked toward the house.

Katie looked at McGaven. "I guess that means we follow."

"I guess so," he said.

Katie could feel the temperature change. Even though the fire was out, there were a couple of firefighters making sure that small scattered start-up areas didn't ignite.

When they reached the front door, which was still mostly intact, with the exception of burned and blackened areas, you could see most of the structure. The smell was different than the previous locations. It had more of a pungent gasoline or kerosene odor.

"Is that kerosene?" said Katie.

"Good nose. Yes, it is. I'll know more when I get the tests back."

"Isn't kerosene more volatile?" said McGaven.

"Depends. It can be if not stored correctly and it has less of a shelf life than gasoline."

Katie saw the enormous living room with what looked like what was left of two large sofas, several display cabinets, tables, and rugs. This home was definitely more upscale than the others. It was one story, the bedrooms in another wing of the house. The primary suite was at the opposite end of the house and was mostly intact. Ames led the detectives to the bedrooms. Heavy burn areas were down the hallway. The farthest side of the home was completely vacant and you could view the outdoors.

The heavy humid smell of smoke and water became stronger and made Katie's stomach churn. She tried not to concentrate on the stench as she moved through the house.

"Did it start here?" said Katie.

"Yes, actually in this room," said Ames as he pointed to a smaller bedroom or office that faced out to the street side.

Katie was confused by what she saw. What was killer trying

to convey? Did he make a mistake? Or was he trying to confuse the detectives?

"Here," said Ames. He walked into the last bedroom, which had windows facing the backyard.

Katie noticed through the gaping holes of missing walls that there didn't seem to be any neighbors that could see the area. She stepped inside with McGaven and they looked around. It was unclear as to where a body could be. There was a bed, dresser, nightstands, and a small knick-knack table.

Ames went to the closet where the door had been taken down. Inside was a small walk-in closet with clothes that now looked like burnt rags.

Katie looked around and expected to see a burned body, but there was none.

Ames kneeled down and opened a trapdoor that led to a crawlspace underneath the house. He turned his flashlight downward and waited for the detectives.

Katie slowly moved next to the investigator and knelt down.

Inside the crawlspace was a woman's body. Her extremities had been burned, but she wasn't scorched beyond recognition. The position of the body was almost in a fetal position with her long dark hair covering her face. She was barefoot. What stopped Katie cold was the fact the body had on a yellow dress. There were still pieces that weren't blackened.

"Can I see this?" she said to Ames and took the flashlight. She got on her stomach, reaching her arms down, and slowly moved the light in a strip grid motion. She wanted to see if there was anything under the house that should be brought to their attention, but there was nothing except the usual support beams and insulation.

She took a closer look at the victim's hands and ankles. She couldn't tell if there were any signs of being tied up or defensive wounds. Her neck was covered by her hair, so it was impossible to see if there were any indications of strangulation. She snapped a few photos with her cell phone for reference until she received official photographs from John.

"Anything?" said McGaven.

"Not that I can see. It's going to be tricky to document the area and body," she said and sat up. "We're going to need to rip away some of the flooring for forensics, but I want John to document everything he can right now. Just in case removing the floor damages the crime scene," she said. "I don't want to disturb anything."

Katie really wanted to get down in the crawlspace, but she needed forensics to do their job and remove the body carefully to preserve any evidence that might be on the body.

"Who's going to oversee the scene?" she asked. "This collection of evidence and body removal is going to take some time."

"Hamilton," said McGaven.

"Okay." She turned to Ames, who had been quiet, allowing the detectives to do their jobs. "What about any other evidence?"

"I just documented and collected what I need for proving arson and testing for the accelerant. It'll be in my report."

"Did you notice anything unusual or that seemed out of place when you first began searching?" she said.

"No, it seemed like any other arson scene."

"Is it okay for us to look around the property and the rest of the house?"

"Of course, Detective."

Katie turned to McGaven. "We need to get this room taped off. No one can enter until John and the coroner arrive."

"I'll take care of it," said McGaven.

Katie continued to look around the house. Searching a home that had been doused with accelerant and set on fire wasn't like any crime scenes she had experienced until the last week. And this was the third one.

As she moved slowly down the hallway and peered into the

other four bedrooms, all she could imagine were the girls' bodies and the fact that the killer wasn't going to stop anytime soon. It was a game to him. More like a need or fantasy. And that's what scared Katie the most.

It seemed he used the yellow dresses in his fake casting call, making the girls model them. But when? The A-1 Talent Agency was like a ghost, nothing coming up through all of McGaven's searching, and yet somehow this person was able to find girls to lure into his game. She knew it was most likely through social media where young girls were looking for this type of opportunity. It wasn't difficult for anyone to talk in private messaging.

But why kill them? Katie thought. She had been running through the psyche of the killer and she kept coming back to the driving force of getting the young girls' hopes up and then killing them while they were wearing the yellow dresses. Was it that they failed him? Why? There was no sign of sexual assault. What was driving him?

Find the million-dollar man... you'll find my Anna...

Katie and McGaven had found Anna, but *who* was the million-dollar man? And did he really exist? Or was it a ruse to give investigators bad information?

Katie continued to walk the house like she was walking a grid, and carefully looked at everything, though most of the contents were basically destroyed beyond recognition, and of no use to the investigation. She observed strange trails of stippling along the floor with darker and lighter burn areas from the fire. Not sure what it exactly meant; she would read about it in the arson report.

She finally made her way to the backyard, which was mostly undisturbed by the fire. Stepping outside onto a large patio area complete with a wrought-iron table and chairs, there was also a built-in barbecue area and two comfortable seating areas with pillows. The landscaping was pristine, with grass, walkways, flowering bushes, and a gazebo. Nothing looked like it had been disturbed. It was a drastic contrast to the house.

Katie turned around and examined the house exterior. There was a large garage that looked to be a three- or four-car structure that, unlike the house, had been completely obliterated by fire. She couldn't help but think that there was a message here that they were completely missing.

She walked around the other side of the house to the front yard. There were still first responders going about their duties. Neither John nor Detective Hamilton had shown up yet, but she knew they would be there soon.

A dog barking interrupted her thoughts. Katie turned to see Ames's dog poking his head out the back window. She couldn't help herself. Looking around, she didn't see Ames, so she took the opportunity to see the dog up close. She stood near the window to look at the sable German shepherd with dark eyes.

"You're a handsome boy." She didn't want to pet the dog due to it being a working animal and not having permission from the handler. Glancing at the decal that read "Blitz," she said, "Blitz, you're a good boy."

"And that he is," said Ames. He had quietly approached.

"I'm sorry, he's just a beautiful dog, I wanted to see him up close," she said and turned to walk away.

"You can pet him."

Katie looked at the investigator.

"Go ahead. I've seen you handle Cisco and I think I can trust you."

Katie decided to move closer to the dog. "You're a good boy," she said, petting his head. The body coloring was gorgeous and she enjoyed seeing him up close. "Thank you," she said and went to meet with McGaven.

Katie waited until McGaven had finished another phone call.

"So what do you think?" he said, looking around.

"I think we're on a tight timeline. Jasmine is still missing. We need to find her now." She could feel her heart rate increase as the anxiety filtered throughout her body.

Katie decided to take some more photos of the scene for them until they received more professional ones. She stood and panned in a three-hundred-sixty-degree move, clicking photos. Walking toward the street, she took more photos of the neighborhood observers and the vehicles that were on the street.

"It's Sunday. You want to go to the office?" he said.

"I think we can work at my house and see what we can come up with."

Detective Hamilton drove up and parked.

"The scene is in good hands with Hamilton and the fire department," she said. "I want to look at these reports from Ames."

"Me too, but first..."

"But first what?" she said.

"Food."

Katie laughed. "Let's go to Stella's Diner."

THIRTY

It didn't take long for the fire trucks to get to the location, which was what he was counting on. As the smoke puffed, swirled, and filled the neighborhood, several people came out of their homes to watch the display. It was his doing—he was responsible and that's what gave him peace. He was doing what was right. It was Cindy's last performance and the girl never realized it was her best. He smiled, congratulating himself. Well done, well done.

What had captured his attention was when the two detectives arrived. They intrigued him, especially the woman. Her partner was also fascinating, with his tall stature and awareness. Although the woman didn't need anyone to validate her, she was strong and shrewd. A bit like his mother. After quietly watching her looking for him at the Pane Construction areas, he had searched the internet on crime news from Pine Valley Sheriff's Department and found out more about her and her partner. They had made quite a name for themselves solving their cases. Until now...

It didn't take long for those precious memories to surface again. After watching the way Detective Scott moved around and interacted with others in a confident and careful manner, it brought his mother to mind. It was a usual day at school and he was in the fifth grade and only days after his tenth birthday. He was excited about receiving an A on his math test. Walking into his house, he was yelling for his mom but didn't see her. She wasn't where she usually was, either in the kitchen or living room. He put his things down and noticed the door to the garage was open. When he went out to the garage, there was his mother... Her beautiful long blonde hair with subtle bangs, dressed in her most favorite yellow dress... She hung lifeless from the rafters with a rope around her neck. Her body perfectly still... her hair and makeup flawless.

At that defining moment everything changed and he was going to make everyone pay.

A ringtone from his cell phone jolted him back to the present. He quickly swiped the screen and settled on a live video feed of Jasmine tied up in his basement. He smiled. She struggled and cried, kicking her feet. The tape across her mouth kept in her screams for help. He wasn't sure why he'd kept her alive, but there was something captivating about her and until he had no use for her—which could be any day or hour—she would stay with him. He put his phone back in his pocket.

Even though his mission was obvious, with the wannabes of the acting and modeling world who needed to be taught a lesson, it still didn't mean that he couldn't have something fun for himself. He deserved it.

He watched Katie speak with one of the firemen and then what looked to be a fire investigator. He observed her movements and body language. It was clear she was concerned and even a bit frustrated. He could only imagine how tough it was going to be when she and her partner couldn't solve these cases. A smile washed across his face.

He had swapped out the sedan for the cargo-carrying vehicle because it was more convenient. He kept it in a safe place. He sat in the van staring through the windshield watching patrol officers move about, knocking on doors, hoping that someone knew something.

His mood changed. What was elated and happy became down and angry. His memories were something that wouldn't give him a moment of happiness. They cursed him and beat him down. It was always her. She dragged him down and laughed at him. Nothing was ever good enough. He couldn't please her. He had gone to his parents to complain about the unfairness, but they said he was being too sensitive. His mother always said that his day was coming. He was the best in the drama club and everyone knew it, but the best parts were always given to overexaggerated, giggly girls who couldn't give the performances that were truly inspired and full of depth. Never. He was always given a role that didn't have a name, merely part of the crowd or chorus.

He had a million voices, a million looks, and was the million-dollar man.

He watched as Katie pet the fire department's K9. She was happy and obviously loved dogs. She had come close to being shot in the head, but he hesitated and wanted to see what she could do. He hated dogs almost more than his teacher.

No matter what he thought or what he concentrated on, he still saw her face. The woman who made his life hell and who never saw his promise as an actor. He continued to struggle with concentration, but that didn't stop him from being an expert disguise artist. He knew no one had to tell him that he was the best. He would continue to prove it over and over again. He stared at his hands, turning them over—front and back.

As he continued to watch Katie, she and her partner seemed to be finally ready to leave after another detective arrived. He decided to follow them after they got in the Jeep, turned the *vehicle around, and drove away. He wanted to know more... and what made these detectives so good at what they did... because now, he would make sure they would never solve these cases—or any others.*

THIRTY-ONE

Sunday 1030 hours

Katie and McGaven returned from a hearty breakfast to her house to work on the cases. She had been adamant about looking at the files from the fire department and wanted to begin connecting the investigation in a more cohesive way. After McGaven did a more thorough background check, he had discovered that Stan Pane had been moonlighting as a private investigator in hopes of putting his business back on track. He had recently obtained a private investigator's license and there were jotted notes in his daily calendar with the name Stella Braxton and something referring to a modeling agency. Somehow he had come into contact with the killer and had to be eliminated.

Katie went into the third bedroom of her house, which she had set up as an office and storage area. She cleared the table and desk while setting up her computer and turned on the printer. There was a large chalkboard along one wall that helped to keep things straight.

Cisco zipped into the room and quickly checked everything out before he left again.

Katie powered the laptop and connected another monitor to it so that the information and photograph would be on a bigger screen. She inserted the flash drive when McGaven entered.

"Okay, this will keep you caffeinated," he said and put down two large iced coffee drinks.

Cisco was on his heels and Katie had a feeling her partner gave the dog a lot of treats.

Katie picked up the drink and took a sip. "Wow, this is fantastic. Thank you. I usually don't like iced coffee."

"Is that the reports?" said McGaven.

Katie looked at the big screen where there were several file folders: *Stagecoach Road—report*, *Stagecoach Road—photos*, *Lost Falls—report*, and *Lost Falls—photos*. She clicked on the photos for Stagecoach Road. The file contained more than fifty photographs. She clicked on the first one, which was an overall view of the property—and kept clicking on each. Most of the overall and longer views were sequential and could be printed and attached together to give a complete view.

"Interesting," said McGaven as he pulled up a chair next to Katie.

"I like the way he does a panoramic," she said.

"It definitely tells a story."

Katie kept clicking until they came to the basement area. It showed the living room and dining area, where the blackened sections were obviously where the accelerant was used. There were different shades of black, some more concentrated than others. The bubbly stippling was prominent around the darker areas. She kept clicking the mouse and then pausing.

The next photos were of the opening of the basement, stairs, and Anna's body at the bottom. It looked like Investigator Ames didn't get close to the body, so the photos were more general.

Katie and McGaven remained quiet, watching the photos flash across the screen.

The next folder was opened. Katie continued with the same process.

"Wait," said McGaven.

"What? Which one?"

"The one in the living room before the closet where Jane Doe was found."

Katie went back.

"What is that?" he said, pointing to an area along the floor.

"I'm not sure," she said and enlarged the photo.

Luckily the pixel count was high and the clarity was good. After a few tweaks of the mouse, an image began to appear.

"It looks like..." said McGaven.

"A shoeprint." She finished her partner's sentence. "There's a good print and two partials showing up."

"Not just any shoeprint, but a specific running shoe. It's a men's Shied running shoe specifically for track running."

Katie turned to her partner. "How do you know that?"

"Because I spent a lot of time shopping for the right running shoe and these are supposedly the best, but out of my price range. They're, like, four hundred dollars."

"But how do you know that tread is a Shied?"

"I looked at these shoes for a long time. I know every inch and that unusual tread that looks like a paisley design is it. Trust me."

"Well, we know it isn't the firefighters or Ames. They were all wearing typical tactical boots," she said. She thought about it. "Wait. Let's go back." Katie keyed up the first house fire and rushed through the slides. She stopped on one photo at the opening to the basement.

"There it is again. What are the odds?" McGaven said.

"Not likely. You know what this means?"

"That the two crime scenes are connected and those shoe impressions put the same person at both locations."

Katie nodded.

"Let me call Investigator Ames and ask him if the debris, smoke, and fire can make shoe impressions more visible to the naked eye," said McGaven.

There was a loud knock at the front door. Cisco started barking.

Katie got up to answer the door.

"Wait. I'll answer it."

"Gav, I'm safe to answer my door in broad daylight."

They both went to the door, where Cisco was sniffing near the threshold. Katie looked out the peephole to see who was standing on the porch. She turned to McGaven.

"It's not a bad guy," she said, opening the door.

John stood there smiling with his laptop and a grocery bag. "Hi. Did I catch you at a bad time? I saw that both you and Gav were here."

"Not at all," she said, opening the door wider and letting John inside. "Is everything okay?"

"Yeah, fine. I went to the location on Oak Lane to help with removing the flooring, but left Eva and Deputy Hansen to finish the documenting and collecting."

"So what's in the bag?" said McGaven.

"I didn't want to come over empty-handed, so I stopped and got some doughnuts and bagels," said John.

"Now we're talking."

"You couldn't still be hungry after that big breakfast," Katie said to her partner.

"There's always room for doughnuts and bagels." He took the bag into the kitchen, followed very closely by Cisco.

"I'm sorry I didn't call, but I figured you would be working since you were at the Oak Lane site earlier."

"No worries," she said. "I thought you'd be still working

too." Katie was glad John had come over; she wanted to show him the shoeprint photos.

"Good. I have some updates for you."

McGaven and John followed Katie to the office area.

"Can you look at this?" she said to John. She keyed up the photos of the footprints that were found at the first two houses.

John studied them for a moment and then enlarged the photos. "I think you're right."

"Okay, just received a text from Ames and he says that it's possible for the prints to show up more prominent from the surroundings and especially with the flashlight source. They appear to be fresh, making them more pronounced. And I'm certain it's a Shied shoe," said McGaven.

"How many of these shoes are sold locally?" she said.

John keyed up stores selling the brand in the Pine Valley area. "It seems there are only two stores in our area that carry them."

"But that's not taking into consideration online stores," she said.

"But we should still check out the stores in case we can get a description of the buyer," said McGaven. "We might get lucky."

John rolled up a chair and keyed up files to show the detectives. He turned to look at them. "We're still trying to match the fingerprints from the Braxtons' home."

Katie nodded.

"The latex pieces that were found are from a type of prosthetic used for Halloween or play dramatizations. But these particular pieces were some of the best, top of the line, and there is only one store that carries it nearby, over in Lost Hills."

"I didn't know there were different grades for makeup prosthetic pieces," said Katie.

"Absolutely. It makes a difference in how long it will last. Lower-end stuff can crack and fall off or is more transparent, while higher-end stays looking very realistic," said John. "I did some research about the people who are very adept in applying such appliances."

"What about Pane Construction?" said Katie.

"We're just getting some lab results. No prints. The rope around Pane's neck was from the barn—we matched it. Couldn't find what the killer used to remove the hands."

"That's not encouraging," said McGaven.

"But... those carpet fibers I told you about. Initially, I told you they were from an old wool carpet from the circa 1950s era. But I also found some petroleum-based oil on one of the fibers."

"Like mechanical or automotive?" said Katie.

"Yes. From the components, I would say with eighty-five percent accuracy they are from automotive," he said.

"So it was in a vehicle?" said McGaven.

"Yes. But since it's from an older era, it would be safe to say a vehicle was recarpeted with this particular fabric."

Katie thought it was good news, but it still didn't point them in the right direction. However, it did indicate that the girls were transported in some type of vehicle.

"So now we know the killer uses latex prosthetics and has a vehicle he transports his victims in that has vintage carpeting," said McGaven.

"These cases are getting stranger," she said, standing up. "Have you found out anything more about A-1 Talent Agency?"

"No, it's just a name that would be used for social media, printed on a business card—no substance," said McGaven.

Katie walked to the chalk wall and started writing a flow-chart of sorts. "Arson fires, all with owners not home, young girls all wearing the same *yellow* dress," she said. "Yellow... there's something important about the color maybe?"

"It reminds me of spring or a color used for celebrations or bridesmaids," said McGaven.

"Yellow usually means something uplifting or happy," she said.

"Or youthful and confident," said John, looking at search results on his laptop.

"Maybe even traditional or innocent?" she said. "So we have someone who's disguising themselves and is probably good enough at it to fool people."

"That's scary if the killer can change his appearance," said McGaven. "Even if someone saw him, he could look different the next time."

"Makes identification almost impossible. And..." said Katie, "he knows it. It wouldn't surprise me if he's been watching us—many serial killers can't help themselves."

"We know that from the shooting at Old Stagecoach Road," said McGaven.

"And that's why the sheriff is concerned about your safety," said John.

"Okay, we've been through this before and I have no doubt we're going to go through this again. It's the dynamics nowadays. Killers and criminals are more brazen, especially with all the information on the internet. These types of people feel that they can do no wrong—and getting close to someone in the investigation is like their biggest fantasy," she said.

"So the sheriff talked to you too," said McGaven to John.

John slowly nodded.

"Is that why you stopped by?" she said.

"Well... no... yes. I wanted to share more forensic results with you. I know this is a horrible case," said John. "But he's just worried about you."

"I know..." said Katie.

"Okay," said John. "The latex found in the woods at Pane Construction definitely has the same components as the other. I can't say for certain if it's from the same batch, but it's consistent."

Katie moved to the chalkboard to add to the flowchart. "Now we have high-end sneakers, latex for disguises, and…"

"I'm sure that you've already thought of this," said John, "but it's possible you've already spoken with the killer. I mean, especially if his disguises are really good."

Katie took a moment. "Yes, we've talked about that."

"My vote, I'm just saying now, is the weirdo guy boss," said McGaven.

"There's definitely something up with him, but I'm not so sure if he's wearing some type of prosthetic," she said.

"Definitely worth checking out," said McGaven.

"Looks like we have several places to visit tomorrow," she said.

The group continued to brainstorm and examine the fire investigator's photographs. Katie knew that something needed to break soon—Jasmine's life depended upon it.

THIRTY-TWO

Monday 0745 hours

Katie arrived at work before 8 a.m. and felt rested and optimistic about what they were going to find out today. She walked into the forensic division and, as usual, was greeted by the soft hum of the air above her head. The atmosphere felt cooler than usual, making her shudder slightly.

Katie knew that McGaven was already there after seeing his truck in the employee parking lot—he was probably conducting searches and digging deep on background checks. He had left early from her house.

Walking down the long hallway, she noticed that all the doors were closed, which was unusual. Slowing her pace, she stood in front of the investigative door before opening it. She was greeted by an empty room. Surprised that McGaven wasn't there, she spied his laptop and notepad filled with scribbled notes that were difficult to decipher.

Katie set her things down and saw a small yellow sticky note that read: *BRB upstairs*. She assumed he was in the detective division. Glancing at her phone, there were no new text messages. If there was any news about Jasmine, she would be contacted.

As she contemplated, the door opened and McGaven stepped inside, shutting the door behind him.

"What, no good morning?" she said.

"I'm sorry, good morning." His face and attitude weren't his usual upbeat.

"What's wrong?"

"Oh, nothing." He definitely appeared to be distracted.

"Okay," she said, rolling out another chair to indicate that her partner needed to sit down. "Something is wrong. What's up?"

He slowly sat.

"I didn't hear you leave. You must've been up early," she said.

"I couldn't sleep so I thought I'd come here to do some more digging."

"Gav," she said softly, "I've never seen you like this. Is Denise upstairs?"

He nodded.

"Did you talk to her?"

"Yes."

"What happened?" She knew the answer was most likely not good.

"She said she needed more of a commitment from me. And if I wasn't wanting to get married... that I needed to find my own place."

"Oh, Gav. I'm sorry," she said. "You know I'll support you in whatever decision you make, but as a friend and your partner..."

He stared at her in anticipation.

"When I see you and Denise together, I don't think I've ever seen such a great couple that truly belongs together. And I would hate to see you lose what you have because of the experience of your parents. One couple has nothing to do with you and Denise. You get what I'm saying?"

"Yeah."

"You want to take a little time—"

"No, absolutely not," he said.

"Okay." She gave a reassuring smile. "I know you'll make the right choice."

"Thanks, partner," he said. He pulled himself together and read through his notes. "We need to check out these Shied shoes. I estimated from the foot impressions that it's a men's size ten or eleven."

"Wow, that's great."

"Well, I had some help from John." He gave a small smile. "There're two stores locally that sell them. Brown's Shoes and Stabler's Shoes. Both are high-end shoe stores located near the Lost Falls area. You're not going to find these types of shoes in a regular department store."

"Interesting," she said. "They're in the area of the second fire."

"That's right."

Katie stood up and grabbed her jacket. "Then let's go."

It never failed to amaze Katie how beautiful the country around Pine Valley was. The landscape changed drastically as you drove along, with the forests, then open areas with ranches and farms, and in some places you could see the valleys dipping in the panorama. Katie drove; McGaven quieter than usual riding shotgun. He wasn't running searches as he usually did when they were heading to an investigation.

"What are you thinking?" she said. It was typical of McGaven to ask her that question.

He turned to her. "I was thinking how it could be possible

we've met the killer. And the more I think about it, the creepier it gets."

"I know what you mean," she said. "I've been focusing on the profile. And for them to be in disguise is a new element—another layer to the psychopathy. Other personalities."

"Maybe there's one personality that doesn't want to kill and he'll turn in all his disguises," he joked.

"Good point, Gav," she said. "But I don't think we're going to get that lucky."

"Probably not."

Katie saw the small shopping area up ahead that housed the shoe store. She had to see what a four-hundred-dollar running shoe looked like. "The killer having such an expensive shoe is telling."

"Where does he get his money?"

"Exactly. It can mean a few things. Maybe he grew up with money. Or maybe he didn't have money growing up and this is a way to make him feel better."

"Or maybe they're just awesome shoes," he said.

Katie laughed. "I can't wait to see them." She pulled into the parking lot. "Seems deserted." Glancing at her watch. "They're probably not open yet."

"It's not quite ten."

"Let's check the area out."

It was a nice sunny morning but the air still had a bit of a chill in it. She spotted two cars around the side of the building and assumed they belonged to employees preparing to open up. The large one-story building housed six businesses, but only four had occupants. It was an older building that was becoming uncommon as Pine Valley, as well as surrounding towns, was updating, remodeling, and building new.

Katie walked up to Brown's Shoes. It was dark inside and she couldn't see anyone moving around. "It's going to be about twenty minutes before they open," she said.

"There's a coffee and doughnut place over there." McGaven pointed a couple of doors down to A Cup of Java.

"That's very convenient," she said. "My treat."

The detectives walked into the small bakery shop. The aroma of baked goods and coffee was overpowering but welcoming.

There was a middle-aged man, dark hair, goatee, and glasses, who was on his iPad drinking a tall coffee with an empty plate next to him. He didn't look up.

McGaven stood at the bakery case where there were all types of goodies.

A young man appeared from the back. He wasn't any older than twenty. "Hi, can I help you?" He stared at their guns and badges. "You cops?"

"Yep," said McGaven.

"Detectives," said Katie.

"We usually don't get many cops in here until around noontime."

"Can we get two large black coffees and—"

"Two of those amazing-looking orange scones," said McGaven.

The young man pulled out the scones and poured two coffees in to-go containers.

Katie put cash down on the counter.

"Oh, no," said the young man. "We don't charge our police officers."

"Thank you," she said and put enough cash into the empty tip jar to mostly cover the food and coffee.

"Thank you." His eyes brightened. Then he said, "Is there a problem you're investigating?"

"No problem. Just talking to some people, that's all," she said, keeping vague, not wanting to talk about their current investigation.

Katie and McGaven left the coffee place. Katie looked

around and there still weren't any new cars, but it was a Monday morning. She sipped her hot coffee... thinking. The small shopping area was convenient for nearby residents and she wondered if the killer lived close to it.

"So something has caused you to ponder," said McGaven. He was beginning to sound like his usual self, even though it was still obvious to Katie that he was struggling with what to do about his relationship.

"Do you find it strange that there is this high-end shoe store in this location?"

He looked around. "Maybe. From what I could find out, it's been here for more than twenty years."

"That would make sense." Katie still looked around. She went to the car and put her scone and coffee inside.

"What's up?" he said stuffing the rest of the scone in his mouth followed by two gulps of coffee.

"I'm not sure, but I want to take a look around."

"Here we go."

"What?"

"You're up to something. Want to clue me in?"

"I'll let you know when I do..." Katie walked around the building.

"Crap," he said putting his coffee on top of the sedan and following his partner.

Katie walked toward the back of the shops. She got that familiar feeling that there was something more about this location, but of course, she didn't immediately know what. She would find out. The leaves crunched under her feet. The area was void of the usual trash that could pile up against a building near a roadway.

She was about to turn around to return to the parking area when something caught her attention. There were two cardboard boxes sitting against the back of the building. They seemed to have been placed side by side. She slowed her pace.

McGaven caught up with her and he too saw the boxes. "What are those?"

"I don't know. The trash dumpsters are on the other side. I saw them when we drove in."

Katie neared the boxes. They seemed to be new, with no markings or printing. They weren't old and damp from the outdoor elements—the flaps were just folded in on each other. She leaned down and gently pulled up one of the flaps and then opened it. What she saw made her stop.

"What is it?" said McGaven.

It took Katie a moment to respond. "Shoes."

"What?"

"Shoes. And I think they're those expensive Shied running shoes."

McGaven moved next to his partner and looked inside. He reached out.

"No, don't touch them," she said. "Just in case."

McGaven retraced his steps to the car and retrieved two pairs of gloves. "Here," he said.

Katie pulled them on and took out one of the shoes. "It says 'Shied' and..."

"And what?"

"It's a size eleven."

"It could be a coincidence. Maybe someone stole them and was waiting to come back for them at another time. Maybe an employee?"

Katie put the shoe back and stood up. "Maybe... but I don't like this." She looked around. Her gut felt like a shadow had passed by them.

"What's in the other box?" he said.

Katie bent over and opened the lid. She immediately stepped back, recognizing what was inside. "How...?"

McGaven leaned over the box.

"How, Gav?" she said. "That's my suit jacket from the

conference. The one I used to try to stop Mrs. Braxton's bleeding."

"Are you sure?"

"Yes, I'm positive. I know my jacket and you can see the dried blood." Katie was breathless and lightheaded. "We need to let Detective Daniels know so he can try to chase down what happened at the hospital after they took Mrs. Braxton in the ambulance. And what happened to the jacket."

"We need John to document and process this," he said. "I'm calling in for a deputy to watch this area until John can get here."

"There won't be any evidence that would help us."

"You don't know that."

"But I do. This killer is playing us. I wouldn't be surprised if he's been shadowing us and has been in disguise every time," she said.

Katie realized there were so many people that could be the killer... and then she remembered the man in the coffee shop. She took off at a full run.

Katie's heart was pounding and she could barely breathe. She rounded the building and ran to the coffee shop, flinging the door open. The man who had been sitting at the table was gone. An empty coffee cup and plate were still there.

"Where is he?"

"Who?" said the young man behind the counter.

"That guy who was sitting here," she said and motioned to the table.

"I dunno. He left, I guess."

"Have you ever seen him before?"

"I don't think so."

Katie looked around the small store searching for cameras. "Are there any security cameras?"

"No, we had one outside, but it hasn't worked in months."

Katie let out a frustrated sigh. She knew the killer would

have been well aware of that. "Don't touch this table or the dishes."

"Okay."

"Got it?"

"Yeah, I get it. I won't touch anything."

"Lock the door behind me and don't let anyone inside until I tell you."

The young man came around the counter with an ashen complexion. Katie ran out, looking from side to side. There was no other car parked when they showed up and the two cars along the side of the building were still there. *Where is he? How did he travel here?*

She heard the door at the coffee shop lock behind her as she ran back to McGaven.

"What's wrong?" he immediately said.

"That guy in the coffee shop. I would bet it was *him*."

"The killer?"

"Yes. The cup and plate are still there and I had the employee lock the door."

"Okay," he said. "How did he know we'd be here?"

"I don't know, but I think he purposely made those shoeprints and waited for us to connect the dots."

"But how would he know we'd do that today?"

Katie thought about it and realized it was so simple. "Not again." She ran back to the police sedan. Dropping to the ground, she diligently searched underneath the carriage. It took barely ten minutes until she found the GPS device. It was a small round apparatus barely two inches wide. She had seen this type of tracker before, but this time it was attached to the Pine Valley Sheriff's Department vehicle. They had been using her Jeep a lot in the investigation, so there had been ample time for someone to attach it to the police sedan.

"Find it?"

"Yes." Katie stood up. "I don't want to touch it until John takes a look at it."

"We need to remove it."

"Wait..." Katie thought about it. "We can use this for our benefit. If the killer doesn't realize we know about it, he'll still follow us, right?"

"I see where you're going with this." McGaven looked around. "That's based on the fact he didn't just see you search for it. He could be hiding close by."

"I don't think so."

McGaven looked hard at his partner. "I don't like that look. Katie, don't let this guy get into your head."

"Gav, we need to find Jasmine. And if the killer can be a chameleon, we need to do whatever we have to in order to find her. This tracker is a free gift." Katie looked around. "He's playing chess with us."

"Maybe. Or maybe he's relying on you to take the bait."

Katie smiled. "Checkmate will always be on our side."

THIRTY-THREE

Monday 1145 hours

Katie and McGaven waited for Brown's Shoes to open after a patrol officer arrived to keep the area contained so no one would contaminate it. Meanwhile, Dr. Dean had called to say he had some information about the autopsy of Stan Pane and so that was their next stop.

The detectives burst inside the shoe store and surprised two employees who had just opened up—one was counting change from the register and the other was dusting the displays.

"I'm Detective Scott and this is my partner, Detective McGaven. We're from the Pine Valley Sheriff's Department," said Katie.

"What do you need?" said the employee counting change. He appeared to be in his thirties, brown hair, heavyset, and seemed to become extremely nervous. His hands shook with the loose bills. "I'm Ted and this is Alyssa."

"You're not in trouble, but we need your help," said McGaven.

"Sure, what can we do?" said a young female in her twenties with purple-streaked hair. She was chewing gum, and her eyes had lit up when she'd found out Katie and McGaven were detectives.

"We found two boxes behind your store. Do you know anything about that?" said Katie.

They shook their heads and looked at one another.

"Not even a size eleven Shied running shoe?" she said.

"No," said Alyssa.

Ted shrugged. "No."

"Look, we're not here to jam you up. What's your business is your business," said McGaven. "Tell us anything you know about that running shoe."

"Besides that it's ugly and I wouldn't be caught dead wearing them," Alyssa said. "But wait... I remember a guy buying a pair recently—well, a couple of weeks ago."

Katie watched the two employees and she assessed they were telling the truth.

McGaven pulled out his phone with a photo of the box and shoes. He turned it toward the employees. "Have you ever seen this?"

"No," they said in unison.

"So what did the guy look like who bought a pair?" said Katie.

"I dunno, just a guy. He wasn't fat or skinny. Brown hair, I think..." she said.

"He had a weird ring, remember?" he said.

"Oh, that's right. He was wearing this gold ring with some type of black stone in a pear shape," she said.

"Anything else about the guy? Did he act strangely? Did he pay with credit or cash?"

"Cash," she said. "And he seemed to count his money slowly. I don't know if that's any help to you."

Katie handed them her card. "Please, if you see him again, call us. Or if you remember something."

"Sure thing," said Alyssa.

The detectives left the store and checked in on the deputy before they left. McGaven left specific instructions until John arrived.

As Katie and McGaven drove back to the police department, they began devising a plan to trap the killer.

"Do you think this GPS tracker was left intentionally for us to find?" said McGaven.

Katie thought about it as her mind spun with all the new things they'd found. "There's no reason for the killer to think we would find it unless he knew about the previous GPS that was put on my Jeep during the time Chad went missing..." She stopped mid-sentence. Just saying Chad's name made Katie stop breathing momentarily and feel as if there was a lump in her throat. It was going to take a while for her to move through her grief.

McGaven remained quiet, giving his partner space.

"So I don't think the killer anticipated us finding the GPS," she finished.

"Okay," he said, happy to agree.

"But we're going to make sure there also isn't one on my Jeep or your truck. That's our backup."

Both Katie's and McGaven's phones chimed at the same moment.

McGaven read the text message. "They've identified both Jane Does. Jessica Grant was the one in the closet and Cynthia Parks was the girl under the floorboards. Looks like Hamilton and Alvarez are going to talk to the families."

"Sounds good." Katie was glad they had more help with these cases. She wanted to go through things slowly and not have to rush around without taking their time examining evidence and conducting interviews. She wracked her brain to try to remember more about the man in the coffee shop, but at the time she'd registered him as ordinary and unassuming.

"Do you think we should also check out the other shoe store?" said McGaven.

"I don't see there's any reason to."

"I was just thinking that this guy seems a couple steps ahead of us. Maybe he went to both? Or left something for us at both of them."

Katie's thoughts were on where Jasmine was and what other innocent girls were being targeted by the killer. Time was ticking down and they had to gain more ground in the investigation.

"Right now we need to keep moving forward," she said. "We can always backtrack if we need to," she said.

McGaven nodded in agreement. "Let's hope we don't have to."

THIRTY-FOUR

Monday 1350 hours

Katie and McGaven had made good time driving back to Pine Valley and to the medical examiner's office. They rushed inside the building and made their way to the morgue. Katie thought about the findings of Anna and Jane Doe, now Jessica Grant. They made her uneasy since they were categorized as accidents rather than homicide cases. The killer was extremely clever, intelligent, and there was no doubt he'd keep committing murders until they caught him.

Standing in the main area of the morgue, Katie felt that familiar heaviness in the pit of her stomach. She had been in the morgue many times, but something was different this time and she couldn't pinpoint why.

"Where is Dr. Dean?" said Katie. Her nerves were on edge and her racing thoughts about the killer kept an endless loop running in her mind.

"I couldn't tell you," said McGaven, his tone seemed annoyed.

It was one of those days, Katie told herself.

"Detectives," said Dr. Dean rushing toward them. This time his lab coat had spots of blood on it, but it still didn't cover his khaki shorts and sandals. "Ah, Detective Scott. Nice to see you."

"Good to see you," she said, but didn't entirely mean it. She was wary of what he would say about Stan Pane.

The detectives followed the medical examiner into the room. Dr. Dean opened a file folder and quickly scanned it.

"Yes, of course," he said. "Stan Pane, forty-two years old, fair health, took medications for an ulcer and ulcerative colitis, and he also had a fair amount of alcohol in his system—0.1 percent—and cannabis."

"Was there anything else in his system that would raise any suspicion?" said Katie.

"Not that I discovered. His cholesterol was high from his poor diet. I found the contents of greasy fast food in his system —hamburger meat, potato fries. It was his last meal." Dr. Dean removed the sheet covering the body.

Katie grimaced. Pane's body looked as if he had been beat up and thrown out of a moving car, with purple and blackish marks all over it, especially around his neck. The missing hands lent more to the horrible condition of the body, giving it a Halloween appearance.

Katie waited for the doctor to clarify the cause and manner of death. She was concerned by the other findings he'd mentioned and wondered if it meant he was trying to keep the results conservative. Although why he would do that she wasn't sure.

McGaven studied the body. It was unclear if he had the same questions or wondered if Pane sustained previous injuries before the hanging.

"I know you're waiting for the final report," Dr. Dean said, looking at the detectives. "First, the hanging wasn't the cause of death. He had been beaten severely around the chest and throat, and it crushed his lungs and thorax area, which is of course where the heart is. And his windpipe was also crushed. Though that could have been during the hanging."

"Can you tell what was used in the beating?" she said. "Was it a weapon, like a bat?"

"See these marks?" Dr. Dean showed the concentrated areas around the chest. "This was caused by something stronger than a bat... something metal like brass knuckles."

"Brass knuckles?" said McGaven.

"Yes. I've seen such injuries from this type of a beating—not very often. This is something 'old school,' if you will."

"What, like the sixties or seventies?" said McGaven.

"Well, it's not something typical today in fights, or even homicides. There're many other ways to kill someone. This seems to be something very personal because it would take time for the victim to die."

"It was torture," Katie said.

"Exactly. This man endured a lot of pain until his heart and lungs couldn't work for him and ultimately his body shut down."

"So it is homicide?" she said.

"Absolutely. Cause of death is homicide and the manner was severe repeated blunt force trauma to the upper body and neck. Hanging by the neck was postmortem, so it definitely didn't cause Pane's death."

"Okay," said Katie, thinking about what Pane went through and, most importantly, why. He was possibly doing some private investigation for the killer, but what would have led to this brutal overkill murder?

"Now," said the medical examiner, "the hands were removed, also postmortem, with something you might find in a garage or working area that would have access to various heavier-duty tools. It wasn't an electric item, more like a hack-saw. The result was effective but left behind definite ragged marks through the arm—the ulna and radius—which left the hands and all the small bones and phalanges completely intact."

"Doesn't that seem strange? Wouldn't it be easier to break and cut through the smaller bones of the wrist?" she said.

"You would think, but it was clear that whoever removed his hands was deliberate and had thought it out. The cuts were perfectly spaced and almost identical on both."

"What about the hands?" said McGaven.

"They were intact. No signs of defense wounds or anything under the nails. But he did have a fair amount of alcohol in his system—could have rendered him weak and unable to fight back."

Katie was reeling with the information. After viewing the body hanging in the barn, she had no idea that Pane took such a beating. Why hang him? Was it to make an example of him? The evilness and brutality of the killer made her shudder, her skin becoming cold.

"We did test for anything on his hands and under his nails, but the only thing that came up was the usual greases and cleaning agents that you would find in the construction trade."

"I see," she said.

"But there was one unusual thing we found, and I'm sure John will explain it in more detail with you, but there were tiny traces of what appears to be some type of latex."

That caught Katie's attention, and she glanced at her partner. The latex seemed to be linking all the cases together.

"I'll send the entire report and findings over," said Dr. Dean.

"Thank you."

"Any other questions?"

Katie was still reeling from the findings and didn't have any immediate questions.

The doctor laughed at her silence, which was an unusual

reaction from him. "If you do have questions, just holler. I'm always available for you."

"Of course," she said.

"Thanks, Doc," said McGaven.

Once they were back in the car McGaven turned to Katie with a serious expression on his face. No smiles. No wisecracks. His eyebrows were furrowed and his mouth straight with no hint of a smile or even a frown.

"What's wrong, Gav?"

"You know I don't usually get concerned about what we're going to run into next. We work the case and every clue, right?"

"Of course." Katie stared at her partner. She had never seen him like this before.

"This case. These *cases* are brutal, and I have a bad feeling about it all. I don't ever say these things, but..."

"We can't investigate objectively if we think there's something bad about it. There's always something bad. That's what we do."

"I'm not worried about me. I'm worried about you, Katie."

"Gav, I'm fine and—"

"I'm not joking around. This killer can change his appearance. He's already leaving us evidence and now your jacket, not to mention he's already shot at you. He's gone from luring young girls who want to become models and leaving them in a burning house, to this... this beating that Pane took and cutting off his hands—that goes way behind the work of a psychopath."

Katie listened to McGaven. Explained like that, the investigation was scary. They were moving into another depth of violent psychopathic behavior.

But Katie remained calm. "Gav, you and I have been through a lot... to say the least. We will find this killer. We just need to keep our wits and have each other's back, okay?"

"It was really creepy that he could have been sitting in the bakery," he said.

"I know," she said quietly. "I have your back, Gav... always. You know that."

"Ditto, partner."

As Katie drove and thought about McGaven's concerns, which he had every right to express, it did give her pause. She knew too that things were going to get dicey, but she also knew they had to keep moving forward. It wasn't just about their safety, but about the unsuspecting girls' safety.

"There's a stop I think we should make," said Katie.

"Jasmine's house?"

"No. Alvarez has point on that and he's been keeping in contact with the family," she said. "Let's go back to the Braxtons' house."

"You know the tracker is working and the killer will know we're going there."

"That's what I'm hoping," she said.

"Let's go."

"Great."

"One more thing. Can we make a quick stop?"

"Sure," she said and smiled. "Burrito or sandwich?"

"Burrito."

THIRTY-FIVE

Monday 1530 hours

Katie and McGaven headed to the Braxton home at 217 Birch Drive after eating quickly and grabbing some bottled water.

"So you're saying that you think the killer has been to the Braxtons' house?" said McGaven.

"It seems likely. The killer had to keep tabs on Mrs. Braxton in order to know she was headed to the conference in Sacramento. And you remember that both Anna's and Jasmine's laptops and phones were missing from their rooms."

McGaven nodded.

"I wasn't entirely sure until I saw my bloody suit jacket in that box behind the shoe store. It connects whoever killed Mrs. Braxton and these cases," she said. "Let Hamilton and Alvarez know we're going back inside the house."

McGaven immediately sent text messages to the detectives.

"You know I always like—"

"To go back to the beginning," he said, finishing his partner's sentence.

"Yep."

"What do you think we'll find?"

She glanced at him. "I don't know, but there has to be more to the fact that Mrs. Braxton had made notes about Pane Construction not long before she was killed."

"You think she hired him to find her daughter?"

"Could be. Just speculating, but it could be what got both of them killed, whether the killer had planned to murder them or if he was covering his tracks."

Katie drove down Birch Drive until they reached the Braxton residence. The small yellow house looked as it did the first time they had visited. John and Eva had documented and searched the residence, so there shouldn't be any issue with them being there.

"They didn't find anything on her phone, which leads me to believe she had another we didn't find," Katie said. She parked a couple of houses down across the street.

"You don't want to park in front?" McGaven asked.

"No, I don't want the neighbor, Clara Taylor, watching. I want to keep her at a distance for a while." Katie took a couple of seconds to study the neighborhood. Everything was quiet and she didn't see the next-door neighbor outside—it was a good time to go back through the home. "So the GPS will show the killer we've been here."

"And?"

"And I think we can set a trap for him that might make him come back."

"That's fairly bold. Maybe he won't want to do that?" said McGaven.

"I don't think being bold is a problem for this guy," she said looking around. "Now I'm not so sure we could bait him. At least not right now."

The detectives exited the vehicle and headed to the house. The flowers across the front were now withering without water and proper care. Katie was surprised the neighbor didn't water them, but since the Braxtons were both gone maybe she thought it didn't matter. But still. It was odd she didn't tend to them since it had appeared she enjoyed gardening.

Katie quickly moved the blue pot where the key had been returned. She picked it up and opened the front door.

Standing in the middle of the living room, the detectives looked around, pulling on their gloves. It was obvious the police and crime scene techs had been there. There were dark smudges along the surfaces and around doorframes. Furniture had been moved and there were plastic and paper pieces on the floor. It wasn't a complete mess, but they could tell the entire house had been gone over thoroughly.

"Where do you want to start?" said McGaven.

"I want to find something that connects Braxton to Pane and any of the victims. I think we should start in the kitchen."

"Really?"

"Yes." Katie went to the counter where items had been pushed to the side toward a corner. More black smudges from dark fingerprint powder remained along the surfaces. She began systematically opening cupboards and drawers. This time, she pulled out the drawers, setting them on the table to go through them. She reached into the openings and ran her hand along every area.

McGaven had opened the refrigerator, sorting through items, looking for anything that might be hidden. He checked the freezer too, including inside freezer bags.

Katie walked through the laundry area, where it was still neat and orderly. She had almost forgotten how organized Mrs. Braxton was and guessed it was most likely due to a strict budget and raising a teenage daughter.

The detectives had searched everything, but didn't find anything of importance.

"Well?" said McGaven.

"The second place women hide things is their bedroom."

Moving to the room, Katie scrutinized the area. It was also neat and minimal. There were no knick-knacks or unnecessary things, which made it easier to clean the surfaces.

Katie could hear McGaven moving around in the other bedroom. She decided to start with the dresser and pulled out every drawer, stacking them on the bed. Just as she did with the kitchen drawers, she examined the slots by visually searching and by running her hand around the areas. Nothing. She moved to the nightstand and repeated it. Nothing once again.

Katie felt frustrated as she put all the drawers back in their appropriate spots. She moved systematically to the electrical items. After finding a metal nail file, she removed the plug and light switch plates. Then she checked the table lamp and then the light ceiling fixture.

Katie stood on the bed, looking around. She knew Mrs. Braxton had to have hidden something important.

McGaven leaned in the doorway watching her, contemplating the options. "Okay..."

"I'm looking everywhere I can think of that people hide stuff and nothing..."

McGaven looked around at the now disarrayed space and his eyes went to the carpet at both sides of the bed. "Did you check along the baseboard area and under the carpet?"

Katie immediately jumped down and dropped to her knees.

"You're crazy," he said jokingly.

"Sometimes crazy can pay off. Obviously she didn't want anyone to find her stuff." Katie pulled at the carpet in the corner and found it loose. She tugged harder and the corner portion flipped back. There were two business-size envelopes with nothing written on the outside. "Gav, you're a genius."

"I try."

Katie stood up holding the envelopes. She put one down and opened the other. Inside was a billing statement from Stan Pane Private Investigations and a report on what he had found out about Anna and A-1 Talent Agency. She quickly read the information, which wasn't any more than what they had found in relation to the company—which was basically nothing. There wasn't anything to connect the two. No receipts. No social media connections. And no other indication of another company that could have merged with the agency.

"What does it say?" he said.

"He found basically what we did about the background of the talent agency, which is that it really doesn't exist. He ran reports for business listings, licenses, tax reports, liens, bankruptcy, and so forth," she said. "But this is interesting. There are initials M.C. with an asterisk notation. Nothing else. I'm not sure where that came from."

"Sounds like an alias. Where did he find that name?"

"I don't know. It doesn't say." Katie gave the report to McGaven and then opened the other envelope. Inside were photocopies of pictures. "This is weird. Wouldn't you send photographs digitally these days?"

"Maybe they didn't want any type of digital footprint?" he said.

Katie looked at the photos, which were dark and grainy. She could see a man walking from a house and to a car. Each photo was from a different location, but there were no notes of who or what the photos were of—no addresses. She spotted a penciled date indicating it was three days after Anna disappeared. "Take a look at this. Here's a notation saying that there had been no information from police."

McGaven studied the photocopies, both front and back. "We need to have John scan these. Maybe it will help with identification of the area they were taken."

"This would have been important for the killer to find. You think he was looking for this?" she said.

"Someone was here looking for something."

"I think they took anything from Anna they could find,

including a potential 'real' journal and any notebooks. Nothing like that was found."

"I wonder what else the killer took?"

Katie looked around the room. "Mrs. Braxton must've had some notes here. Maybe that's where the killer found out about Pane Construction?"

McGaven let out a sigh.

"What's wrong?"

"You know how you sometimes say that things don't feel right or they're staged?"

"Yeah."

"Well I've been feeling that way a lot this investigation, especially after we found the boxes."

Katie knew what he meant—she too was feeling uneasy and as if they were being sent on a weird scavenger hunt with a psychopathic killer guiding them.

. "Let's finish searching—doing our due diligence," she said.

The detectives took extra time to completely go through the house, but didn't find anything more that would help them. Katie put things back into their places before leaving and took one last look around.

The detectives peered outside through the closed blinds. It was still quiet without anyone moving around the neighborhood. They wanted to stay under the radar as far as interested neighbors were concerned. There had been plenty of time for the gossip to begin about the death of the Braxtons.

"Let's go," she said.

When they were satisfied the coast was clear, they quickly left the house, locked the door, and headed to the police sedan.

Katie drove them back to the police department.

"You think we were at the Braxtons' long enough to intrigue the killer?" McGaven asked.

"I hope so."

THIRTY-SIX

Monday 1745 hours

Katie and McGaven arrived at the forensic division at the Pine Valley Sheriff's Department. In the forensic exam room John was organizing evidence and working on the computer. Katie noticed the boxes from the shoe store.

"Hey," she said.

John looked up and smiled. "Didn't think you guys would be back so early."

"We're here to make a plan," said McGaven. He looked at the evidence that had been laid out on the table.

"I heard about the tracker on your car," said John. "You sure you want to keep it there?"

"Absolutely."

"Katie wants to lure the killer," said McGaven.

"Seriously? Actually, that *does* sound like Katie," said John.

"Very funny. I was wondering if you have some kind of a detector we could use, John," Katie said.

"You mean for finding hidden cameras and other technology?"

"Yes. I want to make sure my Jeep and McGaven's truck aren't being tracked before heading home."

"No problem. I'll check them in a little bit and let you know before you guys leave today."

"Great," she said, looking at the box. "Did you find anything?"

"You were correct. The shoes are a match to the prints found at the fire scenes."

"So the person who walked through there before the fire was the killer?" she said.

"I'm not saying that, but it's consistent with the footprints."

"It's another clue tied to the crime scenes," said McGaven.

"The navy jacket is definitely yours, Katie?" John asked.

"Yes."

"I'm testing the blood to see if it's a match to Stella Braxton."

"Okay," she said. "Oh, by the way, we found this paperwork at the Braxton home hidden underneath the carpet in Stella's bedroom. There are photocopies of photographs that we want enhanced if it's possible." Katie gave the envelope to John.

John immediately took special care and sat at another desk with a computer set up with a scanner. With gloves, he carefully unfolded the paperwork. "Let's see what we can do." He loaded the pages into the scanner. Within a minute, the images came across the large monitor. "Okay, here they come. Yeah, these are really poor reproductions. You didn't find the actual photos or maybe a flash drive with them?"

"No, that's it. But there's something familiar about the locations," she said.

With the first image, John adjusted the contrast and lighting. The photo began to look clearer as he went through a process of cleaning up the image. There was the back and side view of a man walking up a sidewalk to a building. At first, the structure appeared as a home but soon they realized it was more a commercial building.

"Where is that?" said Katie.

McGaven leaned in to get a better look. "It looks like the east area of town because of the architecture. I've seen buildings like this when I was on patrol."

John went through different lighting.

"Have we seen this guy?" said McGaven.

Katie couldn't be sure. "I don't know."

The man looked average in build and features. It wasn't clear enough to get a good identification. He wore a jacket with the collar pulled up slightly, obscuring the right side of his face. His hair looked dark, short, and not any particular style.

"Let's take a look at the other three," said John. He took time to run each photo through the same contrast and lighting adjustments. They became clearer, showing ordinary shots of houses.

Katie studied each scene. The man was in only one photo while the others were of locations with structures—the commercial building with the man and the other three were residences.

"Let's try something. I can't guarantee anything, but I have this software program that helps to identify basic things like buildings, cars, landmarks, and anything that can be found in a city," said John.

"Cool," said McGaven.

Katie watched John work—he had an effortless and calm demeanor, but she knew he was wracking his brain to try to identify these areas for them.

"Okay, let's try the first one. I can't help you with identifying the man, but the building might be something we could pinpoint. I put in all the online maps for Pine Valley and Sequoia County."

Within a few minutes a list of areas and streets scrolled

down the page. Katie and McGaven were mesmerized by the outcome.

"Anything seem familiar?" said John.

"Well yeah, but they don't match the image," said McGaven.

John narrowed the locations and types of buildings, which contained areas on the east side.

"There," said Katie, as she referred to 1020 Coal Road. "Does that look the same?" It was identifying commercial structures in a three-block radius from 1000 to 1030 Coal Road.

"Bingo," said McGaven. "I know that area. We would get calls for service for kids partying and homeless fires."

When Katie heard the word "fires," that made her stop and think. "What was along this road before these commercial buildings?"

John keyed up more information. "It looks like there were some small neighborhoods in the 1980s, but a large corporation bought the land for development. It was in a good part of town away from the inner-city areas."

"Can you send this to our phones?" she said.

"On it."

Katie looked at McGaven. "Want to check this area out in one of our cars? We don't want to tip the killer and show our hands if this photo is of him."

He nodded. "Absolutely."

"I'll work on the other photos and send them when they're ready," said John. "And..."

Katie and McGaven looked at John.

"Please watch your backs. If you need more help, just ask."

Katie and McGaven had used John on several occasions because his background as a Navy Seal definitely came in handy.

"We will," said Katie.

John got up from his desk. "I'll scan your cars before you go."

Katie and McGaven went into their office and updated the investigation board. There was plenty of new evidence to incorporate. Katie added the autopsy findings about Stan Pane, the extensive beating, severed hands above the wrist; the shoes found behind Brown's Shoes consistent with the impressions found at the fire scenes; the bloody jacket used to stop the bleeding on Mrs. Braxton (testing of blood in progress); and the paperwork and photocopied photographs from Mrs. Braxton's bedroom.

"Don't forget the tracker on the police sedan," said McGaven.

"Got it," Katie said adding it to the board. As she stepped back, she was beginning to get a clearer picture of the killer's profile. At first glance it seemed all over the place with his personality and behavioral evidence from the crime scenes, but it wasn't. He was a very dangerous and violent individual—and he was escalating with how brutal he could be. That's what scared Katie the most.

McGaven's phoned chimed. He looked at it. "John says the cars are fine—no tracker on either one."

"We should head out to my house and then just take my Jeep," she said.

After a few more minutes of updating the board, they were ready to leave.

"Let's go," McGaven said.

THIRTY-SEVEN

Monday 1845 hours

Katie pulled into her driveway. McGaven had made it back first and he was just getting out of his truck when she cut the engine. She thought about her partner's relationship predicament, even though she didn't see it that way. She still understood his hesitation about, or even fear of, committing and getting married. Getting married was something that she always thought she would do and there was no question it was going to be with Chad. Things change. She hoped McGaven and Denise worked it out—both of them meant the world to her.

Katie stepped out of her car.

"Hey, you looked a little lost in thought," he said. "Everything okay?"

"Of course," she said, trying to sound upbeat. "Just thinking about everything. It has been quite the day."

"That's for sure. And it's only Monday."

Katie unlocked her front door and disarmed the alarm system. Cisco was full of energy and he ran around barking and whining, extremely excited. She walked to the back slider and opened it, letting the jet-black dog run out with lightning speed.

"Seriously, everything okay?" said McGaven as he popped a jelly bean into his mouth from his stash in his pocket.

"Yeah, maybe I'm a bit tired, but I want to check out this building before tomorrow."

Cisco ran around outside and then dropped the ball on the deck demanding some dog play. McGaven threw the ball a few times. Katie went to the kitchen and prepared Cisco's food. The dog was instantly at her side waiting patiently for his dinner, sitting at attention.

"When did you start eating those things? They're so bad for you," she said to McGaven, indicating the jelly beans.

"I can't help it. I like them," he said eating another one. "A lot of officers eat them for energy when on patrol."

"I'm going to change my clothes," she said. "We'll be ready to go in a few minutes."

"Is Cisco coming?" said McGaven.

Katie thought about it; since they were checking out a building it would be a good outing for Cisco. "Sure," she said, hurrying to her bedroom to change into more casual clothes. She heard McGaven talking to Cisco and telling him that he was coming with them.

In less than fifteen minutes, Katie, McGaven, and Cisco were on their way to the commercial buildings on Coal Road. As Katie drove her Jeep, she still couldn't shake the feeling she had about these cases. Finding her blood-soaked jacket had rattled her much more than she'd realized.

The sun was lower in the sky and the light was beginning to fade, leaving a reddish orange twilight. Traffic was beginning to slow down, but after they got off the freeway and entered another area of the county it was becoming less populated with traffic.

Katie turned off at the Coal Road. It was different from what she had remembered of the area, but it had been a while. There was no reason to drive there unless you had business with one of the commercial buildings or you worked there.

"How many houses were there here before all these buildings?" she said.

McGaven looked up the history of the area. "Looks like there were five sections with about a dozen houses in each."

"We're talking about sixty homes. Did the city or county relocate residents or give them time to get out?"

"It says they were given a fair market price for their homes."

"And then they had to move?"

"Looks like it. They probably just integrated into Pine Valley and the surrounding areas," he said.

Katie thought about what it would have been like if she and her parents had had to move. There were still so many people in the area who had been around for decades and generations, and that's what made Pine Valley so special.

"Slow down," said McGaven.

Katie slowed the Jeep, and Cisco took it to mean there was something exciting coming up. The dog circled several times in the back seat, letting out a couple of whimpers.

"Wow, I don't remember these buildings being so big," she said.

McGaven accessed the updated photo on his cell phone. "That one, isn't it? Keep rolling slowly."

Katie complied as she studied the buildings—each had its own personality. Some were basic white and tan, while others had a distinct architectural decoration of unusual windows and rooflines. They housed all types of businesses including computer technology, automotive, offices for various banking and finance companies, and warehouse storage.

Soon they had driven most of the 1000 block and the 1200 block.

"I'm not seeing anything similar," she said. The more she drove the blocks the more she felt defeated. It had been a longshot and maybe they were in the wrong area.

"Maybe we're looking at it all wrong," said McGaven.

"What do you mean?"

"Look at the angle that the photo was taken. As if from a lower viewpoint."

"It looks a little distorted. Like a wide-angle lens was used, making it seem smaller than it really is," she said. Katie tried to look at distinctive things about the architecture. "Wait. Could that be it?"

She was referring to an older building, most likely one of the first ones built. It wasn't as large or distinctive as the others they had first seen.

"I think you might be right."

Katie pulled to the side and parked in a small parking lot with one weak outdoor light. She got out of the Jeep and zipped up her jacket. The evening air was cool and there was a slight breeze, making it even colder. It was quiet. There were only a few vehicles parked, which worked in their favor. Out of habit, she made sure her Glock was secure and that she had Cisco's remote for the pop-door release.

"You good?" said McGaven as he too put on a jacket.

"Yep."

They walked out of the small parking area and crossed the street. Shadows cast across the sidewalk and striped the side of the buildings. Darkness would be with them soon. It would either hinder their walk-around or work in their favor.

Katie stopped and studied the building from the sidewalk— the address was 1020 Coal Road. It had a small area on the side just large enough for three cars. It was a typical three-story commercial building from a few decades ago, which didn't give any indication of what was inside. She didn't see any name or description anywhere.

Behind the triple blocks of buildings was unincorporated land. It hadn't been cleared, leaving the heavily wooded area untamed, and she wondered if they were going to bulldoze it to make room for more commercial buildings, or even come full circle and build residential high-end apartments or condos. It was a great area for people to live away from the central, busier parts of Pine Valley.

"Do we know who owns this area and buildings?" she said.

"From what I could find, two large corporations own most of the real estate here," he said. "I would have to go to the county clerk's office to find out more. Or you could ask Shane."

Katie smiled. "Shane would definitely know." He was the county archivist and researcher she had used on a couple of occasions.

They moved closer to the building.

"There doesn't seem to be any security. Doesn't that seem strange?" she said.

"Yes and no."

"What do you mean?"

"Well, it depends upon what's inside. It's an older building," he said. "And I can't see any cameras, but that doesn't mean they aren't there. They're becoming smaller and smaller these days."

"Then we need to be careful and not break any laws."

"When has that ever stopped you?"

"I only do that when there's a life at stake. There's a difference." Katie walked around to the side of the building where there weren't any windows. "There are very few windows across the front and none on the side. You know, Gav... I don't think this is being used as a commercial building."

"Then what?"

"Maybe residents?"

"Apartments?"

"Not the usual. Maybe it houses people working for one of the businesses?"

McGaven studied the building and tried to see what the windows were across the front. "There aren't any visible lights on inside."

Katie went around back and found two dumpsters. McGaven joined her.

She looked at her partner and then flipped up one of the lids. "You can find out more about who lives in a building by the garbage." She put gloves on, swung her leg up, and pulled herself over the edge. She felt like she was doing military exercises, which dredged up memories—some good and others not.

"That's my partner." McGaven flipped on a flashlight and directed it inside.

"You know you could have done this—your height and all would've made it easy."

"Now what fun would that be," he said and snapped a quick photo of Katie.

"That had better not go on your social media." Katie was annoyed, but she might have done the same thing. "Ugh... it stinks in here. I don't think the garbage has been picked up for a while."

McGaven looked around. "Someone would have to roll the dumpster to the street. I'll look up who pays the bill when we're back in the office."

Katie clenched her jaw and tried not to breathe too deeply. There were five large dark garbage bags—one was partially open. As McGaven directed the light, she could see to open the hole wider. The contents spilled out. There were grocery items: microwave meals, cracker boxes, chip bags, coffee containers, moldy bread, sandwich makings of mayo, mustard, deli meats, along with plastic bags.

"Gav."

"What is that?"

"A peanut butter jar and plastic sandwich bags."

"You mean like found with Anna?"

She nodded.

"You know this isn't enough for a warrant right?" he said.

"Of course, but it's a bit coincidental."

"Do you know how many people have peanut butter and sandwich bags at their house?"

"I know, but..."

"It's not direct evidence. It's not really even circumstantial, but it's intriguing," he said.

"We need to keep digging."

McGaven moved the flashlight beam around in the dumpster. "Then keep digging." There was a slight smile on his face as his partner rummaged around in garbage.

"You are so enjoying this," she said, realizing garbage remnants were on her pants.

"You climbed in first."

"You've got me there." Katie opened the other bags and found typical things that would be from a home in addition to some construction items of broken drywall and part of an interior door. She went through everything and then climbed out.

Going to the next dumpster, they found it was partially filled with more commercial items that would be found in a construction project: old carpet remnants, more drywall, and broken kitchen drawers.

"What about the carpet?" McGaven said.

"It's definitely not antique. It looks like there were stains and threadbare areas." Katie stared at it. She then took her knife from her ankle sheath. "I'm going to cut a small piece where there is a dark substance just to have John test for blood."

"Good idea. He'll probably find some serious food stain... or worse."

Katie pulled at a large piece of carpet and cut out a

ten-inch area. She thought for a moment and then tossed the remaining carpet piece into the forest. "Just for insurance in case these dumpsters get emptied and there is blood on it." She began trying to clean her clothes and stomped her boots to remove kitchen garbage remnants. "Ugh..."

The detectives walked around to the other side of the building where there was a door. There was a small square window at the top that had been painted over so you couldn't see inside.

Katie tried the door, but it was locked. She then knocked several times.

They waited. No answer.

Katie knocked again.

Nothing.

"What did you expect?" McGaven said.

"Someone to answer the door or at least movement. I want to see what's inside."

"We'll have to figure it out another way."

They looked around the area some more and then decided to leave.

Standing at the Jeep, Katie said, "So who was that in the photograph walking to this building? And why did Mrs. Braxton have a copy of it?"

"Is that unidentified man our killer of many disguises?" McGaven said. He retrieved a plastic bag to put the carpet piece into.

Cisco pushed his head through the opening of the window, wanting to be pet.

"And why did Mrs. Braxton think that was so important to keep hidden?" she said.

"Was the photo taken by Pane?"

"So many questions." Katie kept scrutinizing the area and wondered if they needed to come back in the morning.

"When we're back in the office I'll find out more about this property," said McGaven.

"I think it's clear Mrs. Braxton and Pane were murdered for what they knew," Katie said. "And I think they found out too much about the killer, whether it was intentional or part of seeking what happened to Anna. They were collateral damage to keep his identity a secret."

THIRTY-EIGHT

Monday 2310 hours

Katie couldn't sleep. She tossed and turned; her mind wouldn't shut off. She had taken a nice relaxing hot shower to get the garbage grime off her skin, but it didn't help to calm her mind. There were so many things rushing around and around from the cases and where might the clues take them. Her thoughts were never far from the victims and from finding Jasmine.

Katie finally threw her covers to the side and sat up. Her bedroom was dark, but she didn't see Cisco's usual outline on the chair in the corner. Her bare feet touched the floor and she stood up, dressed in lightweight pajama bottoms and a tank top. She contemplated going back to working on the killer's profile— or not.

Katie walked to her door without turning on any lights. She peered down the hallway to the guest bedroom where the door was ajar—she knew Cisco had pushed it open and was snoozing part-time with McGaven. Having a dog to hang out with was the most comforting feeling in the world—and she was glad Cisco could sense McGaven's internal struggles.

Katie smiled as she stepped into the hallway and could hear soft snoring from her partner as she made her way to the kitchen. The glows from the open laptop and oven were the only lighting as Katie's eyes adjusted to the darkness. She thought about a snack, but didn't feel hungry. She looked at the security cameras on the six split screens on her computer. There was nothing that was interesting or that needed to be addressed, so she didn't check the directory of movements. There was usually nighttime wildlife setting off the recordings.

She paused, listening.

There was only the sound of her refrigerator humming.

Having difficulties sleeping wasn't something she typically encountered because usually when it was time to get some sleep Katie was so exhausted she fell into a sound slumber.

Still not turning on any lights, she walked around her living room contemplating, thinking, and trying to connect the clues and people. She kept coming back to the Braxton house.

Why?

It was where everything seemed to have started.

Find the million-dollar man... you'll find my Anna...

That resonated through Katie's mind. And the fact that Mrs. Braxton spoke of "they" before she died.

Could that mean there was more than one person perpetrating these crimes? Did it have to do with the term "million-dollar man" and all the disguises? A million faces?

Katie went to the couch and looked for her briefcase. She didn't find it, so she turned on a small table lamp and kept searching.

"Oh great," she whispered and remembered she'd left it in her Jeep when they came back from Coal Road.

She glanced down the hallway, not wanting to wake McGaven and Cisco. Grabbing her keys and disarming the alarm, she went out the front door quietly.

The porch and the driveway were cold on her feet, so she

quickened her pace and walked around her Jeep to the passenger's side, which was next to McGaven's truck. Katie opened her side door, seeing her briefcase on the floor. Grabbing it, she turned to close the car door—

Before the passenger door shut, Katie was forcefully shoved forward, causing her to drop the briefcase and fall face down against the Jeep seat, taking her breath away. Instinctively, she thrust up her right elbow and struck someone behind her. Her adrenalin kicked into high gear and her mind went into survival mode, doing everything she could to escape.

The person behind her was breathing hard and seemed to whisper something to her that she couldn't make out. Katie tried to turn to face whoever attacked her, but she couldn't. The person—who she knew was a man, based on his strength, build, and prowess—pulled her right arm behind her, which left Katie without another move except... she pushed up from the car seat and used the back of her head to smack the attacker. It was a direct hit that she assumed hit his forehead and face. He pulled her from the car and threw her down, taking off running down the driveway.

Gaining her wits and strength, Katie got to her feet and witnessed a medium-height man dressed in dark sweats and hoodie running down the driveway. Without hesitation, she ran after him. Without her gun, it was a dangerous situation, but she wanted to see where he was running to and possibly what car he was driving.

The man was fast and sprinted like a professional runner.

Katie ran as fast as she could and felt every uneven pavement and rock on her bare feet, but she didn't quit. Rounding the corner onto the street, the attacker had gained more distance. She kept her pace.

The man disappeared around a corner. She had lost visual. A few moments later, she heard a car engine start, rev, and then speed away. As she rounded the corner, she just saw the red taillights of a van but no license plate.

Then the attacker and the van were gone.

"No!" she said as she stopped in the middle of street.

Katie hurried back to her house and called the police, giving the dispatcher all the information she had and the direction the van was heading.

"What's going on?" said McGaven. It was clear he had been woken from a sound sleep.

Cisco trotted into the room.

"I went out to the Jeep to get my briefcase and I was jumped from behind."

"What?" McGaven immediately went to the security laptop, where he pulled up footage of the attack, but there was nothing before that. "They must've been out of view when they arrived, but at least there's footage of the attack."

The detectives watched the video several times before the police arrived.

"Nice move," McGaven said, referring to her headbutting the assailant.

"Yeah, well, I have a headache now."

"Do we need to call paramedics?"

"No, I'm fine."

"Where have I heard that before?"

"Gav," she said. "I'm fine. Let's move on and see if we can get more information about the guy."

"I'm going to send the file to John as well," he said.

"We don't even know if it's the killer we're chasing. It could have been anyone. A burglar. Someone we put behind bars. Anyone."

"Katie, do you really believe that?"

She sighed and thought about the chances it was anyone else but the killer of disguises. "Probably not."

"Did he say anything?"

"No, well, nothing I could understand."

Cisco pushed his nose at Katie.

"Was he going to abduct you?"

"How could he? His van was a block away. That doesn't make sense."

"So he was trying to scare you?"

"There's no other rational reason," she said.

"Except trying to kill you—just like Mrs. Braxton."

"I think he could have easily done that, but he didn't." Katie was shaken and the thought of being stabbed several times in the stomach or kidneys was absolutely terrifying. "How did he know I was going to go outside?"

"Katie, you have to be extremely careful. You understand?" It was clear he was deeply troubled.

"Look, we've had trouble before—" she started.

"Yes, we have, but this *is* different. Bolder. More violent. He's letting us know he can get at you anytime he wants so."

It was true. So Katie needed to change tactics and turn the tables on him.

THIRTY-NINE

Tuesday 0730 hours

Katie updated the investigation board with the findings from the commercial building on Coal Road and the attack on her. Standing back and looking at the layout of the cases, it was clear to her that there were many moving parts but there were also some things that may not even apply to the investigation.

Last night's attack had shaken her up and she wanted to keep busy and moving forward to compensate for it. She wanted to find out more about 1020 Coal Road, and the best way to do that was to visit the county building and meet with Shane Kendall.

"Hey," said McGaven, breathless as if he'd run the entire way from his truck. "Morning." He gave Katie a large steaming coffee.

"Thank you."

"I see you've gotten started."

"I'm going to the county building to see what I can find out about that commercial building."

"Great. I'm going to do some background checking on the property."

"I was thinking," she said. "You know how everything always seems to go back to the beginning?"

"Yeah."

"I want to stake out the Braxton residence—at least for a few days. I don't want to draw suspicion installing cameras. Let's see if our lure worked. Too many killers like to go back to areas where they have either killed or to see the police working."

"Good idea," he said, searching for a number on his phone. "What about Deputy Hansen on the day stakeout detail?"

"Perfect. Set it up," she said. "Let's meet back up later."

"Ten-four. Oh, Katie?"

"Yes, I know. I'll be extra careful." She smiled and left the office.

Before Katie drove to the county building in her Jeep, she checked underneath in case the intruder had managed to install a tracker last night. It was clear.

She enjoyed going to the county building as it reminded her of the wonderful place she lived and all the amazing historical significance within it. Katie had sent a text to Shane and he immediately responded with a positive "sure." She walked past the main area and headed toward the back where there was a nondescript door. Pushing it open, the area revealed an older part of the building that had been original and subsequently added onto over the years.

The old-building smell greeted her as an old friend, making the visit that much more intriguing. She took the winding wrought-iron staircase down to the basement. The first time she visited, it was still old and dark, but it had been updated with good lighting, storage areas for physical maps, light tables, and a computer workstation.

Katie entered the archival and research room, which felt like stepping back in time. She straightened her jacket and looked for Shane. He was sitting toward the corner hunched over several blueprints. His sandy hair was tousled and he wore gold-rimmed glasses.

"Hi, Shane," said Katie.

She had surprised him and he looked up at her and blinked a few times. He had been so immersed in what he was doing that he didn't hear her approach.

"Hi, Detective," he said and stood up.

"I'm always surprised every time I come here. This place is wonderful."

He shyly smiled. "Thank you. It's like home."

"I can see why. Such history."

"Did you have a question for me?" he said.

"Yes. Actually, it's not nearly as old as some parts of the city, but I wanted to learn some information about an area in the east section. The address is 1020 Coal Street."

Shane typed the address in on the computer and after a moment he wrote down some numbers. Katie watched, knowing the routine well.

Next, Shane opened one of the long thin metal drawers that held quite a few blueprints. He pulled out several sheets and took them to one of the large light tables. When the prints were laid on top of the light, the details showed up.

Katie walked over to the large working table.

"This is part of a much bigger area that was renovated around the same time," he said. "It looks like the building you are inquiring about was built and completed in 1982." He moved the prints. "The others on this particular block were built between 1982 to 1984."

"Do you know what was there previously?"

"There were regular homes. Many of them were built back in the 1940s and 1950s."

"Who purchased the land?"

"It was the county—Sequoia County. There was a large project to build commercial buildings at that time with the hopes of boosting the economy. It was first a success, but then they fell on hard times, forcing the county to rent out certain buildings for offices and residences."

"What about 1020?"

"There were upgrades made and it looks like there were four small apartments on the second and third floors."

"When were the permits?"

"It doesn't say on these sheets, but from what I've seen, sometime after 2000."

"Who officially owns it?"

"The name on the deed to this building and two others is DSP, LLC."

"What else do they own?" she said.

Shane sat back down at the computer and keyed up a few search sites. "I don't see anything. Just those three buildings—and it's been owned by them since the beginning."

"What does DSP stand for?"

"Sadly, I don't have the information."

Katie examined the blueprints and knew it was the same building where they had dug through the trash dumpster. What did the photo have to do with the investigation? And why did Mrs. Braxton have Pane shoot the photograph?

"Detective?" said Shane. "Current investigation?"

"Yes. But I'm not sure what this means. At least, not yet."

"I can get a list of all the permits and inspections, and anything else pertaining to the buildings."

"With names? And anything else associated with the project then and now?"

"Of course."

"Would you have the listing of the contractors and any subcontractors that worked on this particular building?"

"Absolutely."

Katie smiled. "It's nice to see you, Shane. As always, I'm impressed with your knowledge and skill set."

"Thank you," he said, not quite meeting her gaze. It was obvious he was slightly embarrassed by the compliment.

She flipped through the blueprints and remodel drawings.

"I can get you copies of everything plus the lists. I'll deliver it to you tomorrow if that's okay."

"That would be great. Thank you, Shane."

Katie climbed the antique stairs and left the county building, heading back to the office. She was mindful of her surroundings more than usual and kept her eye out for a van in the vicinity.

FORTY

Katie rushed back to the forensic division and as she hurried down the hallway she heard McGaven and John in conversation—most likely her partner was telling the story about her encounter last night. She slowed her pace and gathered her thoughts. It was strange to her that the incident made her off balance.

"Detective," said a voice from behind her. It was Detective Evan Daniels.

"Hi, Evan," she said. Lost in her thoughts, she obviously hadn't heard the main door open.

"Everything okay?" he said, searching her face.

He had a way about him that drew Katie.

"Of course," she said. "Just got back from the county archives. Trying to dig up information."

"I see."

She continued toward the office where she ran into McGaven and John. She never said a word or asked why

Daniels was back or for how long. Her mind and focus were on overload.

"There she is... No trouble?" said McGaven with his usual light humor.

"Nope," she said. Walking past them, she went inside the office.

"John had some updates," said McGaven.

Katie turned and looked at the men. "Let's hear it."

"Well," said McGaven, "the carpet didn't have blood on it—human or otherwise."

"What was it?"

"What was left of a chili dinner."

"Yuck," she said, thinking about the garbage she had been covered with. "Okay, what else?"

"The blood on your jacket was indeed blood and matched to Stella Braxton," said John.

Katie leaned back against the table. There was a part of her that had hoped that it was a hoax by the killer to scare them, but in fact it was definitely the jacket she'd used to try to stop Mrs. Braxton bleeding.

"You okay?" said McGaven.

"So he wasn't just trying to mess with us—it's the actual jacket and blood. That's a concern."

"Well you're not going to like what I found out at the hospital," said Daniels. "I tracked down what happens to clothing items when a person is brought in from an ambulance."

"What happened to it?" she said.

"I talked to one of the ambulance drivers and he said the jacket had fallen off the gurney as they were rushing Mrs. Braxton inside the emergency area. When he got back, which was only a couple of minutes later, the jacket was gone along with a few of their supplies."

"Is that protocol for emergencies, to leave the ambulance unattended?" said McGaven.

"It happened in this instance," said Daniels.

"Catch you guys later," said John as he returned to his lab.

McGaven and Daniels were staring at Katie.

"Why do I get the feeling that the sheriff has spoken to you both?" she said.

"Yes, I got a call first thing this morning," said Daniels. "He wanted me to return to Pine Valley and assist on the case."

"In other words, babysitter number two."

"It's not like that, Katie."

"We're talking Sheriff Scott and this is his only niece," said McGaven.

"Well, maybe to help watch over you," Daniels admitted.

McGaven faced Katie. "This is just a precaution. I have to admit I'm on the sheriff's side."

"Can we get back to work?" she said.

"You got it," said her partner.

Katie was really annoyed by this point. She examined the investigation board again to help channel her concentration back to what was important.

"Is Deputy Hansen at the Braxton residence?" she said.

"I should be getting an update soon," said McGaven. "Just so you know, he took one of the confiscated vehicles from our lot, so you don't have to worry that he looks like a cop staking out the place." He sat at the table and opened the laptop.

"What do you need me to do?" said Daniels.

Katie and McGaven glanced at each other.

"How about relieving Deputy Hansen for the next shift—afternoon? And Gav and I will take the evening watch."

"And what am I watching for?"

"Anything. Anyone coming or going or showing any interest in the house," she said.

"I'll let Hansen know he'll be relieved at one. Sound good?" said McGaven.

"I guess that's my cue to leave. Send me the address."

"Will do."

"See you guys tonight." Detective Daniels left.

"Was that kind of mean?" said McGaven.

"No," she said. "If I know Daniels, he's going to check out everything we've been working on before he relieves Hansen."

"Good. Another set of eyes."

"And I don't think he's on the killer's radar."

Katie and McGaven had worked for most of the day on paperwork. McGaven read over Alvarez's reports of family and friends of Jessica Grant and Cynthia Parks. Katie went over the blueprints that Shane had couriered over early.

Katie's eyes were tired after reading lists and going over permits and remodeling plans for the commercial building. She couldn't connect anything useful and it just made her frustration grow. She leaned back in her chair, groaning.

"My eyes are done."

"I'm close to burnout reading these reports. Someone needs to tell Alvarez that he needs to take a writing class."

Katie laughed. "Anything?"

"I've tried to tie the girls to the investigations. The only thing they have in common is the fact they all wanted to be models and actresses. They were good kids, did well in school, and never got into any trouble." He sighed.

"Are they all from here in Pine Valley?"

"They were living here, but not all of them grew up here."

"What about a connection to Jasmine or Anna?" she said.

"No, they didn't go to the same schools and didn't seem to run in the same circles."

Katie stared at the board to readjust her eyes. She was dragging her feet on the profile of the killer. One reason was because his signature, behavioral evidence, and general characteristics were all over the place, making it difficult to pinpoint a background. Obviously he was doing these things on purpose, which was another aspect to his profile. The changing of his appearance to the point of obsessively detailed disguises made him extremely dangerous, due to the fact he could move around easily without attracting attention. Had they already met the killer? That bothered Katie more than anything.

"Earth to Katie," said McGaven. "I would bet you're thinking about the killer's profile."

"If you were a betting man, you would be correct."

McGaven smiled. "Just got a text from Daniels. Nothing new to report."

"Just like Hansen."

"We're not giving up yet."

"Never is not in our DNA, remember."

"Hey, guys," said John at the doorway. "I just sent you both better-contrast pics of those houses."

"Thanks, John," said Katie as she quickly accessed her phone.

"I tried my software program but had no luck. If you have any questions, send me a text; otherwise, I'm going home."

"Wow, it's early for you," said McGaven.

"Unless there's a homicide," said John as he was leaving.

Katie studied the photos but couldn't make sense of the houses. They could be almost anywhere in Pine Valley or somewhere else.

"Anything?" said McGaven.

"I need fresh eyes. Nothing seems familiar."

"We need coffee and some snacks," he said. "I'm negotiating for one of our vehicles in the lot. Trying to change things up so we can't be tracked easily."

"Can it be a car with comfortable seats?"

"I'll try my best."

FORTY-ONE

Tuesday 1800 hours

Katie and McGaven parked and waited in their new four-door sedan a street away from Birch Drive. Detective Daniels slowly drove up and got out. He hurried to the car and leaned down at Katie's window.

"That was six hours I can't get back," he said. "Nothing new, but I'll still have some unimportant information in my report for you to read."

"Okay, thanks," said McGaven.

"Thank you," she said.

Daniels took an extra second and looked at Katie with a smile. "Goodnight." He left.

McGaven drove past 217 Birch Drive and then turned around, parking two houses away where they were secluded enough to not be spotted but still had a direct view of the Braxton residence if anyone approached the front or backyard. There were several cars along the street and they blended in easily.

McGaven tilted the seat back a little and popped a few more jelly beans into his mouth.

"I've never seen you have such a sweet tooth."

"I can't help it. I like all the flavors. Unlike most people, I think all the colors are great."

Katie laughed.

"You want some?" he said.

"No thank you."

He shrugged.

"Did you pack healthier stuff?"

"Of course."

Katie looked into a large grocery bag and the cooler. She found snacks of chips, crackers, and some kind of trail mix. In the cooler there were sandwiches, extra waters, and two containers of potato salad. "Wow, how long did you pack for?"

"As long as it takes." He smiled at his partner. "There's nothing worse than being on a stakeout and being hungry... your stomach growling..."

Katie grabbed a water.

"What do you really think?" he said.

"What do you mean? About what?" Katie wasn't sure if he meant about his personal dilemma or the investigation.

"The case. The killer. I know you have some theories that you don't like to put down because it isn't facts," he said. "Tell me what you think after all we've collected and seen."

Katie took a sip of water. She noticed her shoulder was sore from the scuffle last night but tried to ignore it. "I think everything *is* connected, but we haven't definitely linked it yet. I also think we've come across the killer and I don't know how we're going to identify him. If he has all these disguises and is as bold as he is... he probably has a million IDs. Maybe he's never been put into the system. Thinking about all the possibilities makes my head spin..."

McGaven appeared to think about what she had told him.

"I agree with you. Sometimes it seems like we're grasping at straws but then, wham, we get a hit."

"That's one way of putting it," she said. "I want to get back to that commercial building. It's nagging at me."

"What about the burned-down houses?"

"I've been thinking about them too." Katie fidgeted in her seat. "I've been trying to keep my personal stuff out of my head so I can focus on the investigation. I'm so glad that Hamilton and Alvarez are doing follow-ups and interviews."

He nodded.

Two hours had passed and the detectives were becoming restless and snacking as they waited for something to happen.

A car came up the road and instantly cut its headlights but kept moving.

"What's up with that?" said McGaven.

Katie watched as the small dark-colored two-door car slowed and parked a few houses away. "It may be nothing."

A man stepped from the vehicle and looked around the neighborhood. He walked slowly down the sidewalk toward them.

"Isn't that...?" said Katie.

"Yeah, I think it is."

"That's the manager at Mrs. Braxton's work, Chris Booker," she said. "What's he doing here?"

They watched the man walk slowly and look around every few seconds as if he was trying to evade someone or something. He kept wiping his hands on his pants, obviously nervous and watchful.

"Where's he going?" she said.

"I don't know... the Braxtons' house?"

Booker stopped in front of the Braxton house and stared at it for a few seconds but kept going. He then turned up the path and hurried to the neighbor's house—Clara Taylor's. He knocked on her door; she immediately opened it and let him inside.

"What's going on?" she said.

"Let's go find out."

"No, wait. Let's see what they do, and when he comes back out, we'll stop him."

It hadn't been five minutes and Booker exited the neighbor's house with her in tow.

"Now," she said.

Katie and McGaven got out of their car and walked up the sidewalk.

"Well, this is interesting," said McGaven as he turned on a flashlight and directed the beam at them.

Booker and Clara stopped, stunned expressions on their faces.

"We need to talk to you both," said Katie.

Booker took another look at the detectives, turned, and bolted.

"I got him," said Katie as she took off at full speed. "Stop! Police!"

McGaven waited with Clara, making sure she wasn't going anywhere or made any phone calls.

Katie saw Booker run by the Braxton house and head into the woods. She gained speed as her thoughts flashed to the previous night when she was attacked. Watching this man run, she knew instantly that it wasn't the same person. Booker was heavier, carrying a few extra pounds and running like a scared person and not someone who'd had physical fitness training.

"Stop!" she yelled. As soon as Katie entered the backyard area, it was really dark and she slowed her pace. She couldn't see Booker anymore and knew he was hiding.

She stopped. It was fully dark now but she didn't want to turn on her flashlight just yet. She concentrated on sounds and her surroundings. This was one of the strongest skills she'd honed in the military—it was one of the reasons why she worked so well with Cisco.

She heard a slight sigh. Then it was a straining to stop heavy breathing. She knew it well. It was coming from straight ahead and to the left. It wasn't completely known if Booker had a gun, but she wasn't going to take any chances.

Katie moved like a jungle cat. Her footsteps were quiet and she moved with ease as her eyes accustomed to the darkness. She stopped again. There was no sound, so wherever Booker was—he was staying in place.

Katie pulled her weapon and used her flashlight to direct her way. She moved toward where she had heard the sounds. Within four feet, she said, "Come out now!" She waited. "Come out now! You have nowhere to go. Don't make this harder on yourself."

One, two, and three footsteps.

"C'mon," she said still training her weapon at Booker. She wasn't taking any chances. "Keep coming, show me your hands."

Booker stepped forward with his hands in the air. He didn't look like a crazed criminal, he looked scared and confused. The front of his shirt had dirt and leaves stuck to it.

Once he was close, Katie holstered her weapon and forcibly turned him around. She easily snapped on handcuffs.

Winded, McGaven approached with his flashlight. "Everything okay?"

"Yes. He was hiding. I knew he wouldn't run for very long." Katie looked at her partner. "Where's Clara?"

"She's detained and sitting in the back seat of the car."

"Am... Am I being arrested?" Booker said.

"You're being detained until we can sort this out. The handcuffs are to keep *me* safe, got it?" she said.

He nodded.

Katie escorted him to the front yard. McGaven pulled Clara out of the car.

"Now you both have some explaining to do," said McGaven.

"We can go inside my house," said Clara.

"No, we're going to the police station to sort everything out," McGaven said. He radioed for two patrol cars to take Booker and Clara back to the sheriff's department.

FORTY-TWO

Tuesday 2115 hours

Katie and McGaven prepared for their interviews with Booker
and Clara at the Pine Valley Sheriff's Department detective
division, making a plan for how they wanted to proceed as they
stood outside the interview rooms. The detective division was
quiet at this late hour. The desks were dark and the files had all
been put away in locked cabinets. Being surrounded by so much
darkness made Katie jumpy, which was unusual behavior for
her. The investigation was beginning to weigh heavily—she also
had to worry about her safety more than ever and that made her
tense and irritable.

"How do you want to play this?" said McGaven.

"I say we split up. I'll take Booker and you can talk to Clara.
I think Clara will open up to you and I already have Booker
scared," she said with a slight smile on her face.

"That's my scary partner," he said with a slight smile and
went into interrogation room number one.

After her partner shut the door, Katie went into room
number two, where Chris Booker sat at the table leaning

forward, with his hands on his lap. He kept his gaze downward. The handcuffs had been taken off when they reached the detective division.

Katie pulled out a chair and sat down. She dropped the file folder on the table, which was the only time Booker looked up.

"So, Mr. Booker, why don't you start telling me what was going on tonight? Why did you run? Why were you at Stella Braxton's house? Why were you talking to Clara Taylor? Why don't we start there?" she said, trying to keep him slightly off balance with all the questions.

"No, no, no..." said Booker, shaking his head. He appeared to be a broken man, not the arrogant manager from the accounting firm.

"No what?"

"No, I can't be here. You don't understand."

"Then why don't you tell me?"

Booker put his hands on the table and pressed his palms downward. "Please..."

"Let me spell it out to you. We're investigating several homicides and a missing person, and you don't seem to have been truthful with us. You know what that means? That means you're evading the police and interfering with a homicide investigation. Do you understand that?"

Katie thought Booker was going to cry. His face clouded with uncertainty and sheer terror. She kept the questions coming.

"How do you know Clara Taylor?"

McGaven decided to go down the friendly route. He was concerned Mrs. Taylor would shut down if he pressed too hard, and he needed to get some answers.

Mrs. Taylor sat at the table. She appeared shaken and her eyes were watery. It was unclear if she had been crying or not.

"Mrs. Clara Taylor," began McGaven. He took a seat across from her so his height wouldn't be deemed as intimidating. "We need to go over some things. We're investigating several homicides in addition to Stella Braxton's death."

She nodded. Her fingers were interlaced; he thought to keep her hands from shaking.

"You do understand how serious it is to have not told us information related to the Braxtons' deaths?"

"Yes."

"How long have you known Chris Booker?" He remained calm but stared directly at her.

"I really... don't know him."

"What was he doing at your house?"

"He called me and said he needed to talk to me."

"Didn't you think that was strange? Mrs. Braxton's boss, who you don't know, needed to talk to you after she died," he said.

"Not really... well, yes, I guess it was unusual."

"What did he want from you?" said McGaven. He was careful how he worded his questions and he kept his tone calm and even.

"He said he'd left something at her home and needed it back."

"What?"

"I don't know."

"He left something or she had something of his?"

"I... I don't know... He said there was something in the house that was his."

McGaven pushed back in his chair. "You realize Mrs. Braxton's house is still considered part of an open homicide investigation, right?"

"I didn't think of it like that."

"Had Mr. Booker ever contacted you before?"

"Once. It was right after Anna disappeared. He said that he was worried about Stella."

"What else did he say?"

"He just asked questions, like how was she doing, was she going anywhere... things like that."

"Did he talk about the deaths of Stella and Anna?"

"No."

McGaven felt she was lying.

"I'm going to ask you one more time," said Katie. "How do you know Clara Taylor?"

"Um, I can't remember. I think I met her at work," said Chris Booker.

Katie leaned forward. "Why do I think you're lying?"

"I dunno."

"Mr. Booker, people are dead. One of your employees, one of your clients, three girls."

"Client?"

"Yes."

"Who?"

"I'm not at the liberty of discussing an open homicide case," she said as she watched Booker squirm and wring his hands. She decided to use another tactic. "Is something wrong?" she asked more kindly.

He shook his head.

"Look, I'm trying to get to the bottom of things. Can you understand that?"

He nodded.

"Why were you back at the Braxton residence?"

He sighed. "I was looking for something."

"What?"

"Stella had some photos and I needed to get them back.

They weren't in her things from work. So I asked Mrs. Taylor if she could let me in. I know she helped out over there."

"I see," she said. Now she was getting somewhere. "What photos?"

"Just stuff from the office."

Katie watched him for a few uncomfortable minutes, trying to push him into explaining more, but it didn't happen.

"I don't know what to say," he said.

Katie knew he wasn't going to tell her any more. But she and McGaven were sure going to dig deep into this guy's background.

Katie stood up. "Okay, Mr. Booker, thank you for your time."

"I can go?"

"Of course. You weren't in custody. You were free to go anytime. This was just a friendly interview," she said. Leaning on the table close to his face. "But I warn you, the next time you're brought in—it won't be of your free will."

He stood up.

"I'll have an officer take you back to your car."

"Mrs. Taylor, we're trying to get to the root of things. We're investigating homicides and suspicious deaths. If you know anything, now would be the time to tell us," said McGaven.

"I understand, Detective, I really do. I miss Stella and Anna."

"We're trying to find their killers."

"I... I... miss them so much. I've been a widow for five years and they've been such wonderful neighbors. There's a hole in my heart now," she said.

That hit a chord with McGaven, but he didn't let it show. "Had Mr. Booker contacted you before?"

She looked down. "Yes, he came to my house once before

and then tonight. I swear on my husband's grave they're the only times."

"Okay. Please, if you know anything, even if it seems small, call us please." He handed her a business card.

"Of course," she said and took the card.

"I'll have an officer drive you home."

Katie and McGaven walked out to the parking lot. Both were visibly tired and had things weighing heavily on their minds.

"So what's your take on Mrs. Taylor?" said Katie.

"Honestly, I think she's telling the truth. She doesn't know anything. She said she had spoken to Booker only one time before tonight—and I believe her," he said. "What about Booker?"

"He's scared. He knows more than what he's saying. What? I don't know for sure."

"You think he knows something about the killer?"

"There's something—I just can't get to the truth. I didn't want to burn that bridge, so I took it easy on him."

"Detective Katie Scott taking it easy on a person of interest?" He laughed.

"What? I did."

"I'll get the background checks started in the morning. I don't know about you, but I'm exhausted," said McGaven.

"It could be all those jelly beans."

"I can see you're funny even when you're tired."

"I'll see you back at the house," she said. Katie got into her Jeep. Her body was exhausted, but her mind was racing with all the new information. She sat in her car and watched McGaven get into his truck and pull out of the parking lot. She watched to see if anyone followed him or if there was a van in the vicinity. It was all clear.

Katie drove home.

FORTY-THREE

Wednesday 0815 hours

Katie stood with her arms crossed in front of her, staring at the investigation board as if she would solve the case just by looking at it. She wanted to put together a more detailed criminal profile than just a threshold assessment, and she wanted to see what had changed during the course of the investigation as they'd gathered new information and evidence.

The killer profile had changed. He was bolder and hadn't a care in the world over his killings, which had been brutal and sadistic. He was a man of many faces, both in the physical and psychological sense. It gave Katie pause. How were they going to catch him? They had to be smarter and stay a step ahead of him. The GPS tracker was a start. Appealing to his arrogant and high-minded side was also a tactic. If the killer was made to think he was winning and made a mistake because of that, they could catch him.

"Okay," said McGaven.

His voice almost startled Katie; she was so deep in thought

about the killer. She'd delved so deep into the psyche it was almost like he was in the same room as her.

McGaven kept speaking. "As far as Clara Taylor goes, her background is clean and is what you would expect from a retired, widowed schoolteacher," he said. "I think she's been caught up in something she's unaware of, trying to be nice and neighborly helping out Mrs. Braxton's boss." He paused. "But Christopher Robert Booker, known to most as Chris, has a scattered past. He's been in jail for assault, trespass, and shoplifting."

"What was the assault for?" Katie asked.

"It was a party at a private residence. A fight broke out, three people went to jail," he said.

"That's a big leap to serial arsonist and killer."

"Yeah, well there's more. He has a long history of work-places and they don't seem to have been positive departures."

Katie thought about it. "With all his ups and downs, he might be the type of person who would get into the wrong crowd."

"Wrong crowd?"

"What I mean is... when people become desperate... Maybe he's having trouble making ends meet and that can make people do things they normally wouldn't."

"Well, you're correct. His credit rating is in the dumpster and it looks like he's in debt. And money seems to be missing from his account."

"Twenty thousand?"

"Yep."

Katie thought about what he had said last night, admitting he was looking for something at the Braxtons' house. He'd also seemed surprised that one of the homicides was one of his clients.

"After what I saw when we were at the accounting firm, I

doubt that the working relationship between Mrs. Braxton and Booker was good."

"Probably not, but what I briefly saw of Mrs. Braxton, she seemed to be a strong woman who could handle a guy like Booker."

"I agree," she said.

Katie's cell phone rang.

"Detective Scott," she said.

"Yes, hello, Detective. This is Ray Hudson from DSP Incorporated. I'm returning your call."

"Thank you, Mr. Hudson."

"What can I help you with today?" His voice was deep and congenial.

"We've been conducting an investigation that has brought the building 1020 Coal Road to our attention. It was in some papers belonging to a murder victim."

"Oh, I'm sorry to hear that. What can I do for you?"

"What is the building used for? Commercial or residential?"

"It was commercial for many years and then we turned the top two floors into apartments for workers or anyone visiting our companies."

"Is anyone living there now?" she said.

"No. There was someone residing in the top apartment, but he has since moved out."

"I see," she said, thinking about the food in the garbage dumpster.

McGaven looked up from his paperwork at Katie.

"Was there anything else?" said Hudson.

"Would it be possible to view the inside of the building?"

There was a pause.

"It would help us cross this off our list."

"I don't see why not."

"Great. Can I make an appointment?"

"I'll do one better. I have a lockbox being put on the side door. Hashtag 3 1 3 3. It will be available from today."

"That would be great," she said, jotting down the access number. "Thank you."

"Anything else I can help with please let me know," he said and ended the call.

Katie looked at her partner. "We're in. A representative for DSP Incorporated is having a lockbox put on the side door—and he gave me the code."

"So we're not going to meet him in person?"

"I don't think so," she said.

"And I didn't hear you mention that we might take some samples for testing—if, and only if, something appears to be suspicious."

"No, why would I?" she said and smiled. Since the detectives had been given permission to look at the building by the owner's representative, if anything were to indicate something illegal had happened there, they would have the legal right to take a sample or even close the building until it was straightened out.

"I couldn't find much on DSP except that they have been in business since the commercial buildings went up and they seem to be the only projects they have. There were a few names associated with the company." McGaven sorted through files. "And I'm not entirely sure what DSP stands for, but it's what's on the legal documents."

"Could be the initials of whoever began the company," she said.

"Maybe."

Katie decided to add more names to a list of people they had interviewed and spoken with.

Chris Booker (Mrs. Braxton's boss)
Clara Taylor (Mrs. Braxton's neighbor)

Stan Pane (owner of Pane Construction, Mrs. Braxton's client, did some private investigation work.)

Kip Johnson (house-sitting neighbor's house next to arson fire in Lost Hills)

Kayla, Deb, and Trevor (kids at mall who knew Anna)

Tom and Patrick (security officers at mall)

Ted and Alyssa (employees for Brown's Shoes store)

Unknown Guy at A Cup of Java

Unknown Guy (photograph of 1020 Coal Road)

Unknown Assailant (mall hallway, Katie's house, and shooter at Lost Hills arson site)

Raymond Hudson (Representative for DSP Incorporated for commercial building 1020 Coal Road)

Arson Investigator Luke Ames (Pine Valley Fire Department, PVFD, new from Northern California)

McGaven stood next to Katie, reading her list. "I get what you're doing, but Ames... Really?"

"I'm just brainstorming. He's new to the area, and arrived just at the same time as the arsons began. And—" she said.

"And we've been fooled by people before who we thought were on our side."

"I'm just keeping all the players straight in my mind. And, no, I don't think Ames is the killer," she said.

"Who's lied to us?" said McGaven. "Who has reason to try and push us in another direction?" He continued to study the board.

Katie remained solemn.

"You know that Ames, the three teens, and Pane, who is dead, are not the killer."

"But one of the others on this list could be the killer in disguise."

FORTY-FOUR

Wednesday 1105 hours

Katie drove up to the commercial building at 1020 Coal Road
and pulled into the small parking lot. There were no cars. She
turned off the police sedan.

"You really think it's a good idea to use the GPS-tracked
vehicle?" said McGaven.

"Why not?" she said. "We're letting the killer know where
we are."

"Yes, is that a good thing?"

"Not the optimum, but we need to force him to make a
move."

McGaven sighed as he opened the car door and stepped
out.

Katie knew it was bordering on reckless, but something had
to change in the investigation. The detectives walked around to
the side door where there was indeed a lockbox. Katie punched
in #3133 and it dropped open, revealing a key. Katie looked at
her partner and inserted the key, opening the door. It stuck
slightly and then swung inward. Immediately, they were met

with a garbage smell of old food, reminding her of the dumpster she had climbed into the night before.

"Ugh," said Katie. "When was the last time someone was here?"

The building was three stories and it appeared that the first floor had been an inside parking garage, which now had walls divided into office areas. It was cold and dark, as if you were trapped in a basement garage with no escape. With no windows and poor lighting, strange shadows loomed around every corner.

Katie switched on her flashlight. McGaven stayed behind his partner as they searched the area for anything suspicious. There were odd rooms and corridors without closets or storage areas, just cement walls.

"This is odd," she said. Her voice made an unnerving echo around them.

"Bizarre," McGaven agreed.

Once Katie was satisfied with their search of the weird first floor, she and McGaven went to the back of the building where there was a staircase leading up to the second and third floors. Oddly, the steps were wooden and very narrow. Katie thought it would have been difficult to move furniture up there. The building made her jumpy, which was irrational—at least she thought so. It was old, vacant, and smelled horrible. The lack of windows gave the impression that the building was closing in on them.

At the second floor there was a long hallway, with a door on each side. Obviously to the two apartments the representative had spoken about.

Katie and McGaven spun around at the sound of a door closing. It didn't slam; rather, there was a creaking of hinges along with a scraping sound. They readied themselves for anything, but everywhere remained quiet. Katie's hand was on her Glock, but she didn't pull the weapon yet.

"What was that?" she barely whispered to her partner.

He shook his head and pointed up to indicate that the sound had come from the top floor.

Katie nodded. She'd thought that too.

The detectives retreated from the second floor, pulling their weapons as precaution, and headed back to the staircase. Katie didn't like the fact that they were bypassing the second level to search, but they needed to proceed to where they had heard the sound.

Katie took the lead and cautiously climbed the next section of the stairway. McGaven was two steps behind and his approach was quiet, but she knew he was watching the downward stairs for anything—or anyone—that might sneak up or possibly ambush them.

The top floor was different from the second. There was a white door with a glass window taking up half of the entrance. Katie could see the hallway behind it clearly; it had two dark garbage bags leaning against the wall. She glanced back at her partner and he nodded, meaning it was clear to move through the door.

Slowly turning the knob, Katie pushed open the door. As on the second floor, there were two doors on each side of the long hallway, plus there was another door at the end of the hall, which she assumed to be a storage and maintenance area.

The old outdoor carpeting felt spongy under Katie's shoes and made a soft squishy noise. She heard McGaven's footsteps behind creating the same sounds.

Katie took the left door and McGaven the right. They made eye contact. Knowing they were on the same page, and without any words, they moved into the apartment areas.

Katie forcefully opened the apartment door. Standing at the threshold she kept her gun directed out in front, fanning from left to right. She could see the entire area, which was larger than she had imagined. The living room, kitchen, and dining area were open. The two bedrooms, separated by a bathroom, were at the other side of the area with open doors. Indentations in the carpet in the living room suggested the room had once housed a sofa and some type of table with two chairs. There were only two windows on each side of the entire living space, giving what would normally be a pleasant floor plan an overshadowing of darkness.

After seeing the front area was clear, she moved in deeper, still vigilant and hyper-focused. The apartment smelled, but not quite as bad as the entrance. Katie could see the apartment was dirty and that a couple of dishes were still in the sink. The faucet dripped with regular timing. The refrigerator hummed and made a clunking sound as it cycled off its temperature setting.

Katie opened the fridge a few inches to find some old food and two dishes containing some type of puree. The stench of the spoiled food hit Katie, causing her to choke back an urge to vomit.

She heard the scraping sound once again.

Katie moved quickly toward the bedroom, clearing the first one, and then the bathroom. When she entered the second bedroom, she noticed a built-in shelving unit and, sitting on one of the top shelves, a petite gray cat.

Relieved, Katie returned her weapon to its holster on her hip. "Who are you?" she said. "And why did someone leave you here all alone?" She approached the friendly cat who was more than happy to receive pets.

"Hey," said McGaven at the doorway. "Making friends I see."

"We can't leave him here."

"Well he's not riding along with us today."

"Nothing?" she said.

"No. It looks pretty much like this apartment except the walls are scuffed and it looks like no one has lived there for quite some time. The refrigerator and stove are gone."

"This one hasn't been cleaned, but I take it that the garbage smell is from the trash bags that no one has taken out," she said as she picked up the cat. "You are so sweet. Why would anyone leave you here?" Looking around, she said, "He must be starving. There're no cat bowls or a litter box."

"That's why there's an undertone of ammonia with the rotten garbage." McGaven pet the cat. "He is cute, but I'm a dog person."

"Aw, wouldn't Lizzie love a cat," she said. Then realized she had brought up the topic her partner didn't want to talk about. "I'm sorry, Gav."

"No biggie," he said. "Let's look in the garbage bags in the hallway for due diligence."

Katie nodded. "This place didn't offer anything further to the investigation." She was disappointed, but at least it was crossed off the list. "Your turn with the trash."

The detectives went out to the hallway.

"I'll flip you for it?" he said pulling gloves on.

"You're on your own." She found a cup and filled it with water to let the cat drink.

McGaven pulled out all the bag's contents in the hallway. "This is disgusting."

"You're not going to get any sympathy from me."

He finished checking the contents only to find that it was the usual trash. There were no notes, writings, mail, or anything that might identify the person the garbage belonged to. It was food and take-out containers from nearby pizza restaurants.

After repacking the bags, McGaven said, "Well, this was a bust." He looked at his partner holding the cat. "You can't bring him."

"I'm not going to leave him here to starve to death. Obviously, no one is coming back for him."

McGaven sighed and pulled out his phone, dialing the Pine Valley Animal Shelter. He was good friends with one of the managers. While he coordinated with the shelter and explained the circumstances of the cat, Katie took the time to look around the other apartment. She immediately saw what McGaven had meant. There were black scrapes on the walls and some of the drywall had been punctured with holes. She tried to figure out what had caused the damage—it appeared to have been done on purpose. There were black smudges and strange lines throughout.

The cat happily followed Katie around the apartment, giving a few meows.

Katie's attention stayed on the walls. There was something strange about the marks and holes, so she decided to take some photos from the middle of all the rooms, panning around. It reminded her of something, but she couldn't think of what it was. Most likely it was just wear and tear of an apartment. Her senses were heighted, making her more alert and skeptical.

"Okay, everything is all set to drop Mr. Whiskers off at the animal shelter. You can leave a message with the representative at DSP Inc. about the cat being found and that we took it to the shelter."

Katie picked up the cat once more. "Will do."

FORTY-FIVE

Wednesday 1330 hours

The killer contemplated whether to kill Jasmine or to let her die at another location slowly burning to death, which was what she deserved.

He stood over her, watching the terror in her eyes and in her body movements as she followed every move he made. There was something about the teen that mesmerized him and had done from the beginning. It was something he had never experienced before. Had the evolution begun?

She was indeed beautiful. Tears running down her cheeks, her long blonde hair with wispy bangs resting softly against her face, accentuating her eyes; and the lovely tone of her skin reflected in the yellow dress—it was almost perfect.

Was it perfect?

Had he finally found the one?

He wasn't sure what that would feel like—it was completely new to him.

As he continued to stare at Jasmine, her face seemed to

morph into Mrs. Drysdale—judging, jealous, and mean to the core. He knew it wasn't physically possible, but the vivid memory of the teacher's face loomed in his mind's eye. He would never forget her dark dead gray eyes and teeth that looked like they had been carved from a block of wood—the complete opposite of his mother's angel face. He could still feel her hate-filled stare no matter where he was.

The killer removed one handcuff from Jasmine's hands so she could drink water and eat a peanut butter sandwich.

"Think about what you've done and how you could do better," he said.

Jasmine reacted with cries of fear, flailing her loose arm around in a feeble attempt to free herself.

He moved away from the girl and climbed the few stairs, shutting and locking the door behind him. The sound of the locks still gave him chills and almost forced an involuntary reaction from his throat and bowels, but that was a memory from another time.

Once inside the main house, the killer snapped back into the moment, thinking about everything he had learned about Detective Katie Scott. She was going to be a problem—and due to her tenacity and skill, he knew she wouldn't stop in her efforts to find him. He'd devised a plan that would shake her to her core until she would be unable to think, work, and live in the way she had become accustomed to—it would be devastating.

There were two computers set up on an old folding table. One had the tracking details for her police sedan while the other one showed several loops of Katie working crime scenes. The more the killer watched and studied her closely, the more he grew to hate her.

The killer knew the detectives had found out about the GPS tracker and were rotating cars when they went to specific locations and conducted interviews.

He leaned close to one of the screens showing Katie as she went about her duties. He whispered in a hateful manner, "You can't trick me... You can't beat me... You can't outsmart me... I'm the million-dollar man... You are already dead but just don't know it yet."

FORTY-SIX

Wednesday 1700 hours

"And then she throws the lid open and climbs into the full dumpster," said McGaven. "It was priceless."

"What, no photos?"

Katie laughed along with her partner and Detective Daniels and John. They were sharing a couple of pizzas Daniels had brought to the office. It was a nice moment away from the investigation and the rest of the world. They sat around a conference table in forensics, away from the work, so they could have a little bit of a break.

"I'm not surprised," said John.

"Katie can be pretty scrappy if she wants to," said Daniels.

"Yeah, she can, but she always has my back," said McGaven. He looked at her. "I can't imagine having any other partner."

"Hear, hear," they said in unison as they raised their beverages in the air.

"Thank you, Evan, for bringing the pizzas," said Katie. "You know how Gav can get when he doesn't eat on time."

They laughed.

"Oh yeah, but Katie can be a softie when there's a cat involved," said McGaven.

"Did you really find a cat?" said John as he ate another bite of pizza.

"Absolutely," she said. "And big softie Gav made sure the cat was going to be taken care of."

"Awww..."

The detectives and John spent a little more time eating and sharing stories before they all went their separate ways.

Katie drove home and didn't feel as frustrated with the investigation as she did the day before, but she had to figure out a way to draw the killer out without putting lives at risk. She didn't know how to do that or if it was possible. It seemed the killer was pinpointing her for some reason. It was easy for criminals to fixate on the police or detectives working their case and to blame them instead of themselves. She wanted to use that to their advantage, but her fear was that there would be more deaths before she could catch him and that the safety of everyone around her would be in jeopardy.

Katie pulled into her driveway next to McGaven's truck. She wondered if her partner had decided yet about what he was going to do about his relationship. Was he going to move out and break up with Denise? Or was he going to make wedding plans?

Katie entered the house to be greeted by a rambunctious Cisco. McGaven was working on his laptop at the counter.

"Anything interesting?" she said, putting her things down.

"No. I got an email from Denise."

Katie stopped and stared at her partner. "And?" she said hopeful.

He didn't immediately answer.

Katie patiently waited while she fed Cisco. She didn't want to pressure him.

"She wants to talk," he finally said.

"That's a good sign."

"And she's been updating me on what she and Lizzie have been doing."

"That's a really good sign. I think it means she misses you."

He looked up and for the first time Katie saw sadness in his eyes. It pained her to see him this way.

"I hope you're right. We're going to meet tomorrow night."

"Gav," she said. "It will work itself out."

He forced a smile.

Katie let Cisco outside and she joined him. The cool air as the sun was setting made her feel a little bit better as she thought about how she was processing Chad's departure. After a while, she and Cisco went back inside. She was headed down the hallway to change her clothes when McGaven yelled from the kitchen.

"Clara Taylor just sent me a text and said she's in trouble."

Katie returned to the kitchen. "Did you try and call her?"

"Yeah, went straight to voicemail."

"Call for patrol, but let's get over there right now."

Katie drove her Jeep and they sped over to Mrs. Taylor's house as fast as she dared to drive.

"See anything? Any car out front?" she said.

"No. I don't see anything unusual, but that doesn't mean anything."

"It's dark too," she said.

Katie parked in Mrs. Taylor's driveway and the detectives sprang out of the car and headed to the house. Katie glanced over at the Braxtons' house, which was dark and seemed quiet as well. She moved to Mrs. Taylor's porch and knocked.

"Mrs. Taylor? It's Detectives Scott and McGaven."

There was no sound or movement.

Katie knocked again. "I'll go around back."

"I'll go in through the front," McGaven said.

"Patrol should be here any minute, but I don't like this," she said. She glanced at her partner before she hurried around the house. She heard McGaven knock on the door again before it slammed open as he forced his way inside.

Katie ran through the backyard gate and around the house to the back door. It was a slider and partially open, which made the back of her neck prickle. She pulled her Glock as she slowly moved the door wider. It was almost silent as it glided on its smooth track. She cautiously stepped inside. She expected to see McGaven, but her instincts told her to stay quiet. She didn't hear her partner, no footsteps, no movement of any kind, and strangely no voices.

Katie's adrenalin skyrocketed. She felt as if she were moving through a bomb-ridden battlefield, waiting to take a wrong step. Her senses were off the charts. She could smell the remains of a cooked dinner, so where was Mrs. Taylor?

Katie cautiously cleared each area. Where was patrol? They should have arrived by now. The only lights were two nightlights that gave everything a funhouse effect. The book-cases and chairs seemed askew and out of place. She approached a large sofa sectional in the middle of the room. Shadows obscured the corners and areas of the floor, making it difficult to decipher what was real and what was created by the lack of light.

Katie felt a slight cool breeze coming from the open front door. She finally decided. "Gav," she whispered. "Gav," she said again.

As she rounded the couch and neared the long wooden coffee table, she saw boots. They were the tactical boots police officers wore. "Gav," she said again. This time she knew the body on the other side of the coffee table was her partner. "No, no, no," was the only thing she could say. She ran to her partner and immediately dropped to her knees.

McGaven was lying on his back with his Glock still in his right hand. At first, Katie thought he was dead, but she could see his chest moving up and down.

"Gav," she said again and touched his face. "What happened? Gav, can you hear me?"

McGaven remained unconscious, but his pulse seemed to be strong.

For a brief moment, the only thing she thought about was her partner. Looking next to his body, she saw a long object, which she realized was a stun baton. He had been ambushed and hit with thirty thousand volts. She had to get an ambulance dispatched right away.

Katie stood up to retrieve her cell phone just as someone grabbed her from behind, placing something around her neck. It was quick and efficient. Her Glock and phone dropped to the floor. She grabbed at her throat; it felt as if it were collapsing into her body. Her air restricted as she gasped for breath. She tried to use her elbows and feet to free herself, but the person who had sneaked up on her was extremely strong. Even as they thrashed around the room with her, the attacker didn't make any sound or a say a word.

Katie gathered all her strength, using self-defense moves she learned in the military to try to free herself and turn the tables on her attacker, but her dwindling power was taking hold of her. The lack of oxygen made the room spin so much, she didn't know if she was standing upright or lying face down.

Excruciating pain fired straight through her throat and chest, eviscerating her ability to breathe. She tried desperately to take another gasp of air, but she felt her body weaken and then go limp. She couldn't feel her arms and legs. Her body hit the floor, and just before her eyes closed she saw her partner lying there unmoving. She reached out for his hand as everything went black.

FORTY-SEVEN

Wednesday 1930 hours

Excited voices conversed all around. Heavy footsteps moved from one area to the next. There were noises that sounded like plastic closing and papers crinkling.

Katie opened her eyes, feeling an immense pain in her chest. She saw unfamiliar faces above her and immediately sat up.

"Take it easy, Detective," said a paramedic.

"Gav," she said with a strange hoarse voice.

"Lie back down."

"No, where's McGaven?" Katie moved herself a couple of feet along the floor so she could lean against the sofa. She looked around the room and saw three deputies and two paramedics. She remembered she was in Mrs. Taylor's home. "Where's Mrs. Taylor?" she said.

One of the paramedics shook his head to indicate that the woman was gone.

"Where's McGaven?" she said again, barely able to with her sore throat.

"He wasn't here when we arrived," said one of the deputies.

Katie looked around frantically. "He was here and there was a stun baton right next to him." She looked at the location and saw a green jelly bean that must've fallen out of his pocket. "He was right here."

Detective Daniels arrived at the scene and immediately knelt down next to Katie. "Are you all right?"

"I... I don't know... but..."

"I heard on the scanner about two detectives at this address. I knew it was you and McGaven," he said. He seemed to gather his emotions, looking at Katie's wounds. "What happened? Those are strangulation marks."

"Please help me up," she said.

"Detective, you need to be taken to the hospital," said the paramedic.

Daniels helped Katie to sit on the sofa and he kept close to her.

"I'm fine, really. I'm feeling better." Katie got up and looked toward the hallway and saw the body of Clara Taylor. She was covered in blood and reminded Katie of the condition in which she had found Mrs. Braxton in the parking garage. It pained her that they couldn't prevent this from happening.

The paramedic sat next to Katie on the couch. "Let me put on a bandage and make sure everything is clean."

"Fine," she said.

The paramedic wiped the area around her neck, put gauze on it, and then wrapped it with a bandage.

"Gav received a text from Mrs. Taylor that something was wrong, so we came immediately after calling dispatch to send patrol," she said to Daniels in a whisper.

"It's okay, take your time," he said.

Katie began to feel some strength return, but the harder she tried to talk the weaker her voice became. "We have to find Gav.

Every minute that goes by is more time for the killer to..." Her voice choked up.

John walked in. Katie was surprised.

"I called John when I heard the radio dispatch," said Daniels.

Katie didn't say anything. She was trying to figure out how she was going to make this right.

"We're going to find him," said Daniels.

There was movement among the first responders in Mrs. Taylor's living room. They shifted. There were several "sirs" spoken. Sheriff Scott entered, his face drawn, as he hurried to Katie. His usual leadership demeanor had taken a hit and now his priority was his niece. The sheriff was extremely fit for a man in his late fifties.

"Uncle Wayne," said Katie hoarsely.

The sheriff sat down next to Katie. "What happened?" he said.

Katie told her uncle everything leading up to their entering the Taylor residence.

He gently moved part of the bandage and it was clear he was pained by what she had gone through.

"I'm fine. A little shaken. We need to find McGaven right now," Katie said.

"We will. I'm putting together a task force with the best."

"Good. Where are we meeting?" she said.

"Katie, you were nearly killed. You can't be on the task force. You're too close to it."

Katie wanted to scream in protest, but she remained calm. "Gav and I have been chasing this killer. Of course I'm close to it. You can't leave me off this now. Please..." She felt better as the oxygen flowed throughout her body. "If the killer wanted to kill me, he would have done it. But he didn't. He's made it seem like he was after me, but he remained in control. Now he's taken someone close to me... Don't you see I have to be part of the task force—I know how he thinks." She looked at her uncle imploringly.

The sheriff said, "You have two choices. You either go to the hospital to get checked out or go home and stay there to rest."

"But..."

"I'm giving you an order, Detective. Two choices—pick one." The sheriff was firm and once he made a decision it was to be obeyed.

"I'll go home."

"Detective Daniels and John will escort you and stay with you—because I know you, Katie," said Sheriff Scott.

FORTY-EIGHT

Wednesday 2355 hours

Katie rode home with John in her Jeep, and Daniels followed. She wasn't in much of a talking mood and she couldn't confide her thoughts and plans. The last thing she wanted to do was to get anyone else in trouble or fired or—worse—killed.

As John drove up Katie's driveway, he said, "I can only imagine how you're feeling. But, Katie, you have to realize that it's best to let the task force do their jobs. I know you've done some tactical maneuvers in the past, but not under these conditions."

Katie knew John was sensible and levelheaded, but she was going to do whatever it took to get McGaven home safe. "I know," she said. "Thank you for being here."

As they were walking up to the front door, another car pulled in. Katie recognized it. Denise stepped out and hurried up to the porch.

"Katie," she said. "I heard. Are you all right?"

"I'm fine, Denise."

She looked around. "Is Gav on his way? He's not at the hospital."

Katie realized Denise didn't know about McGaven's abduction. "Denise," she said softly, "they didn't tell you?"

"Tell me what?"

"He was abducted."

"No... no that can't be..."

"The sheriff is assembling a task force with the best deputies, SWAT, and the fugitive apprehension team."

"No. Why are you here then?" she said sobbing.

"Denise, come in and..."

"No, I've got to go," she said and ran back to her car.

"Come inside, you shouldn't be alone," called Katie.

"I have a neighbor watching Lizzie and I've got to get back." Denise got in her car and drove away.

Katie sat quietly on the couch with Cisco at her side. The big dog pushed his body closer to hers; he wasn't going to leave her. She was bored and was desperate to help find her partner, but she was being careful about what she did due to the fact that both John and Daniels were watching her closely.

Katie picked up her cell phone, looking for any new texts from her uncle, but there was nothing. Then she went through her email to bide her time. She decided to view again the clearer images of the photos that were found in Mrs. Braxton's bedroom again. Scrolling through, she looked at the houses. They seemed average, all except one, which was a larger home on acreage.

Katie shifted her position as Cisco grumbled from the movement. Why did the house look familiar? Had they seen it before? She didn't think so.

"Katie, you okay?" said Daniels.

"Yeah, I'm fine. A bit tired," she said. "Have you heard anything?"

"No. But as soon as they have a plan in place or as soon as anything changes, we'll know."

She nodded. Her world was crashing all around her but she had to stay strong, alert, and physically and mentally efficient. Petting Cisco helped to calm her nerves. She had noticed her hands were shaking slightly and growing tingling sensations were rearing their ugly heads throughout her arms and legs. The post-traumatic stress had been awakened and was plaguing her.

Katie rose from the sofa. "I'm going to bed. Wake me if there's any news."

"Of course," said Daniels.

"You'll be the first to know," said John.

Katie moved to her bedroom followed closely by Cisco. She looked at the bed and no matter how comfortable it seemed and how tired she was, she knew she had to come up with a plan. She had visited all the crime scenes and knew more about the killer than anyone. Reports aren't the only thing—but standing in the areas and seeing the bodies firsthand made her closer to him than anyone else in the investigation.

Katie opened her closet and stared at the contents. Her clothes were hanging neatly and there were shoes and accessories stacked around. She looked specifically at a certain duffel bag. Its contents were Army clothes: heavy-duty shirts, pants, and boots. There were belts that would carry more than just a gun. In the corner was a gun safe and inside were various rifles and extra handguns.

Cisco nudged her hand.

"I know... we've got to get him back safe."

The dog softly whined. It was as if he knew McGaven was in trouble.

Katie contemplated her options for several minutes. If she pursued the killer to find McGaven she would be suspended and perhaps relieved of her duties—permanently. But she couldn't put a price on a friend or family member if she could do something to save them.

Walking to her dresser, there were still photographs of her with her parents, friends, and Chad. There were photos taken with her military and blue family too.

Katie looked at a photo that had been taken not too long ago of her and Chad when they had gone camping. The memory came back to her with vivid recall of a neighborhood near the crime scene. She remembered how Chad joked that it would be a great house for them after they were married. It was a bitter-sweet memory, but she knew where the house was located.

She pulled her phone and looked at the grainy image of the larger house, now remembering where she had seen it before. She was one hundred percent positive. It was near the fire location at Lost Falls, where Jessica Grant's body was found in the closet. They had passed this other property on their way up the drive.

Katie began filing through her mind all the crime scenes, evidence, and autopsies—in addition to the attacks, various homes, and commercial buildings they'd visited. There was something that she wasn't processing—some link she had missed.

She sat down on the bed, pushing for a clue or memory of the one thing that would fill that last piece of the puzzle. Her tiredness caused her to struggle to remember everything about Old Stagecoach Road and Lost Falls. Still, she backtracked through her memory. She remembered talking to a neighbor who had said he was house-sitting nearby. There was no other close house it could have been.

"What's your name?" she said.

"Kip. Kip Johnson."

"You said you're a neighbor?" said Katie.

"Well, actually, I'm house-sitting for a friend."

Katie watched the man. She couldn't ignore her instincts. "Do you always run this trail?"

"I have a few times—sometimes the longer one on the north side."

"Have you seen anything out of the ordinary over the last few days?"

"Like what?"

"People? Cars? Anyone that might be scoping out the place?"

"No... it's pretty quiet out here."

"Have you seen any teenagers?" She watched him with curiosity.

"No. I don't think so."

Katie closed her eyes, recalling Kip Johnson's voice, running it over and over. Opening her eyes, she realized that the voice on the phone of the representative for the commercial building was the same. Could it be? Her thoughts raced and skyrocketed through all the people who had been questioned and interviewed... the man sitting in A Cup of Java had the same build as the older jogger in Lost Falls. But if some type of prosthetic had been used to either make him look old or young... If she had to guess, Katie bet the real person would be older like the jogger.

Katie tiptoed to her bedroom door and quietly opened it. She listened for John and Daniels. John seemed to be moving around in the kitchen and Daniels was talking about something she couldn't quite hear.

Looking at her friends and family smiling happily in those photos, Katie knew exactly what she had to.

"Okay, Cisco, we're going on a mission," she said softly.

The dog knew exactly what she meant.

Katie didn't want to waste any more time. She grabbed her duffel bag and opened her gun safe, taking an AR-15, Beretta, and ammunition. Cisco's tactical gear was in her Jeep. Opening her bedroom window, she carefully and quietly popped out the screen and climbed out. She gave Cisco a command of *hopp*, meaning "to jump" in German. The black dog easily jumped through the window. He glided as he flew through the air, not touching any part of the window frame.

Katie hoped John wasn't watching the cameras as she and Cisco hurried toward her Jeep.

"And where are you going?" said the same man, who was standing at the front porch.

Katie spun around.

John's arms were at his side, relaxed, his expression difficult to read. Katie couldn't tell if he was angry or not. But she was caught in her actions and now she had to recalculate her plan.

John glanced at her bag and then back to her. "You weren't going to leave without telling us, right?" He clenched his jaw.

"I..."

"You found something out. Right? I've known you long enough, Katie. How could you leave us in the dark?" He kept eye contact with her.

Katie put down her pack. She knew she was being selfish, but she still wanted to protect the people she cared about. And that meant finding McGaven before it was too late. "I'm not leaving you in the dark, but I'm disobeying the sheriff's order and I don't want to put you both in jeopardy. Whatever happens to me—I take full responsibility. I was going to update you..."

John nodded. "Are you done?"

Katie remained quiet.

"We're talking about one of our own. I can't speak for Daniels, but I can tell you that I will do everything I can to rescue McGaven and bring him home. We're a team. A family."

That sentiment hit Katie hard. "Okay, I'll update you."

Katie took the next fifteen minutes to update John and

Daniels about her theory of where McGaven was most likely located. It was going to be a lot of ground to cover.

The three of them worked out a plan. Katie and John left with Cisco, and Daniels headed to the police department headquarters to speak with Sheriff Scott. They had prepared for just about anything.

FORTY-NINE

Thursday 0300 hours

McGaven kept dozing off and waking up each time with a jolt. He had been hit hard and he felt the intensity of the electricity going through his body—he actually felt as if he was going to have a heart attack. His mind kept going through the time he and Katie arrived at the Taylor house.

He finally opened his eyes and stared out in almost pitch-blackness. His wrists and ankles were shackled. It was cool and he couldn't feel his legs due to lack of movement and wasn't sure if he could stand up.

Once he felt more awake the pain kicked in. His head and right shoulder seared with agony that moved throughout his body like Taser volts.

A soft whimper came out of the darkness from his right side. He thought he had imagined the sound. Then he heard it again.

"Hello?" he said.

More crying.

"Is somebody there?"

"Yes..." came weak voice.

"What's your name?" he said, the throbbing in his head coming in bursts.

"Jasmine."

McGaven's mind cleared. "Jasmine MacAfee?" The missing girl.

"How do you know that?" Her voice sounded even more frightened. "Did he put you in here to hurt me?"

"No, I'm a police detective." He remembered riding in an enclosed vehicle like a van. And Katie... oh, Katie. He hoped she was okay. Or maybe she was in another room. He had no way of knowing where she was.

"Okay..." Her voice trailed off.

"Is there anyone else here you know of?" McGaven asked.

"No, it's been just me. I'm so thirsty."

McGaven was extremely thirsty too. "It's okay, Jasmine. We're going to get out of here." He thought more about it. "Who is *he*?"

"I went to an audition and he was there. He said his name was Maxwell something."

"Is he the only one?" The name Maxwell didn't sound familiar and he doubted it was the man's real name.

"I think so... but..." She paused.

"What?"

"Sometimes it seems like it's someone else, but it's him. I know it."

McGaven knew exactly what she meant. They were in the house of the man with all the disguises.

Moving his body, he tried to get to his back pocket where his keys were. He could feel them but couldn't quite reach them. He had to rest but would try again.

"What's wrong?" Jasmine said, her voice shaky.

"I'm trying to figure out how to get us free."

Jasmine started to cry.

FIFTY

Thursday 0500 hours

Katie and John made it to the house in Lost Falls next to the arson site and where she had spoken to the supposed house sitter named Kip Johnson the day they went to the crime scene. They'd had some trouble finding the house due to the area it was in, and once there they'd had to find something to break the padlock on the metal entry gate. She used infrared binoculars to see if anyone was there.

"Anything?" said John.

It seemed vacant and there had been no movement of any kind for almost twenty minutes.

"No, it looks clear," she said. Katie walked back to her Jeep where Cisco waited. "Like old times, huh, Cisco?"

The dog whined and his tail thumped against the seat while he watched Katie with his intense yellowish wolf eyes. He was in tune to her change of moods, her actions, and when something big was about to happen. He was ready.

John geared up, as he followed Katie's cue. It was as if he too were getting ready for battle.

Katie watched the sky begin to brighten; it was going to be daylight soon. She took the opportunity of darkness to organize her gear and change into something more appropriate. The key to the success of any mission was wearing layers and being able to carry everything she would, and might, need.

She thought it would have been good to have a bulletproof vest instead of just a reinforced one with pockets, but it was too bulky and heavy to bring. Two handguns, a rifle, spare ammo, and a field knife were her important means of defense. She didn't have any idea of what she was going to walk into—but she was going to be ready.

Katie tried not to think about the reality of Cisco's safety and instead focused on his extensive training. He most definitely would prove to be an important aspect of hunting down the killer and freeing McGaven—that's what he was bred and trained for.

Once Katie was finished, she checked and double-checked Cisco's tactical vest and support pieces. She kept a leash hooked to her weapons' belt, but Cisco definitely knew she was preparing for the worst. She had to be prepared to go force on force if it came to it. The killer had already proved he was brutal, ruthless, and capable of just about anything. If they were going to be able to get through this, they had to play the killer's game.

Katie and John got back into her Jeep and drove through the gate. John made sure the gate was closed after her. As they got closer to the house, the more doubt crept in. What if she couldn't find a clue to find McGaven? What if they weren't there? What if this was a mistake? What if?

She pulled into an open-ended carport by the front door. It was important the Jeep wasn't visible from the outside if someone wasn't looking specifically for it.

The sky was brightening.

Katie and John had studied the property before entering

and noted that it looked like no one had been there in a while. It was most likely a second home. She hadn't had time to search for the owner identification. The house appeared to have not been inhabited in a while. The garden was overgrown, with weeds, and the furniture she could see through the windows was covered in sheets.

She didn't expect the killer was there now, but she suspected he had been.

Katie tried doors and John tried various windows for access. Cisco heeled next to Katie. She wasn't going to leave him in the car for any reason—they were all going to stay together until it was over and McGaven was brought home.

They found a back door that didn't fit properly in the lock area, and Katie and John were able to push and pull at it until it gave way and opened.

They entered.

FIFTY-ONE

Thursday 0600 hours

McGaven knew it was only a matter of time before his attacker came back and killed him. Why would he need him alive? Unless it somehow fit into his diabolical and psychopathic fantasy to stash him with Jasmine.

He had been trying for at least an hour to get to his keys, but the handcuffs were making it impossible and Jasmine was secured and too far away to reach them.

"Sean?" said Jasmine.

McGaven had told her to call him by his first name so he seemed more like a friend than a police detective.

"Yes?"

"I'm scared."

"I know. I am too. But I'm going to get us out of here."

"How?"

"I'm not sure yet."

There were footsteps above, quick and purposeful, and they were coming closer—it sounded like the noise was right above them. He unconsciously flinched.

The sound of locks being disengaged and a creaking door opening made light blast into the holding area, blinding McGaven and Jasmine. He couldn't see anything and felt as if he would never see regular light again.

"How do you like it, Detective McGaven?" said a man's voice from above. His tone a sneer.

McGaven still couldn't focus on anything much, but he managed to see an outline of a man standing at the top of the stairs, obviously looking down on them. It reminded him of an alien apparition in a science fiction movie.

"What do you want?" said McGaven.

"I never really want anything because, you see, I always get what I want."

"What's your name?"

The man laughed with an eerie pitch that didn't seem to belong to him. "Names can be changed, dropped, rearranged, so my name isn't important."

The riddles made McGaven think the man lacked a grasp on reality. But he was strong and cunning, and along with his other personality traits he was also extremely dangerous.

"We're going on a field trip." The man came down the stairs one step at a time. With each movement there was a distinctive creak or squeak. "But first things first," he said and he shoved a rod into McGaven's chest, forcing another thirty thousand volts through his body.

The last thing McGaven heard was Jasmine screaming.

McGaven woke to the sound of an eight-cylinder engine roaring as the van traveled at a decent speed on uneven terrain causing it to shift and bob and weave. He lay on his right shoulder, pain shooting down his arm and up through his neck after every hole and ditch they drove over. His chest felt tight and heavy from the two jabs of electricity flooding throughout his body.

He rolled onto his back and then his left side, his wrists and ankles still securely fastened and making his arms and legs hurt. He saw Jasmine lying on her side with her back to him—at least she was still alive.

They were in some type of a cargo van, but he couldn't see the driver and there was no opportunity at this point to escape or overpower the killer. If Katie was still alive, he knew without any doubt she was doing everything she could to find him. He shut his eyes and said a prayer as memories of investigating previous cases with Katie, as well as good times with Denise and Lizzie, played through his mind. He loved his life and would do everything he could to make sure he made it through this.

Suddenly, the van stopped. Both McGaven and Jasmine slid forward on the old rug they were lying on.

They waited their fate.

Soon the back doors opened and the intense aroma of the dense pine forest swirled in the air. The killer grabbed Jasmine's legs and pulled her out, dumping her on the ground. She cried and pleaded, but he paid no attention to her words. It was as if he was unaware of the teen's agony, making the experience of the last moments of her life that much more terrifying.

McGaven knew they were in one of the most wild, dense, and rural areas in Sequoia Forest. No one would be able to find them.

He suddenly became enraged. He knew he could find the strength that was needed. He had a deep love of life and survival. He wouldn't let this be his last moment on earth.

The killer grabbed McGaven's ankles and easily pulled the detective out of the van. The strength of the captor was impressive, and in great contrast to his unassuming appearance. That was what was truly frightening.

McGaven hit the ground hard, causing a shooting pain from his shoulder and down his back. His strength was declining, but he was determined not to give up. Looking up, the killer stood over him, just staring, and McGaven wasn't sure if he was going to kill them now or was thinking about when he would do it.

"Sorry I had to Taser you twice, but you're such a big fella and I wasn't taking any chances," the killer said. His voice sounded robotic and rehearsed.

"You think you're tough?" said McGaven, surprised by how different his voice sounded, hoarse and tired.

"Tough isn't important."

McGaven glared at him.

"You're definitely tougher than I am, but I'm here and you're, well, on the ground wondering when you're going to die."

Jasmine started to whimper.

"What do you want?" McGaven asked.

"To rid the world of people who are being posers."

McGaven wasn't sure if he'd heard the killer correctly. "And who gave you that authority?"

The killer laughed. "Authority? No one. It's because I can." He walked to the van's passenger door and returned carrying a rifle and a handgun.

McGaven knew what his fate was going to be and he was going to take it with courage. His emotions were running high as tears flooded his eyes. There was no one he hated more than the killer standing over him.

The killer pointed the rifle at Jasmine and readied it for fire.

"No!" yelled McGaven.

The killer stopped and looked at McGaven as a small smile appeared on his face—it soon turned into a full-face grin. "You know, Detective, as I've watched you and your partner, I mistakenly assumed you weren't very interesting, but I can see that I was wrong." He paced. "I have something much more interesting for you both. Something that has been a fantasy of mine for a very, very long time."

The word "fantasy" clicked in McGaven's mind as a word

Katie used to describe what drives a serial killer—trying to obtain a personal fantasy. "And what's that?"

The man pulled Jasmine to her feet. She wobbled because her ankles were shackled together. He unlocked the handcuffs from her wrists but left her ankles secured. Still terrified, she backed up against the van's cargo area.

"We're going to play a little game," the killer said. "I'll let you two go, but there's a catch." He laughed. "I'll give you a ten-minute head start."

McGaven knew what the killer had in mind. His blood ran cold. It was to make their deaths, if they were ever found, look like an accident. There would be no evidence to track back to him—he would make sure of it.

"And you, big guy," the killer said. He quickly released the detective's legs.

McGaven could barely feel his feet; he knew he couldn't get the jump on the killer.

"I'm feeling generous today. I'll give you another couple of minutes before I come after you. Starting now…"

McGaven struggled to get to his feet with his hands still cuffed behind his back. He wavered, wanting to attack the killer, but the cards had been dealt. He took several steps and waited for Jasmine. The girl could make only tiny steps, using her arms to help keep her balance.

"C'mon," he said to her, knowing it was their only chance to survive. He estimated that they were going to be moving eastward. He knew it was possible to get to an area for help before being shot, but what he couldn't figure out was why the killer was giving them a head start. Were there traps in the forest? Was he leading them into something much more terrifying? Or was he using them to bait Katie?

The killer pointed the rifle in the air.

"Oh, and I'm sure your partner will try to find you," he said, his mood rising.

"You can bet on it." McGaven gritted his teeth and hoped that Katie would find them before they'd been killed.

"That's exactly what I'm counting on. Betting your lives on it." The killer laughed and fired the rifle. The sound echoed around the forest as the morning light began to brighten the sky and surroundings. "Go!"

McGaven assisted Jasmine to a wooded area, moving as fast as they could, and soon they disappeared. They could still hear the killer laughing.

FIFTY-TWO

Thursday 0630 hours

Once Detective Daniels was satisfied and had rehearsed what he was going to say to the sheriff, he left Katie's house, taking everything he could to show Sheriff Scott. He too knew that they were gambling, but he agreed they needed to track down McGaven as soon as possible.

His thoughts were on the detectives and John. This killer was volatile and didn't seem to follow one single aspect of his profile, but rather changing the rules as he went. That made him an extreme enemy—a lethal killer.

There were dozens of first responder vehicles, including police and fire, at the Pine Valley Sheriff's Department. Qualified volunteers were on standby. Daniels hurried to the department's conference and meeting room, which could hold the most people. He updated the sheriff on everything about Katie, John, and Cisco leaving the house. The sheriff clearly wasn't happy, but he pushed through his personal feelings and updated the men and women he had called in from the city along with county police officers, detectives, local and county available firefighters, SWAT, and the fugitive apprehension teams to cover all bases.

To Daniels, the sheriff said, "What about her phone?"

"She has it on, but the signal is sketchy. John was going to try to send info every fifteen minutes. The area they're going to cover is immense."

"From Katie's and McGaven's reports, it seems the killer likes rural and deserted places. If I know my niece, I would say she's going to follow up on the previous arson sites and that commercial building," said Scott.

The group had mostly assembled with all available officers and volunteers. The sheriff addressed them.

"By now everyone should have their assignments. I want all the locations covered and searched. Some of you will go and interview people who Detectives Scott and McGaven have spoken with during their investigation. SWAT, fire, and fugitive apprehension teams head to Sequoia Forest. You will receive updates as they become available. I want the detectives to start back at the Taylor and Braxton homes and move out from there." He looked at the crew. "Stay in contact and report anything out of the ordinary. Until further notice."

The officers dispersed, mostly in pairs, to their assignments.

"What can I do to help?" said Daniels.

"Go with SWAT and keep me posted," said Sheriff Scott.

"On it."

FIFTY-THREE

Thursday 0700 hours

Katie took caution and extra care to search the house, making double sure she and Cisco weren't walking into a trap, but it seemed to be just a house that hadn't been occupied in a while. That being said, there were signs a person had been there recently. One of the big overstuffed chairs had the white sheet removed and it appeared that someone had sat in it.

John took safeguards as well, moving in the opposite direction in the house. He was cautious and took time to address each area. Cisco searched too. He would alert to something unnatural, suspicious, or an item that could potentially have the killer's or McGaven's scent on it.

Katie tried hard not to think about what McGaven was going through; she knew her partner was strong and resilient— he'd had her back on so many occasions she had lost track. He would be able to survive anything. They had gone through some terribly difficult moments since they had worked together on cold cases. She smiled as she remembered the first day they had met when McGaven's orders were to ride along with her. They didn't see eye to eye at first but grew to respect one another and have each other's backs—no matter what.

Katie walked through each room, slowly searching the spaces, up, down, and around, considering anything that might indicate the killer had been there and where he might be headed. She could feel the clock ticking down. It was a calculated risk, but she had to do something to get closer to the killer —if she found him, she would find McGaven.

Based on the crime scenes, she knew their killer was brutal with his victims and showed no remorse, but every move he made was thought out and completely adhering to his belief and perspective of what he felt was right. It made it difficult for Katie to pinpoint his conclusive profile—what made him tick and what would set him off. He showed different signatures, like the many faces he wore. It became a delicate balancing act for Katie, which would make her decisions problematic, if and when she found him.

"Anything?" she said.

"Not yet," said John.

Katie loved the fact that John was positive and hopeful. It was nice, almost a relief, to have him with her.

Katie, with Cisco heeling at her left side, maintained focus, moving strategically throughout the house. Looking through the four bedrooms, two bathrooms, rest of the living areas, and kitchen, Katie felt a dark feeling come over her. There was nothing indicating where the killer was headed or if he had been there. It was extremely disheartening.

She thought about the locations he had specifically chosen to commit arson—they were always rural spots and highly unlikely to have anyone witness the events. What did these places mean to him? Something from childhood? His favorite parts of the state?

John approached Katie and Cisco, his expression was strained and concerned. "Are you all right?"

"I don't know..." Katie's neck began bothering her with a dull throb. When she put her hand up to it, there was a small amount of blood. She went into a bathroom near the kitchen and looked in the mirror. She was pale and her eyes were glassy —her stare wasn't the usual lively and get ready for anything, but rather, tired, scared, and frustrated. Basically, she looked how she felt. She knew her strength had been waning, but she had chosen to ignore it.

After redressing her neck, Katie sat down in the big burgundy chair for a few minutes to rest. John joined her, sitting in a chair facing her.

"What are we going to do?" she said to John.

"Look, you've done everything you can," he said.

"It's not enough. We have nothing to report and we don't know where Gav has been taken—or if... he's..."

"Don't let your mind go there," he said. "We have to keep pushing forward. The sheriff has put everyone out and they're tracking down all the leads and places where the killer has been."

"That's the usual plan and protocol, but—"

"You can't start doubting yourself now, Katie. Let's keep moving forward... at least you don't have to worry about someone having your back." John paused and captured Katie's gaze, his dark eyes seemed to peer into her soul. "I'll always have your back. I'm not going anywhere."

"Thank you, John," she said. Katie knew John meant what he said and she trusted him.

Katie leaned back in the chair, running her hands along the sides of the plush cushion. There was a piece of paper between the seat and the cushion. Pulling it out, it appeared to be from a printer.

Katie unfolded the paper.

"What is it?" John asked.

Cisco pushed his nose against it and took extra time to smell it.

"It's from a website advertising camping, hiking, and sleeping under the stars in the most beautiful forest in the state —Sequoia Forest." She passed it to John to look at. "Of course," she whispered. "It makes sense that the killer would take full advantage of the most lush, dense, and remote area near Pine Valley. It's a magical place for anyone who visits—an experience of a lifetime."

"We need to let the sheriff know," John said.

Katie nodded and sent a text message to the sheriff. Still holding her cell phone, she took a deep breath. "It says there's a sixty percent probability of rain, but they never seem to get this possibility right."

"Okay, good to know. But we need to move now. We can prepare for the storm on the way."

Katie nodded. "Okay." She hoped the rain would hold off. "Well, Cisco," she said. "Looks like we're going to Sequoia Forest. It's going to be the biggest search of your lifetime..."

FIFTY-FOUR

Thursday 0730 hours

The sun was up peeking through the large pine trees, but there was a cluster of dark clouds moving in as well that could bring some showers. The morning warmth took the chill away, which made it easier for McGaven and Jasmine to move through the forest.

McGaven had finally been able to retrieve his key ring, where he had a handcuff key, and they were able to release their remaining shackles. Without wasting another moment, McGaven took the handcuffs and put them in his back pocket. His body felt as if he had been thrown out of a moving truck. Every muscle and joint had soreness.

His priority was to get them to an area where there was a park entrance or an adjacent roadway and flag down a vehicle for help. He wasn't sure of the direction to go but concerned they might be going deeper into the forest instead of out to the perimeter.

"You have jelly beans in your pocket," said Jasmine.

McGaven couldn't help but chuckle, thinking about Katie

giving him a hard time over the candy. "Yeah, I can't help it. I like them." He put his hand in his pocket and popped one in his mouth, hoping that the sugar would give him more strength. He gave one to Jasmine.

She took it gratefully. The girl looked exhausted.

"Jasmine, we need to make better time. Okay?"

She nodded.

McGaven zigzagged around trees and bushes, making their progress more difficult but also making it harder to be followed. He instinctively put his hand in his pocket again and could feel at least a dozen jelly beans still there.

McGaven suddenly stopped. He took a jelly bean in his hand and rolled it back and forth, and then he set the candy on a log where it would hopefully leave a scent and a possible trail. He also carefully bent over some low-lying twigs and pressed down a weed area with his foot.

"What are you doing?" Jasmine asked, looking around the forest, expecting the worst.

"Leaving a trail."

Katie and he had developed subtle ways to leave a trail, and how it might work if their colleagues were looking for them. There was a chance the killer would be able to pick up on it as well, but they had to take the chance. He had to do everything he could to get both him and Jasmine to safety.

"Keep going," he urged the girl.

McGaven estimated that they had been moving for fifteen to twenty minutes. He'd helped Jasmine get over downed trees and through tight spots whenever he could in order to keep up their pace. And they had stopped once in a while for a few seconds to listen for any noise behind them—footsteps, rustling of leaves, or anything that wasn't natural to the forest. Since it wasn't the official summer months anymore, he wasn't too worried about encountering a bear, but there were other animals they could come across. They weren't traveling a typical well-worn hiking trail—they were off the grid and moving through the inner belly of the woods.

Jasmine suddenly stopped. "I can't go any farther."

McGaven grabbed her arm to force her to keep going. "Yes, you can. You're strong and we're going to get through this to safety. You will be with your family again," said McGaven as he left another jelly bean.

She looked at him and nodded.

They continued to move through the trees, but not as fast as McGaven would have liked. The low-lying branches scraped their arms and faces. Downed trees made it especially difficult, as they had to climb over them instead of taking the time to go around. It sapped their strength.

The sun made the deep shadows of the forest more pronounced and McGaven wondered if they should hole up, hide in between tree trunks. But that would be a dangerous tactic. They could end up trapped without enough space to get ahead of bullets. The best thing that they could do was to keep going to find help.

They stopped for a minute for Jasmine to rest.

"It's okay," McGaven said, looking back, expecting the worst. He tried to find something that could be a weapon, but there were only branches and it wouldn't be enough to fight off a killer with a rifle.

McGaven and Jasmine carried on as fast as they could. They were quiet and didn't speak in order to conserve strength as they navigated through the woods and slight hills. They had to keep going. It felt as if they had been at it for hours, but only a little over forty minutes had passed. McGaven wasn't going to give up hope—he would keep moving with every ounce of strength in his body.

Just then a shot rang out in the forest. It was some distance away—a warning. McGaven couldn't help but think the next would be directly at them.

FIFTY-FIVE

Thursday 0800 hours

It took a little longer than expected to get to the main entrance to Sequoia Forest. It was an amazing drive and location—under different circumstances it would have been a lovely trip. Katie kept vigilant watch in her rearview mirror. Nothing was going to slow her down. Katie realized a command unit was in full force to find McGaven, but she hoped that she and John could expedite the search—and be able to find McGaven alive.

Katie pulled into the empty parking lot. She thought the best pursuit would be on foot, so she drove the Jeep a little bit off road to camouflage it.

John was studying the map of the area on his phone. "I think there are three main places someone could drive into if they were hiding something or had a hostage." He continued to scroll and swipe. "This is a good spot, and if we continue to move north, it'll be a solid place to start."

After parking, Katie turned and looked at Cisco. His eager face, intense expression, and ears pointing north gave her pause. She didn't want anything to happen to him—he was a retired military working dog and should be enjoying life, not hunting down serial killers. There was so much at stake, but was she making things worse? Was she giving the official search party more to deal with?

"Katie," John said.

She turned to look at him.

"I know there are several variables in play here. You have to be strong."

"I know."

He studied her. "I know you're exhausted, but we can do this together."

She forced a smile, knowing he was right. His support helped her to keep the faith and move forward.

"And," he said, "I think we need to separate to cover more areas."

"But—"

"No, I've been thinking about this ever since we left the house. We can keep in touch, but because of this terrain and extreme rural location it would be the smart way to approach this. It'll be like I'm shadowing you and Cisco."

Katie knew John was right. "Okay."

They got out of the Jeep and Katie opened the back, allowing Cisco to join them. She was ready to set out to hopefully catch a scent of McGaven if he was out there. It was a long shot, but she had confidence in them and Cisco.

Katie grabbed her lightweight daypack with extra supplies and made sure there were emergency items for Cisco as well. She put the pack on. Once satisfied with her gear and Cisco's fitted vest, she was ready.

John fitted Katie and himself with the high-tech walkies. Katie was impressed by how he took the difficult task of getting ready when they didn't really know what they were going to run into—either way it was going to be the most difficult track they had ever done.

"Thanks," she said, not knowing exactly what more to say to express her gratitude. Or her concerns. Everything seemed to press down hard on her. The danger. The reality. And potentially the death of her partner. Words weren't easy right now.

"I know," said John, as if he knew what she was thinking. He moved closer to Katie, adjusting her headset. "Can you hear me?"

She nodded. Smelling the faint scent of soap on him from an earlier shower, Katie closed her eyes and wanted to remember something nice.

Katie put a tracking device around Cisco's flat tactical collar that would buzz when she pushed a button, alerting him to return to her. She used it in case they were separated or she wanted to call Cisco to her from any location up to half a mile away. She dropped the remote into her pocket.

John stood next to her as they took a moment before setting out. He had made sure her phone was synced with his.

Katie stopped at the top of the trails and looked out at the view. She closed her eyes and took a deep cleansing breath. Even though it was morning and sunlight filled her view, the forest seemed dark and foreboding—an entrance to a deep abyss. There were also some darker clouds in the distance that seemed to be approaching.

Katie took a small Ziploc bag from her pocket that had one of the McGaven's gloves in it and turned to Cisco so he could take in the scent. The dog took extra time smelling the glove and seemed to recognize it as his tail began to wag in recognition. Katie looked up at John, who was watching. She then hooked the long lead on Cisco and said, "*Such.*"

They headed down the main trail at a moderate pace. The terrain was fairly smooth, with some unevenness and rocky areas.

John put his hand on her shoulder. "I'll go this way, but I won't be far in case you need me. I can't track you." He smiled.

Overwhelming feelings rushed Katie, but she nodded and continued to follow Cisco. The K9 took a sharp right and continued down a side trail. Katie followed, watching in every direction, expecting the worst. She glanced back as John went another path and disappeared.

There were areas that seemed too narrow for them, but Cisco easily maneuvered his long sleek body around bushes, limbs, and tree trunks as he kept his direct focus on the track. Katie watched the dog while making sure she wasn't going to step on anything that might prove to be dangerous or unsafe. The last thing she needed was to get hurt.

She felt good considering everything she had been through, not to mention the lack of sleep. It would eventually catch up with her. She knew she was primarily functioning on adrenalin, her symptoms of post-traumatic stress close to the surface, but in their own way they helped her to keep moving. Having John nearby made it even better. He had been a good friend and colleague through all their cases.

They made considerable distance in the first ten to fifteen minutes, which was a good sign, at least that was what Katie told herself. One of the first things that a K9 dog handler learned when they began any type of training for protections, searches, and tracking was to trust your dog—as simple as that. If there was ever a time for Katie to trust Cisco—now was it.

After another ten minutes had passed, Katie stopped in an area with many tree trunks on the ground. She and Cisco drank water to hydrate and to rest for five minutes. She leaned against one of the downed trees. Cisco moved closer to her, extremely interested in something on the log. The dog continued to sniff loudly and fast. He then sat down as an alert.

Katie looked down to refocus and to see what he had found, and that's when she saw it. There was a smashed green jelly bean sitting on the log. She told Cisco to search in case the food alone had attracted him. He seemed to increase in enthusiasm the more he sniffed. He spun around and gave low whimpers.

There was only one explanation that made sense. How was that possible way out here?

"Gav," she whispered.

Katie looked around for more clues and that's when she noticed two low-lying branches that had been snapped. It wasn't the usual result of an animal or person stepping over them—it had been done on purpose. She took a bit of extra time to search around for anything else her partner might have left and then decided to update John.

"John, you copy?" she said.

"Affirmative."

"I found some clues that seem to indicate Gav has been here."

"Keep going."

"Ten-four. Out."

Katie's pulse elevated. It was the first time since Mrs. Taylor's house that she had felt positive.

"Okay, Cisco, let's *such*."

The K9 team proceeded for half an hour and with each minute her heart became heavy again, worried they might be tracking McGaven's last moments.

Cisco stopped and stuck his nose near a bush—he slowly downed.

Katie's heart stopped. Upon closer inspection, she found another jelly bean. She also saw more indications of purposely broken foliage. She updated John. She could see he was following her direction, parallel approximately a quarter of a mile away from her.

"Gav, keep 'em coming."

There was a rumble in the distance.

The storm was coming.

FIFTY-SIX

Thursday 0935 hours

They couldn't go any farther. Jasmine had slowed her pace so much McGaven worried she might faint from exhaustion and he didn't think he could carry her for very long. They were no closer to a main road and he couldn't push the teen any farther, so the next best thing would be hide out. He remembered the killer tucking into a wooded area near Pane Construction and Katie and Daniels missing him. They would do the same.

McGaven could feel his strength declining and his chest hurt—he was concerned his mind was playing tricks on him, that he couldn't navigate them through the forest. He scoured the immediate area as Jasmine leaned against a tree. Medical attention was far away—and they didn't have any way to communicate to call for assistance.

"You okay?" he said.

"I don't know..." she said, breathing heavy. "I feel weird. Dizzy."

"Stay there. I'm going to find a place where we can hide and wait it out."

She nodded and immediately sat down.

McGaven hadn't heard any gunshots or movement in a while. He was worried what might be in store for them and concerned there might be booby traps. All these thoughts ran through his mind. He also thought about what he was going to do if the killer found them. All police officers thought about it—what if you had to give your life to save someone else? He knew exactly what he would do without hesitation.

He finally found what he had been looking for: a perfect hiding place. It was a hollowed-out area in a downed tree with dense foliage, but it was hidden by other trees and no one would be able to see you unless they knew you were there. The horizontal tree trunk was also near a ravine, which made it even better. Thunder rumbled in the distance and the sunlight was diminishing due to the dark overhead clouds, making the forest even darker—hopefully that would also work in their favor.

"Come here," he said to Jasmine. "I want you to hide in here. There's only enough room for you, but I'll be nearby. I don't want you to say a word or come out unless I tell you to, okay?"

Her face conveyed fear. "Please... no."

"We can't keep going. We have to stay hidden until it's safe."

Jasmine looked at the hollow and nodded resolutely. "Okay." She crawled in.

"You'll be safe. Don't make a sound until I tell you it's okay. No matter what."

She nodded again.

McGaven would never forget her pale face and blue eyes staring back at him, as if he was giving her to the devil.

He turned away to search for a space large enough for him to hide in, and that's when he heard the rustling. It wasn't from an animal—it was footsteps from a human—the killer.

He moved as quietly as he could and found a cluster of trees with a good hiding place he could squeeze himself into, but still see who was approaching the area. He slipped into the trees and prayed that Jasmine stayed quiet.

He heard more heavy footsteps. They were getting closer.

Katie and Cisco slowed their pace. Katie's sixth sense, or cop instinct, appeared to be working overtime. Every sound, every footstep she thought she heard made her question everything. She kept flashing back to the battlefield—all the death, destruction, and horrifying images. They had never left her mind and she had never completely recovered from her traumas, but she had healed and learned how to manage them and would for the rest of her life. But now she felt the presence of someone or something. It was eerie and almost had a demonic quality to it, making her skin prickle.

Katie reeled in Cisco so he was at her side. The dog's steps were almost silent and he didn't make any sound. She wondered if he'd had the same instinctual reaction that she was experiencing. There was definitely something strange about where they were. She glanced down at the dog and saw that his ears were forward and his body tense. He didn't make any audible sounds as his breath was shallow, barely visible, but he too seemed to know there was something very close.

Katie wanted to update John, but decided to remain quiet. She moved to the side of the makeshift trail, kneeled with Cisco, and used her binoculars to peer into the forest for any movement or sightings. Cisco tucked in close to her side. She could feel the dog's heartbeat next to her ribcage.

Katie saw it. There was movement. It was subtle at first, but she could make out the slight outline of a person—a man. A rifle was slung over his right shoulder. It could be a hunter or maybe a hiker with personal protection. But Katie didn't think so.

Could it be the killer?

She watched him move and the way he kept touching the rifle grip. There was something familiar about him and she wondered if he had one of his disguises on—probably not. So this man was the killer who been so prolific—such loss of life with the teenage girls, Mrs. Braxton, Mrs. Taylor, Stan Pane, and who knew if there were more.

She could target in on him and kill him—then it would be over. But she didn't know where McGaven was and she couldn't take that chance. She worried that maybe McGaven had been left somewhere else to die—the images of the girls after the fire haunted her.

Katie shuddered at the fact that this killer had touched her, been to her house, and almost strangled her to death at Mrs. Taylor's home. She absently touched her neck, remembering the force that had tried to extinguish her life. He was stronger than most and that might be a problem. She had to be ready.

Anger didn't fill her soul, it was rage. She wanted this person to pay; she wanted to stop the carnage and to halt his unfulfilled fantasy. Violent psychopaths don't realize that their fantasies will never be satisfied. Not ever. It would eventually come down to the fact—live or die.

She made a judgment call—there were too many unknowns in this situation and she had to get a better vantage point to shadow the killer.

"I have subject in view...wait for confirmation," she barely whispered into her microphone.

She then heard the distinct sounds for dash, dash, dash... pause... dash, dot, dash. It repeated again: "OK" in Morse code. It suddenly occurred to Katie that John was also near the killer if he didn't want to give away his position. She had to move fast.

Katie showed Cisco hand signals to indicate to him to retreat into a brush area and to stay until released. The dog knew these commands well, but they hadn't had a use for them in a while. Nonetheless, he obeyed. She couldn't look directly at Cisco's eyes, so she turned to leave him. She hated doing that more than anything, but there were more things at stake, too many lives, too many unpredictable scenarios, and she couldn't balance his safety as well. She kept Cisco safe the best way she could.

Katie moved up to the greener areas where her movement and footsteps didn't make a sound. She kept a direct visual on the killer and continued to move through the wooded area, stalking him.

McGaven could feel his heartbeat drum faster, making his head pound. He wasn't sure if it was just his adrenalin gaining momentum or if his heart had taken too many volts of electricity, but he couldn't worry about that now. He strained to listen for Jasmine, but he was relieved she was staying silent.

Daring to move slightly in his position, he leaned forward and to his surprise he saw the definite outline of a man with a rifle directed forward, moving slowly through the brush and tree limbs. He knew it was the killer. He must've estimated that he and Jasmine would drain their energy and need a place to hide. He'd calculated the risk of letting McGaven and Jasmine go into the forest, but he must've done a risk assessment and he had been right. The killer wasn't worried at all—it seemed to be more like a relaxing walk in the forest to him.

McGaven became mesmerized watching the man. He moved and kept hidden like a chameleon, which was an added trait to his million-dollar man disguises.

McGaven's view zoomed in closer and closer to the killer. He didn't think anyone could see him or even search for him—but as he watched and waited it was clear the killer was coming for him. There was no doubt about it anymore. He had no weapons, no cell phone, and no one knew where he was. Not many options, but he would at least try to stop the killer from finding Jasmine.

The killer had come so close that McGaven could see the details on the bottom of his jacket, the make and model of his rifle, and the brand of boots he was wearing. He kept moving closer as if pulled by a magnet or an unknown and unseen force.

"You are so predictable," said the man as he pointed the gun directly at McGaven's hiding place, as if it were completely transparent.

McGaven could barely breathe as the barrel of the gun zeroed in on him.

"Bang, you're dead." The killer laughed.

Katie saw the killer pointing the rifle directly at a location in the trees. He said something she couldn't quite hear.

She wanted to just kill the man right where he stood, but her life wasn't in immediate danger and therefore it wouldn't be a legal shot. She knew in her bones, in her soul, and in her mind that it was him, but she couldn't afford to make a catastrophic deadly mistake.

The killer appeared to be talking to someone and laughing.

Katie kept inching forward.

It began to rain. Not sprinkles or light rain, but huge drops, gaining momentum. Katie kept her eye on the man. He backed up and...

McGaven emerged from the dense tree-stump area.

Thankful that he was alive, Katie's momentary happiness snuffed out as she watched in horror as the killer got ready to shoot her partner. He was making McGaven kneel on the ground with his hands on his head. The killer was planning on executing him.

Katie, with no other choice, sighted her scope and fired.

The shot echoed around the forest and throughout the valley.

Katie ran as fast as she could, filled with pumping adrenalin, toward McGaven.

The killer lay on his side holding his upper arm—his weapon a couple of feet away. The bullet had hit precisely where Katie had aimed, disarming him. She wanted the killer alive to make sure he would spend the rest of his life in prison and to interrogate him for any other victims he might be holding or have murdered.

McGaven could barely stand; he was exhausted and looked ill.

"Gav," she said, still with a hoarse voice. Katie was relieved to see her partner and turned her rifle downward.

"Bravo, Detective Katie Scott," said the killer. His eyes looked sunken, giving him a haggard appearance, even demonic. He was much older than Katie had first thought.

McGaven tossed a pair of handcuffs to Katie.

With precise timing, the killer grabbed Katie's ankles, pulled hard and she went down.

It was such a quick movement she didn't have time to think.

She kicked at the man as he tried to overpower her; they tussled and wrestled to get the weapons and control.

Within seconds, as the rain poured down, Katie and the killer slid over the edge behind where Jasmine was hidden. And disappeared.

FIFTY-SEVEN

Thursday 1200 hours

Katie felt the earth leave her body as she slid over the edge, feeling every uneven part of the hillside. Her world went upside down then righted itself again. Her fall shook her like a ragdoll and all she could think about was getting to her Glock as fast as she could.

Mud covered her vest and her gun belt, feeling like heavy cement. It was difficult to see with muck flowing down her face. She clambered to get up and draw down on the killer, but he wasn't anywhere to be found. She could hear McGaven yelling from above, but couldn't make out his words.

The rain kept pounding down, causing mud to slide from above and rush by her, making it difficult to balance. It was exceptionally cold, sending shivers down her spine.

Katie was tackled from behind again. She went down and wrestled with the killer once more. This time she was prepared for his moves and was able to adjust for what he was going to do next.

The killer punched her and tried to strangle her again. She

reached into her holster, but the killer was lightning fast and was able to grab her gun and push it into her face.

Katie watched the rain roll off the killer, flattening his thinning hair. She could see his true identity. He was in his forties but looked to be in his sixties. His eyes said everything she needed to know, in that it was clear the man was desperately searching for something that was never going to happen—to right whatever went so wrong in his life.

"I knew you would be trouble! You ruined everything," he said.

Katie didn't say a word, watching his hands; she knew he would tell her everything she needed to know.

"You ruined my life. You think you're so smart. But you can't have happiness... You're just like *her*. And... and... people like you take lives... so perfect... and she was..."

Katie watched him fill with an anger that began to spill over. He was going to kill her. She saw his right hand begin to shake as the thunder roared overhead—as she slowly moved her hand to her pocket and pressed Cisco's remote.

Katie couldn't fight him, and if she moved the wrong way, she knew he would fire directly at her head. She closed her eyes.

"You will never interfere in my life again! They were posers, pretending, and they deserved to die. I should have killed Mrs. Drysdale when I had the chance. But the most important woman in my life took her own because of people like you. No one! Is ever going! To do that to me again!"

He began to squeeze the trigger.

Through the heavy downpour and in the battering thunder, a black streak made its way down the side of the ridge effortlessly, almost flying. The large paws and head made direct contact on the killer's arm, making him drop the weapon. Cisco sank his teeth into the man's shoulder, making him cry out in extreme pain, which was heard over the roar of thunder.

The strength and unrelenting bite of the dog overpowered

the killer, which allowed Katie to grab her weapon and take control as she stood over the now weak man. She let Cisco have a few more bites before calling him off.

Katie looked at the pitiful excuse for a human being writhing in pain. She took zip ties from her backpack, which she had managed to keep on. The killer was secured and wouldn't be hurting anyone ever again.

"Good boy, Cisco," she said as the dog stood valiantly next to her.

Katie looked up and saw her partner along with John standing in the rain, looking the worse for wear and giving her the thumbs-up sign.

It was done—finally over.

After the rain subsided, Katie and McGaven were able to get a steady signal to call from her cell phone and give their location and an update to Sheriff Scott. It took another hour before the cavalry of law enforcement arrived along with a helicopter to fly out Jasmine and McGaven to the hospital to get checked out.

Katie and John stayed at the location with the killer until they received their orders to accompany the man to waiting police who would take him into custody. The rain had subsided to a consistent mist, but more thunder cracked in the distance.

The storm wasn't over yet.

The killer remained quiet while he was secured and didn't seem to have anything more to say. His wrists and ankles were hog-tied for extra security while he waited. His face was down and turned to the side away from Katie and John.

"Your instincts were correct," said John.

Katie remained still, Cisco at her side. "I'm just happy it turned out the way it did. Not only did we find Gav, but we found Jasmine alive." Many emotions were running through her mind and her heart. It was difficult for her to separate how she was feeling about the case, McGaven, and what was next for her.

She looked at John who was soaked, his shirt clinging to his body, his baseball cap drenched, but his eyes told the entire story of who he really was besides a forensic expert for the Pine Valley Sheriff's Department. He was a soldier, ready to defend, and a lifelong friend.

"Thank you," she said, finding it difficult to tear her eyes away from his.

"Not necessary," he said.

"Yes, it is... thank you for believing in me and having my back."

He looked at her. "You would do the same for any of us. You're nothing less than amazing."

She smiled, slightly embarrassed by the compliment.

"You think you've won?" said the killer from the ground. His words seethed with disdain and he'd turned his face toward them. His voice was different, but that wasn't anything unusual based on his MO.

At first Katie was going to ignore him, but then her curiosity got the better of her. She walked up to him and looked down. He now resembled a pathetic man, who preyed upon young girls, but she saw the demon in his eyes and the unrelenting drive that he would have never stopped—ever—to get what he desperately needed.

Katie looked back at John and Cisco standing side by side watching her. It struck her hard that she witnessed the true meaning of strength, honor, and bravery by looking at them. Everything she had been through with McGaven, John, and Cisco was miraculous. She knew she couldn't do what she had done without them.

Katie looked down at the killer again. "I would say we have won."

The killer laughed.

"Looking at the position you're in—we won," she said.

"It's only the beginning... I could have killed you at any time... there's so much you don't have a clue about."

"Then why don't you tell me?"

"You think you're so smart... figure it out yourself," he said.

"Just like I thought—once a coward always a coward."

"You think just because you caught *me* that you're safe? You think I'm alone? You think there aren't more like me?"

"I think you're desperate and you'll say anything at this point," she said. "I think... whatever happened to you to create the monster you are will haunt you forever. Who is she? She obviously didn't care about you." Katie wanted to rattle the killer, to get a glimpse into his psyche, and find out what drove him.

"Never talk about her like that!"

"Who? Someone you came across? Girlfriend? Family?" She paused. "Your mother?"

"Never speak of my mother! She was beautiful, perfect, and didn't deserve—" He abruptly stopped and turned his head the other way.

"And?" she said. "Tell me more. Why cut the hands off Stan Pane? Did he steal from you? Was he going to give you up? Or were you just feebly trying to cover your tracks in an attempt to confuse us?"

Katie waited and asked more questions, but the killer never spoke another word. She realized that not only had he suffered a tragedy in his past, he had also suffered some type of abuse that broke him and created the monster he had become. They may never know what exactly drove him, but Katie was confident the truth would eventually come out.

After the killer was successfully taken into custody, Katie, John, and Cisco managed to backtrack to her Jeep, where several more law enforcement officers waited—including Sheriff Scott and Detective Daniels.

"So glad you're okay," said an almost tearful sheriff as he hugged her tightly. "I cannot imagine what I would do without you." He held her longer and it was clear he was thankful things didn't go down as they could have.

Katie saw a look of relief on Daniel's face too.

"I'm sorry I wasn't truthful from the beginning," she said.

Daniels hugged Katie. "I'm so glad you're all right," he whispered in her ear.

They were all soaking wet, but it didn't seem to matter as they reunited. Katie knew she was in serious trouble and was prepared to take her punishment, no matter what it was going to be. But, for now, she and everyone were safe. She'd never felt so much love after such a terrifying ordeal. Cisco jumped up and down and stayed at her side until they got home later that day.

FIFTY-EIGHT

Thursday 1845 hours

Katie and Cisco watched from the Jeep as two deputies and another car with a woman from social services drove up to Jasmine's home and walked her to the front door. Katie hadn't been home yet; she wanted to see Jasmine reunited with her family—safe and sound.

When the door opened, her mother was the first to cry and fiercely hug Jasmine. Then her dad and siblings followed. It was a wonderful spectacle of love and relief. The family cried and thanked the deputies. There wasn't a dry eye, including Katie's as she observed the reunion. The woman went inside with the family and hopefully everything would be straightened out and perhaps counseling would be appropriate.

Happiness filled Katie's heart that they were able to save Jasmine, but knowing that Anna was lost made her deeply sad. It was something she'd have to live with. Katie's life was always a flux of bittersweet reality when it came to her work.

She slowly drove away and headed home. Cisco whined and pushed his large head toward her.

"We're going home, Cisco… we're going home."

FIFTY-NINE

The Night Owl was extra busy that Saturday night. Katie was ordering another beer at the bar. She watched McGaven and Denise sitting at a table together and they were clearly happy working things out. They held hands and were talking intimately. Katie was thrilled to see them back together—especially after such an ordeal as they'd had. The thought of losing someone you love usually brought people back together—and sometimes new people together.

"So you thought you were going to be fired," said John, grabbing a couple of shots and two beers for his group of friends. He paused putting down the drinks.

"Not fired, per se. But I was worried what the consequences would be. I have to take some of my accumulating vacation days —and take responsibility for my actions. And... a reprimand that will be on my permanent record."

"Oh yeah? It could be worse, you know." He smiled at her as his usual intense dark eyes seemed to soften.

"It always could be worse." She absently brought her hand

to her bandaged neck. "I'm glad Jasmine MacAfee is home safe with her family and that they have the opportunity to work things out."

"I heard they finally got the killer's real identity?"

"Maxwell Carter. I won't forget that name for a while. No sheet or arrests, but not just an ordinary guy. They found his real residence, and tons of forensic evidence, as you know. There were laptops from victims, lots of various types of theatrical makeup, and different types of clothing including yellow dresses. It's not completely clear from old reports, but it seems that his mother committed suicide due to high expectations she had set for herself, and when she felt they weren't achievable—she thought dying was a better choice than being mediocre. And... she was wearing a yellow dress. Young Maxwell Carter had found her body."

John sighed. "Wow. Losing his mom and then finding her body..."

"He had been creating this façade and becoming different personalities for quite some time," she said.

John leaned toward Katie. "I'm glad everything turned out in the end and that I could help... and you're safe."

Katie smiled and couldn't help but appreciate the man John was—she was glad that he was not only her friend, but together with McGaven and Cisco—they were a team.

"His home was creepy that's for sure," said John.

They are going to be questioning him for quite some time—and the FBI has him in their sights to answer for other crimes," she said. "I'm glad it's over."

John moved closer to Katie. "You'd do anything for the people you care about, wouldn't you?"

Katie took a sip of her beer. "Without question."

He smiled and gestured to his table. "Come join us." He grabbed the drinks.

"Thanks, but I'm on my way out. Another time?" she said.

"I'll hold you to that," he said and paused a moment. "Well, Detective Katie Scott... I look forward to working with you after your vacation."

Katie gently tapped his shot glass. "Until then."

John left and returned to his friends. Katie was happy with how everything had turned out as she glanced around the bar seeing all the people who had each other's backs. They were family. That was partly why she felt guilty for feeling down. Her entire life was changing and she could actually feel it as well as see it. She hung around a few more minutes to finish her beer but wanted to go home to peace and quiet—and to begin her much needed vacation.

Katie put down her empty bottle and got up, just as Detective Daniels approached her. She thought he had returned to Sacramento and was surprised to see him.

"Hi," she said.

"You leaving so soon?" he said.

"I'm tired and my neck is still uncomfortable." She had a difficult time keeping his gaze.

"You know you're the talk around the police department."

"You're teasing me."

"No, I'm serious."

Katie walked to the door to leave and Daniels accompanied her. She turned back to see everyone having a great time and made eye contact with Investigator Ames, who raised his beer and nodded in her direction.

She smiled.

Katie and Daniels walked to her Jeep.

Daniels moved in close to her, but she turned slightly. It was clear he wanted to kiss her, but she wasn't ready to begin any relationship right now with anyone—no matter what a nice thought that was. She needed to be okay alone and single before beginning a new relationship. Everything was still so raw in her personal and professional life, and she had some healing to do—both physically and emotionally.

"I'm sorry," he said. "I just didn't know when I was going to see you again."

"It's going to be a few weeks before I get back to work," she said. Looking at him, she remembered their previous time together and how enjoyable it was. "Evan, I really like you and we definitely have chemistry together, but I'm in a tough place right now. I hope you understand?"

"I know you need your space and time to heal," he said. "When and if you're ready, I'll be here. You know where to find me." He smiled.

"Thank you for understanding," she said and gave him a kiss on the cheek. "Bye."

She got into her Jeep and left the Night Owl. Her thoughts were full and she had things to sort out. She was warming up to the idea of taking some time for herself and not having the demanding schedule of cold cases—or killers around every corner. No matter what sadness she felt, things did have a way of working themselves out. She smiled, thinking about everything she had—and even the things she would like to have, including a solid relationship. Her life was changing, but she was okay with that.

SIXTY

A Month Later

Inside the maximum-security prison where Pine Valley as well as surrounding smaller towns housed the most dangerous criminals, they had a new inmate. He paced and yelled all the time, driving the guards crazy. He wasn't deemed insane, so he had to do his time in a regular prison. It was always the same. Sometimes they would put sedatives in his food to keep him calmer.

"I'm Maxwell Carter and I will be back! I promise!"

He would rattle the prison doors and fixate on the same things, repeating them over and over.

"Detective Katie Scott, you ruined my life! I'll be back!"

"Shut up, Carter," said one of the guards as he walked by.

"I will never be quiet about Katie Scott. Never. She is to blame for everything. *Everything*. She will be set free! Are you listening, Katie Scott?"

A LETTER FROM JENNIFER CHASE

I want to say a huge thank you for choosing to read *Find My Daughter*. If you did enjoy it, and want to keep up to date with all my latest releases, just sign up at the following link. Your email address will never be shared and you can unsubscribe at any time.

www.bookouture.com/jennifer-chase

This has continued to be a special project and series for me. Forensics, K9 training, and criminal profiling has been something that I've studied considerably, and to be able to incorporate them into a crime fiction novel has been a thrilling experience for me. It has been a truly wonderful experience to continue to bring this series to life.

One of my favorite activities, outside of writing, has been dog training. I'm a dog lover, if you couldn't tell by reading this book, and I loved creating a supporting canine character, Cisco, to partner with my cold-case police detective. I hope you enjoyed it as well.

I hope you loved *Find My Daughter,* and if you did, I would be very grateful if you could write a review. I'd love to hear what you think, and it makes such a difference helping new readers to discover one of my books for the first time.

I love hearing from my readers—you can get in touch through social media or my website.

Thank you,

Jennifer Chase

www.authorjenniferchase.com

 facebook.com/AuthorJenniferChase

X x.com/JChaseNovelist

instagram.com/jenchaseauthor

ACKNOWLEDGMENTS

I'm grateful to all my law enforcement: police detectives, deputies, police K9 teams, forensic units, forensic anthropologists, and first-responder friends—there's too many to list. Your friendships have meant so much to me over the years. It has opened a whole new writing world filled with inspiration for future stories for Detective Katie Scott and K9 Cisco. I wouldn't be able to bring my crime fiction stories to life if it weren't for all of you. Thank you for your service and dedication to keep the rest of us safe.

Writing this series continues to be a truly amazing experience for me. I would like to thank my publisher Bookouture for the incredible opportunity, and the fantastic staff for continuing to help me to bring this book and the entire Detective Katie Scott series to life.

Thank you, Kim, Sarah, and Noelle for your relentless promotion for us authors. A thank you to my absolutely brilliant editor Jessie and the amazing editorial team—your unwavering support has helped me to worker harder to write more endless adventures for Detective Katie Scott and K9 Cisco.

PUBLISHING TEAM

Turning a manuscript into a book requires the efforts of many people. The publishing team at Bookouture would like to acknowledge everyone who contributed to this publication.

Audio
Alba Proko
Sinead O'Connor
Melissa Tran

Commercial
Lauren Morrissette
Hannah Richmond
Imogen Allport

Cover design
Head Design Ltd

Data and analysis
Mark Alder
Mohamed Bussuri

Editorial
Jessie Botterill
Nadia Michael

Made in the USA
Columbia, SC
14 February 2025

53846939R00209